THE
RELUCTANT
PIMP

THE
RELUCTANT
PIMP

Rochelle Padzensky

HERO
PUBLISHING

The Reluctant Pimp
Published by HERO Publishing LLC
Denver, Colorado

Library of Congress Control Number: 2020914099

PADZENSKY, ROCHELLE, Author
THE RELUCTANT PIMP
ROCHELLE PADZENSKY

ISBN: 978-0-9985034-4-8

FICTION / Coming of Age
FICTION / Women

QUANTITY PURCHASES:
Schools, companies, professional groups, clubs, and other
organizations may qualify for special terms when ordering
quantities of this title. For information,
email heropadz@q.com.

This book is printed in the United States of America.

To my husband, Herb, my teammate,
who cheers me on and
is always there during bad times.
And to those many survivors of dark times
who teach us what grit, determination,
and perseverance can do.

PROLOGUE

You're not born to be a pimp. You don't go to school to become a pimp. A headhunter wouldn't tell you your resume qualifies you to become a pimp. You won't find an ad in the paper that says "Help wanted: pimp." So how do you become a pimp?

I can't answer that question. I can only tell you how I, Edward Allan Anderson, became one. Life is a series of events that often shape who you become and why. This is my version of those events in my life and how they affected me.

ONE

MY MOTHER WASN'T A PROSTITUTE, and my dad wasn't a pimp. My early childhood was much the same as that of most working families. Dad went to work every day and mom was a housewife.

My earliest memories are when I was somewhere between two and three years old. We lived in an apartment in Denver, somewhere east of downtown. Our apartment had big windows. I looked down into the street from what I remember as a large living room. I loved to climb on the sofa and look out onto the street to see the grass, the trees, and the brightly colored flowers in summer.

The apartment had one bedroom with a large alcove that contained my bed, a tall brown wooden chest, and a brown wooden rocking chair. My favorite memory is of my mother sitting in that rocking chair reading to me. My mother was soft and comfy, and I remember arranging her breasts to create a comfortable pillow for me to lie against as she read to me every night.

Her favorite author was Edgar Allan Poe, which is how I got my name. She wanted to name me after him, but as she used to tell it, my father said, "No son of mine is going to be named Edgar." So, they settled on Edward Allan.

My dad worked five days a week. I don't know what he did back then, but I remember that on Saturdays when the weather was nice, he'd put me on his shoulders and say, "Eddie, Eddie, it's time to wash the car."

My dad had a secondhand 1956 Chevy Bel Air that he purchased in 1960, the year after I was born. It was turquoise and white. He had a love affair with that car and took tender care of it. We would go down in the back of the apartment building where he kept it parked. He'd give me a rag and after he'd soap up the car, he'd give me the job of washing the chrome bumper in the back.

In the trunk, he always kept a spare tire, a spare battery, a bottle of water, jumper cables, chains, and a can of gas. "Eddie," he'd say, "you always want to be prepared. In case you're someplace where you can't get to a gas station and the battery dies, you run out of gas, or the radiator boils over, you're prepared."

Of course, I had no idea what he was talking about, but I listened and memorized what he said. When we finished washing the car, he'd take the hose and help me rinse off the bumper, and then it was my job to polish it until the sun shining on it would blind you.

When we finished, we'd go upstairs for lunch. He'd kiss my mom, sniff the air, and say, "So my darling Betty, what have you been up to while we washed the car?"

"Well, now Cliff, just what do you think I've been up to?"

"From the smell of things, I'd say fried chicken, potato salad, coleslaw, and maybe some cake."

"You're just so smart, aren't you?" And then they'd laugh and kiss again. This happened every Saturday during the summer. Then we'd have lunch. I'd have my pbutter n'jelly samich (that's what I used to call it) and milk, and they'd have bologna sandwiches. Then, tired out from the morning's activities, we'd all take a nap.

When we woke up, we'd get dressed. Mom would pack a picnic basket with all the things she'd made in the morning and we'd drive over to City Park. Sometimes we'd take a ride on Miss Denver, the boat that went around the lake. If we were lucky, the fountain would be on and we'd watch and catch the spray. If I was super lucky, the captain would let me ring the bell. Sometimes Dad would rent a rowboat and we'd paddle around the lake. Sometimes we'd just feed the ducks and then find a place to put our blanket and picnic basket.

Lots of kids were always around, and we'd run and play until we got tired, and the grown-ups had our dinner ready. After we ate, we kids would run around and play some more. Our parents would settle down and listen to the band concert. When the band played a march, the kids would march around and play parade. On the way home, I'd lie down in the back seat and immediately fall asleep. Saturdays were my favorite days, but sometimes we also did special things on Sundays, like driving Dad's car into the mountains. During our drive, we'd stop in little towns and look around and drink cherry cider from one of the roadside stands.

That time in my life will always stand out in my mind as some of the happiest days I lived as a child. Dad and Mom were happy and the three of us had lots of fun together. But then life began to change.

One day my dad walked in, ran over to my mom, and said, "Oh, Betty, I've lost my job. Business has been bad lately, but I didn't know it was that bad. Bud had to lay off three of us. What'll we do, Betts, what'll we do?"

My mom put her arms around my dad and said, "Oh, Cliff, I'm so sorry. It'll be alright, honey, you'll find another job."

I had no idea what losing a job meant. Sometimes I'd lose a toy that I might find later. Or sometimes I'd lose something and never find it. It didn't seem to be any great problem, though. So maybe my dad would find his job.

Every day, my dad would read the paper and go out looking for a job. Every evening, he'd come home dejected. "Nothing yet," he'd say to my mom, and she would smile back at him. Soon, he began to work at odd jobs—a day here, a day there.

One night as I lay in bed, I heard my parents talking. I crept out of bed so I could hear what they were saying. "We're at the end of our rope, honey. We have no more savings. I don't know what we're going to do," I heard my dad say to my mom. His voice sounded funny, and it scared me a little.

"I'll get a job," my mom said. "I'll go looking tomorrow. Shh, it's settled." She put her fingers over my dad's lips. Mom seemed to make my dad feel better—listening to her, I didn't feel so scared either.

The next morning, my mom looked at the ads as she drank her coffee. "Now, Eddie, you be a good boy for your dad. I'll be home later."

She arrived home late in the afternoon. Excitedly she announced, "Okay, boys, you're looking at a working woman!"

"You got a job, honey? Wow!" my dad shouted. "Details, where, what, when?"

"Now, don't get upset, Cliff. I got a job as a waitress at Rocky's Diner on Colfax. I know it's not the greatest, but it's a beginning. I'll work different shifts every month. To start, I'll work breakfast. I'll start at five in the morning and finish at about one in the afternoon. When you get a job, I'm sure Mrs. Wilson next door will watch Eddie until one of us gets home." She took a breath and looked at my dad.

"Well, honey, I hope it won't be for too long. I should be able to find something soon."

Our life then settled into a new routine. I'd stay home with my dad unless he found day work, and then I'd stay with Mrs. Wilson until one of my parents came home.

We didn't go to the park and we didn't go to the mountains anymore, but we still washed the car on Saturdays when the weather was nice. And my dad still instructed me on being prepared for an emergency.

TWO

I REMEMBER MY FIFTH BIRTHDAY. Mom brought home a small chocolate cake from the diner. Mom and Dad sang happy birthday to me, and I got a new book, *The Little Engine That Could.* The next month, I started school.

Dad still hadn't found a job, so he took me to school each day. I'll never forget that first day. I'd never seen so many kids in my life. We didn't have many kids around the apartment building where we lived, so I never really had any regular friends. The only kids I'd ever played with were the ones at the park.

At first, I wasn't sure about having to go to school each day. There were so many things I'd never done before. Some of what we did was fun, like painting. Initially, I was uncertain about what I was doing, since I'd never had any paints, but I soon found out how much fun it was to create my own paintings.

Other activities I didn't like so much, especially when they were things I already knew how to do, like recite the alphabet and my numbers. My mom had taught me letters and numbers, and we read together each evening, so I didn't like that we had to work on them at school too. I did like snack time, which was graham crackers and milk, but the rest period we had to take afterward annoyed me. I didn't understand why I needed to rest when I wasn't tired.

Every day at school, we participated in outdoor games. Sometimes we played kickball. Not having played with many kids before, I didn't understand what it meant to be a team player. Whenever the ball came to me, it seemed like someone was always yelling at me to pass it. I especially hated when one of the teachers yelled at me to "pass the ball, pass the ball."

This is pretty much how my first year of school went. Eventually, I got used to what we did at school, even though I still felt like I'd rather be at home. The one other big change that happened during the year, though, related to my dad. He started to act differently and his breath smelled funny most of the time, especially when I got home from school. I would soon learn what that meant.

The summer after kindergarten passed, and I spent most of the time learning how to read with the help of Dad and Mrs. Wilson. The odd jobs Dad did seemed to be getting fewer, and I noticed that he always had a cold drink in his hand. I also noticed that Mom and Dad were fighting more often.

Unfortunately, we had no family and no one to help us. My mom had been abandoned as an infant at St. Anne's Orphanage in North Denver, and she was brought up by the nuns there. I wasn't sure what happened to Dad's family, but I did know that his parents were dead. If Dad had any other family, he didn't have relationships with them.

Mom and Dad used to hold each other and me and say, "Remember, all we have is each other." Mom would then say, "We should be grateful; it's more than a lot of people have."

It made me feel warm and happy when we hugged like this. I knew that no matter what happened, Mom and Dad loved me.

I started first grade a lot more in tune with school. My teacher, who I thought was the oldest person I'd ever seen, was Mrs. Cox. She wore her hair in a tight bun on the back of her head, and she must have had a million wrinkles. She was a good teacher, though, and I began to get the hang of things and even got to know a couple of kids in the class.

One night after Halloween, I was sound asleep in my bed when Mom came and quietly woke me up. "Shh," she said. "Be very quiet, don't say a word, and get dressed."

When I looked around, I saw that our apartment was basically empty. *Where could all our things have gone?* I wondered.

Mom carried me out to the car while Dad quickly packed up my mattress and took apart my bed. This was my first experience with moving in the middle of the night. Little did I know then that I would become a master in the art of moving from one place to another, like a ghost breezing through a room; now you feel him, now you don't.

I fell asleep in the car in the front seat between my mom and dad. The back seat, the trunk, and the top of the car were bulging with all our possessions. When I woke up, we were at our new apartment. It was much smaller than our old one. My bed had to be set up in a corner of the living room because the bedroom was so small there was only room for my parents' furniture.

The next morning, Mom took me to register in the new school I would be attending. My stomach clenched and I wanted to cry. I didn't know anyone, and the teacher didn't seem as nice as Mrs. Cox.

I got confused all over again—just like when I first started school. With Mrs. Cox, we had been learning addition, but in this class, they had already moved on to subtraction. I felt totally lost and stupid. They were also reading from a different book, and everything else they did seemed to be different too. I wanted to crawl into a hole and just stay there. I didn't want to go to school anymore. I hated school, and I hated our life. All I wanted was to go back to our old apartment so I could be in Mrs. Cox's class again.

As the year progressed, things at home got steadily worse. Dad's odd jobs were almost nonexistent, and he seemed to always have a cold drink in his hand. He and Mom had begun to argue loudly at all times of the day and night, and I'd heard Mom say that she hated that Dad was drinking alcohol and getting drunk all the time. I figured out that being drunk had to do with why Dad didn't act or sound much like Dad anymore. Mom also seemed tired and cross all the time.

Then a bad thing happened. One evening when Mom came home from work, Dad came out of the bedroom with a shopping bag full of his clothes.

"I'm leaving, Betts. It's no good anymore. You'll be better off without me. Best I leave now before things get even worse."

Mom began to cry, but she didn't say anything. I think she knew it would be futile.

My dad turned to me and said, "Don't forget, Eddie, take good care of the car and always be prepared." Then he left, without saying goodbye, without a kiss or a hug or anything. He just left.

Mom and I hugged each other and cried until we had no more tears.

Abandoned. By my dad. At six years old. It still hurts.

==

AFTER DAD LEFT, THINGS GOT even worse over the next few years. Mom and I moved several times in the middle of the night because we couldn't pay our rent. Each time, we left more of our possessions behind. Anger was building up inside me. How could my dad have done this to Mom and me?

By the time I was thirteen, we made our last stop. The Stout Street Arms on 22nd and Stout Street. To me, it couldn't get any worse than this. It was a small three-story building, and we had a one-room apartment on the second floor, 2B. The bathroom was down the hall and shared by all the tenants on the floor.

As we moved our few remaining possessions into our apartment, my nostrils were overcome by the stench of cabbage cooking, stale cigarette smoke, rotting garbage, and the smells of something even more gross than rotting garbage. The dim bulb in the ceiling made it difficult to see where we were going. It was, however, light enough to see the paint peeling from the walls and the dirt that clung to the carpet.

Our apartment had one small closet; a few open shelves for kitchen cabinets; a small, filthy sink; a small apartment-sized stove, and a refrigerator. The kitchen floor consisted of rotting linoleum in a pattern that was no longer discernible because of the embedded dirt.

"I see we have serious scrubbing to do," my mother observed.

I remained silent, revolted by the smells and the filth. Quietly, we began the task of first cleaning the apartment and then unpacking our few remaining possessions.

"I know you're angry, Eddie, at how things are going. Bad things happen to everyone. We just have to keep going, and things will get better, I promise. And just because things are bad doesn't mean you can do bad things. Don't forget, we still have each other. That's the most important thing. Do you understand me?"

Keeping my head down, I said, "Yeah, Ma. I understand." *Yeah, sure, things are going to get better. When cows fly.*

The bathroom down the hall was truly disgusting. Mom cautioned me about using the toilet and forbade me to use the bathtub. "We'll just have to wash up the best we can in the sink. Try to use the bathroom at school as much as possible and avoid using this one."

The next morning, I reconnoitered the neighborhood. How can I best describe it? Gray. Gray concrete sidewalk. Brown. No grass. Just dirt, gray-brown dirt with lots of broken glass from empty whiskey bottles. Even the weeds were brown, choked of all color for lack of water. The air smelled of alcohol, decay, and poverty. The entire landscape and the people in it looked as if all life had been sucked out. What remained was an empty husk.

Mom registered me in a new school, and once again, the curriculum was different from the last school I'd attended. I felt lost, confused, and furious with my lot in life. How could this be my life?

When I needed new clothes for school, we shopped at Goodwill. No matter what, though, Mom made sure I always had new underwear and socks.

"Clean underwear is a must, Eddie. Never be without clean underwear and socks. You have to keep your feet in good shape because they take you where you need to go."

Then she'd scour the racks and bins to find the best shirts and pants. I never did have a regular pair of shoes, only tennis shoes. Mom did her best to find a pair that was not too worn. Same with a winter jacket—she looked for ones that would last through the school year. "It's important to stay warm in winter, especially since you walk most of the time."

Of course, she never bought anything for herself. There was never enough money. Her clothes were so worn they were almost rags, not that it mattered that much since she usually wore uniforms.

We subsisted, not existed. A couple of nights a week, Mom would boil water and we'd wash the best we could from a large pot. We barely had enough to eat.

I hated everyone, and I was sure they hated me. That year, I barely got passing grades in my classes, except for reading.

The only good thing in my life was that Mom took me to the library at least once a week. I had become an avid reader; it became my only escape.

THREE

ABOUT TWO BLOCKS AWAY ON 24th and Stout, there was a small grocery store, Greenstein's Cash Grocery. The owner, Mr. Greenstein, fascinated and amazed me.

He was a short, rotund man, balding with a few tufts of hair on either side of his head. He wore round, gold-rimmed glasses. The amazing thing was his pipe. I never saw it lit, but he kept it clamped between his teeth and spoke and performed his duties with it hanging out the side of his mouth. Once or twice, I did see him put it in his shirt pocket.

The store didn't have the same appearance as a supermarket. Round barrels greeted you inside the entrance. One barrel always held potatoes. Another contained onions. A third barrel often was filled to the brim with chili peppers, the aroma of which permeated the entire store. A few smaller barrels held different varieties of dried beans, walnuts, or peanuts, depending on the season.

A small counter in the center of the store held a limited variety of vegetables and fruits, adding an aroma of citrus to the air. The wooden floor creaked when you walked around the counter.

A small chilled case in front of one wall held a small selection of inexpensive meats and cheeses. The walls were covered with shelves stocked with canned goods, and in the rear was a walk-in refrigerator where Mr. Greenstein kept the dairy products and other items that needed refrigeration.

In the front of the walk-in was a counter where Mr. Greenstein bagged and checked out the groceries. First, he'd tear off a small piece of wrapping paper and write down the amounts of each item with the small stub of a pencil he always kept behind his ear. He'd lick the end of the pencil, write down the amount of each item, and then add all the items up so fast his fingers were almost a blur. He never made a mistake. It fascinated me to watch him do this. He'd ring up the amount on a huge brass cash register that made a loud "ka-ching" with each purchase. Every kid who entered the store got a sucker or a piece of licorice from one of the glass canisters on the front counter. Mr. G never charged for those.

My mom would send me there to pick up a few groceries every week, so I became well acquainted with the grocer. Hungry for social contact, I'd hang around and chat with him, enjoying the aromas emanating from the small store—visceral smells of comfort and safety.

AS IF THINGS WEREN'T ALREADY bad enough, my mom came home one day in tears. The diner had gone broke and closed, literally overnight. Now, what were we going to do?

"Don't worry, Mom. You'll find another job, I'm sure. In the meantime, I'll see if I can find a job after school."

My words echoed my mom's words to my dad, years before. Except that I was sure my mom wouldn't abandon me and become a bum like my dad. Just thinking about what he had done to us made me angry.

My mom dried her tears and said, "You're a wonderful son, Eddie. You're right, I will find work."

It was then I had the idea of approaching Mr. Greenstein for a job. Immediately after school the following day, I went to the store.

"Good afternoon, sonny boy. How's things today? What can I get for you?"

"Hi, Mr. Greenstein. I'm here because I was wondering if maybe you needed some help around the store. My mom lost her job and . . . and . . . so I need to help out. I can work every day after school. I'm strong—"

"Okay, sonny boy. I understand. And yes, I could use a little help. It would be good to have someone help me move and load these barrels, and clean the case, and stock the shelves. Yes, a good helper, I could use."

So it was settled. I'd be Mr. Greenstein's helper. I felt happy for the first time in a long time. Now I could be of some help to my mom. I could hardly wait to get home and tell her.

At home, Mom greeted me with a smile. "Guess what?" she said. "I found a new job working for a commercial cleaning company."

I grabbed her and said, "Well guess what else? I have a job as Mr. Greenstein's new helper. I'll work every day after school and on Saturdays."

We were both so happy and relieved that we wouldn't be out on the street, and we danced around the room, laughing and crying at the same time. Life was surely about to get a lot better.

⸺ ⸻

WORKING FOR MR. GREENSTEIN PROVED to be a real education. I never realized how physically difficult the job could be. I'd watched him move those barrels around with great ease, but the first time I tried moving one of them, I almost killed myself. He taught me how to lift and turn by using the strength in my legs and arms.

Different goods were delivered every day. Lugging and loading those boxes proved to be another challenge. Unloading canned goods and shelving them also strained my arms and legs and made them ache. I learned a new appreciation of this little rotund man as my body adjusted to the demands of the job.

I also gained a new understanding of math. Learning how to mark up goods and adjust for spoilage, breakage, and theft impressed me. Being able to work with the numbers the way Mr. Greenstein did gave me a clearer picture of math than I'd ever achieved in school.

A big priority was making sure the perishables were kept fresh. Mr. G was scrupulous about keeping things at the right temperature and either selling items about to spoil at a reduced price or disposing of them so they wouldn't cause anyone to become ill.

I soon came to understand how Mr. G ran such a successful business. He knew every regular customer by name, and all the while he filled their orders, he kept up a running conversation, pipe clamped between his teeth, asking about their kids, their jobs, the weather, and other topics. A great *schmoozer*, that was Mr. G.

I couldn't wait to get there every day after school. In addition to moving and lifting, loading and unloading, and stocking the shelves, my job consisted of keeping the floor and the produce counter clean. It was a lot of hard work, but it made me feel important—like what I did made a difference.

Every evening before I left, I helped Mr. Greenstein put the food from the case into the refrigerator and then thoroughly cleaned the case. Now, besides being a middle-of-the-night master mover, I became a master cleaner.

Although a tough taskmaster, Mr. Greenstein was also a kind man. Being no fool, he knew how tough things were at home. Before I'd leave for the evening, he'd grab a bag, put in a couple of potatoes, onions, some produce, and maybe some canned goods, saying, "So, sonny boy, take this home to your mom. It'll maybe save her a trip here." Thanks to him, we were eating better than we had in a long time.

Occasionally Mrs. Greenstein would come into the store. I thought Mr. G was fussy about keeping everything clean until I met Mrs. G. She'd go over the store with her sharp eyes and spot even the minutest bits of dirt.

"Get the Clorox, hot water, a bucket, and a scrub brush. Germs! Do you want *someone should get sick* from something they bought at Greenstein's? I think not. Get busy." Even Mr. G scurried to do her bidding. She was the Queen of Clean.

Like her husband, she also had a kind heart. She could bake bread, cakes, and sweet rolls that tasted to me like a feast for the gods. Whenever she came, she always brought us big brisket sandwiches on her freshly baked bread and an extra loaf for me to take home, as well as a cake or some intoxicating smelling sweet rolls.

When Mom came home, we'd gorge on these delicious goods, savoring every bite, and for just a moment, it would take the bitter edge off our life.

As much as my job invigorated me, I started to notice that my mom's job was taking its toll on her. The company she worked for did all kinds of cleaning, including residential, new construction, and office cleaning. As the new person who had to fill in for whoever didn't show up, on any given day, she could never be sure what shift she might be working. Sometimes she'd work during the day doing residential or construction cleaning. More often, though, she worked cleaning offices, which meant that she started at four and finished sometime around midnight.

Some nights after riding the bus home, she literally dropped into bed without even taking off her clothes, she was so exhausted. It hurt me to look at her; she had become rail thin and looked old. I wished I could do something to ease her burden. Once again, I would damn my dad for what he'd done.

Between our two schedules, we didn't see each other much, and I spent most of my evenings alone doing homework and reading. On Sunday mornings, she slept in and usually didn't get up until noon or later. Then it was time to do the washing and get ready for another week.

＝＝

EVENTUALLY, I FOUND SOMETHING NEW to do on Sunday mornings. I never remembered us going to church, so I decided to make a list of churches in the area and experiment going to different ones. Why? I don't know. I was searching for something; I just didn't know what.

The experience proved to be quite interesting. Each week, I put on my best pants and a clean shirt and either walked or took a bus to the church I decided to visit. The services in each church had similarities. They all had prayers they said in unison, songs they sung, often accompanied by a choir, and, of course, the weekly sermon. In some churches, the atmosphere was cold and unforgiving. Others seemed warm and friendly. I always looked at the bulletin boards first to see what kinds of activities they offered.

One Sunday morning, I found myself at a Baptist church that seemed very friendly. I looked at the bulletin board and saw they were having a potluck lunch following the service. After the service, I ventured down to the social hall and stood at the door, looking in.

A plump lady in a pink dress and matching pink hat came over to me.

"Hi hon, waiting for your parents?"

"No ma'am, I'm here alone. It's only my mom and me, and she usually works a night shift. So on Sunday she tries to rest and get ready for a new week."

"Well then, you just come right on in and have some lunch."

"But it says potluck, and I didn't bring anything."

"Oh, pooh, don't worry about that. There's plenty of food. Now you just come over to my table and I'll introduce you to my family and you'll eat with us. What's your name, hon?"

"Eddie, ma'am, Eddie Anderson."

"Well, Eddie, it's nice to meet you. My name is Madge Johnston." As we spoke, she guided me through the crowded room to a table where a man and five children sat.

"Mom, Mom, let's eat already," shouted the three boys over the noise in the room.

"Okay, kids, just settle. I want to introduce you to Eddie. He's new here and he's going to have lunch with us today." She turned to me and said, "Eddie, first let me introduce my husband, Ted."

"Hello, Eddie, welcome," Ted said, as he waved a hand at me.

"Now then, the oldest girl there is Julie. Next to her is Frank. He's the oldest boy. Next to him is Tom and then there's Joe. Angie is our baby girl."

I said hi, glad to meet you all, and then Madge said, "Now you just sit yourself down and I'll go get some food for you and me. The rest of you can go ahead and start eating."

Angie took her plate of food and came and sat next to me. "Here Eddie, you can have a bite of mine while you wait for Mom."

"Thanks, but I can wait. So, tell me, Angie, do you go to school?" I asked.

"I go to preschool. Next year I'll start real school. Where do you live? Where do you go to school? Where's your folks?"

"Now, Angie, stop peppering Eddie with questions. You never let a body rest. You exhaust your mom and me and everyone else with your constant questions."

"I'm sorry, Daddy. I just want to know about Eddie."

"It's okay, Mr. Johnston, I don't mind."

Madge arrived with a huge plate heaped high with ribs, chicken, salad, some kind of bean salad, Jell-O, and potatoes. My eyes feasted on all that delicious-looking food.

"Gosh, that looks so good and smells fantastic. Thanks."

"You're welcome. Now dig in. Everyone else has."

I attacked the food. I didn't realize how hungry I was. I ate silently but listened to the family chatter about their week and about the week to come. How normal and happy it all seemed. For a moment, it made me feel even bleaker about my own life. But at least my stomach was filled, and that went a long way toward making me feel better. By the time I'd finished eating everything on my plate, Madge had returned with a piece of lemon pie, a piece of chocolate cake, and a bag in her hand.

"Ready for dessert?" she asked.

"I'm always ready for dessert," I answered. As I dug into the pie, I realized I was pretty full already. "Would it be alright if I took the cake home to my mom?" I asked Madge.

"Absolutely. And I made a plate of food for you to take home to her too," Madge said.

I felt so grateful, I kinda choked up, and like an idiot, I stammered some kind of thank you. What a kind woman.

Madge patted me on the back, "No problem, hon, there's plenty of food. Hate to see it get wasted. Now it's time for us to go, but you come back here again. You're always welcome."

"I will. And it was nice to meet all of you, Mr. Johnston, Julie, Frank, Tom, Joe, and Angie."

They waved their goodbyes and left. I sat there for a moment longer, gathered up the food Madge had packaged up for me to take home, and left.

The next thing I had to figure out was how to explain the food to my mom. She had no idea how I was spending my Sunday mornings. Would she be upset that I was going to church when she had given up religion after my dad left? Would she wonder what I was seeking? Or think that maybe I had done something wrong? I weighed my options and decided on a half-truth. I would tell her the food came from a church bazaar that I wandered by as they were cleaning up and they were kind enough to give me some leftovers. Good enough.

After that, I attended church whenever I had a chance and became better acquainted with the Johnstons. I even began to feel like they were my family.

Suddenly and unexpectedly, at least to me, Mr. Johnston got a new job, and they moved away.

Abandoned. Again.

FOUR

THINGS HAD GOTTEN A LITTLE better. We were more stable financially, able to pay the rent and take care of the basics. With the additional groceries from Mr. Greenstein, we definitely weren't starving. Still, Mom hardly drove the Chevy since we couldn't afford to buy gas, and she carried the minimum amount of insurance.

If Mom had a Saturday off, we'd take care of the weekend chores and then get into the Chevy and drive to the downtown Denver Public Library. We'd load up on books, and if it was a nice day, we'd sometimes wander around Civic Center Park or drive to another park that was close. We never went to City Park anymore. The memories of Saturdays with Dad were too painful for Mom.

Maybe once every month or so, we'd drive downtown and go to a movie. We both loved the movies, so it was a special treat.

Sometimes we'd go to the ice cream shop and get a cone. We were careful not to drive too much or too far.

Heeding my dad's words, I kept check on the car daily. This, at least, was the one piece of good advice he gave me. We kept it parked behind the apartment building. Mom taught me how to start it, so each day I gave it a good start and checked the radiator and oil. And, just like Dad, I washed it on weekends when the weather was nice. Mr. G had an old tarp that he gave to me so I could cover the car when it rained or snowed. The Chevy continued to be our most precious possession, a means of escape, if necessary, so taking good care of it remained a priority.

Mom still worked for the cleaning company, and I continued to work for Mr. G. After I got my driver's license, I was able to drive the car on weekends when we took an excursion. Finally, we had ceased moving in the middle of the night. We couldn't go down any further except to become homeless.

I was now a junior at Manual High School, where I'd been going for the past three years. The fact that I'd been able to stay at the same school had helped improve my grades. I continued to be an invisible guy, though—a true loner. I didn't have close friends. Almost no one knew who I was or cared what I did. Each school day, I walked to school by myself, came home by myself, and then went to work for Mr. G. After work, I went home, studied the best I could, and then went to bed. God. I. Hated. My. Life.

I often changed the route I took to school so I could walk down different streets and look at different houses and apartments. I thought maybe Mom and I could move into one of these apartments or houses one day. The neighborhood close to the school was full of old houses with grass, nice yards, and big trees. I always felt safe as I walked down those streets. It was much different than Stout Street, where you could watch drug deals going down, see drunks pissing on the street, and watch the prostitutes hoping to find one last john.

On a beautiful spring-like morning in March, I decided to walk down 25th instead of 28th. When I came to Lafayette, I turned and started to walk down the block. As I walked, I came up to a house with a sign in the yard that read:

Help Wanted

Handy Man and Yard Work

Inquire Within

The house seemed pretty rundown. The fence needed painting; the yard was overgrown and full of weeds. It looked like the house needed repairs and painting too. *Probably some little old widow lady who just can't take care of it by herself*, I thought.

Recently, I'd been thinking about finding another job. Now that I was a junior, it was getting more difficult to work for Mr. G. By the time I got home from work, I hardly had any time to study. I had more homework than ever, and I desperately wanted to graduate from high school. I decided I'd stop by after school to ask about the job.

═ ═

ONE OF THE GOOD THINGS about school was gym. Afterward, we got to take showers. This was the only opportunity I had to get my entire body wet and washed. Even though the water was usually lukewarm and the soap didn't lather well, it felt great to stand under the water and get wet. Since it was gym day, I was feeling pretty good when I left school—clean and ready to present myself for a possible new job.

When I reached the house with the sign, I took a deep breath, opened the gate, walked up the battered stairs, and knocked on the door. I was totally unprepared for what greeted me. I found myself staring into the most beautiful set of boobs I'd ever seen. They were set into a T-shirt with kind of a scoop neck so that they peeped over the top.

When I finally managed to raise my eyes from those boobs, I found myself looking into a cascade of long brown hair with golden glints, and a pair of big baby blues. *Wow! Some little old widow.* She sure didn't match the outside of the house.

"Yes," she said. "Can I help you?"

I swallowed and tried to get some saliva in my mouth. Finally I stammered, "I'm here about the sign, 'help wanted.'"

She smiled through luscious-looking pink lips and straight white teeth. "Of course. Come in." She opened the screen door. "Follow me into the kitchen and we'll talk about it."

As we walked through the house, I felt surprised by the interior. It didn't seem to fit with the outside, either. Since the outside was run down and old-looking, I expected the inside to be old, too, and filled with ratty, dusty furniture. Instead, in the entryway was a black contemporary modern table with a different kind of mirror over it. As we passed the living room, I got a flash of plush gray carpet and more modern furniture. The dining room also had black furniture. We reached the kitchen, which also looked very modern: gray tile with yellow trim. The kitchen table and chairs were gray too. Wow! Not what I'd expected at all!

Not only that, but looking around, I felt dirty even though I had showered. I checked my clothes and realized how filthy they were and how unkempt I looked. I didn't belong in such a nice house.

We sat down at the table. "So tell me, what is your name and tell me a little bit about yourself."

"Eddie Anderson." I hesitated, not sure what else to say.

"Nice to meet you, Eddie. My name is Francesca VanMaster, but everyone calls me Ches. So, do you go to school?"

"Yes, ma'am. I go to Manual. Right now I have a job working at Greenstein's Cash Grocery every day after school and on Saturday. I'd like to find a job where I don't have to work as late every night so I have more time to study."

"I see. And do you have family?"

"It's just my mom and me."

"And what does your mom do?"

"She works cleaning office buildings, which means she works a night shift, so we don't get to see each other much."

Ches clucked sympathetically. "Tough, isn't it?"

"Yes, but we manage."

"Um. Well, let me tell you a little bit about the job and myself. I'm a widow. My husband, Rob, was killed in an auto accident two years ago, and I've had a hard time ever since. About two weeks ago, I woke up and said to myself, 'This is not what Rob would want you to be doing. He'd want you to get your life together and start a new one.' I looked around and realized I'd neglected everything for the last two years. So, the first place to start would be to clean up the house." A tear ran down her face. She swiped at it.

"I'm sorry about your husband," I said. I waited.

She smiled. "Thank you. Anyway, there's a lot to be done. The yard needs cleaning up. There's a couple of broken steps on the front porch. The fence and house both need painting. The windows need washing, the attic and basement need to be cleaned out . . . you get the picture. There's quite a bit to be tackled. Would this be something you might be interested in doing?"

"I could do all those things. How many days a week and how many hours would you want me to work?"

"What time do you get out of school?"

"School is out at three-thirty, but I have study hall last period and I could get excused from that for a job and be out at three."

"Okay, I was thinking maybe Monday, Wednesday, and Friday. Let's say from about three to six or six-thirty."

"That would work great for me."

"Okay, today is Monday. We can give it a trial run. Would you like to start on Wednesday?"

"Sure, that'd be fine."

"Would you like to know how much the job pays?" She smiled.

Of course, dumbass me would like to know how much. "Yes," I stammered.

"Would twenty dollars a week be satisfactory?"

I calculated the total in my head. "That'd be okay."

She held out her hand. "Then, it's a deal. I'll see you on Wednesday."

I smiled, took her hand, and said, "Thanks Mrs. VanMaster. You won't be disappointed."

Since we're going to be working together, Eddie, call me Ches. She showed me out and waved. As I walked home, I thought about seeing those great boobs three times a week. *Yeah!*

FIVE

I ARRIVED AT MR. G'S over an hour late.

"So, sonny boy, you're late. Anything wrong?" Mr. G looked concerned.

I came down from my cloud really quick. I had to tell him that I got a new job and wouldn't be working for him every day anymore. He'd been so good to me. How could I do this to him? All of a sudden, I felt bad. I didn't know how to start.

"So," he prodded.

Guess I just had to spit it out. "I was looking for a new job. Now that school is getting tougher, I need more time to study. But, I could still work for you on Saturdays and maybe Tuesday or Thursday too."

"That's it, sonny boy? You had me worried there for a minute. I was afraid you were in trouble. A different job to study more . . . that's good." He took the pipe out of his mouth and said, "I like that. And, yes, you can still work for me on Saturday."

I felt relieved. *Good old Mr. G. He's become a good friend.* "Thanks, I appreciate it."

Mr. G took off his glasses, carefully wiped them with his hanky, put them back on, and said, "So, enough standing around, time to get to work."

If I wasn't mistaken, he was wiping away a tear. "Yessir, Mr. G. Right away."

≈ ≈

I COULD HARDLY WAIT FOR Mom to get home so I could tell her about my new job. I finally fell asleep around eleven. It seemed I had only been asleep for about five minutes when I heard her come in. I woke up immediately.

I sat up and said, "Hi, Mom." Startled, she jumped.

"Eddie, why are you awake?"

"I have some news to tell you, Mom. I found a new job today doing some handyman work for a widow. Her name is Mrs. VanMaster."

"A new job? Why? I thought you were happy working for Mr. G, and he's sure been so good to you."

"I am. I just need more time to do homework, that's all."

"Of course, you're right. Shame on me for not noticing. I'm glad. So when will you be working?"

"Monday, Wednesday, and Friday about three hours a day. And Mr. G said I could still work for him on Saturdays."

Mom hugged me, gave me a kiss, and said, "I'm really happy for you. Now, I'm bushed. Let's go to sleep."

"Right, Mom, goodnight." I immediately fell asleep and dreamed about those boobs all night long.

≔ ⹀

ON WEDNESDAY, I MADE ARRANGEMENTS to leave school last period. I got to Mrs. VanMaster's in about five minutes. As the doorbell rang, I felt a sense of anticipation.

"Hi Eddie, come on in."

Once again I felt my heart thump as I looked at this beautiful woman. She was wearing a sweater that made those boobs look especially delicious. I did my best to be casual. "Hi," I said. The day had turned gloomy and rainy, so I guessed we wouldn't be working outside.

Once I got inside, we went into the kitchen. She sat down and motioned for me to sit down. "I thought we'd start in the basement today. So, the first thing I'd like you to do is bring in some boxes from the garage." She pointed to the back door. "Bring in as many as you can carry."

I headed out to the garage and fumbled around until I found a light. It took a few minutes for me to locate the boxes. They were all folded flat and stacked against the back wall. I picked up several and headed back toward the house. Ches grabbed a stack and helped me carry them downstairs.

We walked into a large, messy rec room. Obviously, she hadn't been down there in a long time. Off the rec room, down a hall, was an office, and next to it a small bedroom and bathroom. A door led to the rest of the basement, which was unfinished and stacked with boxes, old lamps, old furniture, suitcases, and more. Wow, I'd honestly never seen so much stuff in one place. Heck, I never knew that anyone could even have that much stuff.

As we worked packing up things to be given away and reorganizing what Ches wanted to keep, we talked about our lives. She told me that she and Rob had been married for ten years at the time he was killed. I asked what Rob did and how they met.

"Rob was a consultant," she said. "He had expertise in setting up medical and research laboratories. He advised them about what equipment they'd need, where and how much to purchase, the best possible layout for their lab, what amount of money they'd need to get started, and where to find financing. I was a sales associate at one of the equipment companies."

"So you met because of your jobs?"

"That's right. Rob was as smart as they come, but he wasn't obnoxious about it. In fact, the reason I liked him so much right away was that he was charming and funny and always had a good time no matter what he happened to be doing. He loved every minute of life."

It was obvious she missed him terribly. I felt bad for her but didn't know what to say. We worked silently for a while as she tried to choke back her grief. Finally, she seemed to collect herself, and she said to me, "So, enough about me, tell me about your life and what you do."

"My dad left when I was six and we've never heard from him since. It was hard on my mom and so we had to keep moving around for a while. Now she has a job that pays pretty well and I work at Greenstein's Grocery every day after school. Then I do my homework. That's about all."

"So when you get home so late, what do you do for dinner?" she asked.

"Oh, sometimes my mom fixes something for us but because she works so much, I usually just open a can of soup. Sometimes I might make myself eggs or a sandwich. I keep it easy so I have plenty of time to study and go to bed."

We continued working and then Ches said, "You know, if there's anything I have in the giveaway pile that you want, you're welcome to take it."

I had been eyeing an old table and lamp I really wanted, so I was glad to hear her say that. "Thanks," I said. "I would really like that table and lamp. Maybe I can come back with the car after I finish here and pick them up."

"That would be fine."

After we finished for the day, Ches told me she felt a sense of accomplishment and thanked me for my work. "Take the things you want upstairs and I'll see you in a bit when you come to pick them up."

When I brought the stuff home and put them in our apartment, I smiled and thought how surprised Mom would be when she saw the new acquisitions. Our place was so small that it seemed to fill up by adding just those two small items. It made me feel good to have added something we needed that contributed to our comfort.

=== ===

FRIDAY TURNED OUT TO BE another chilly day. I guessed we'd be working in the basement again. Perhaps we'd finish cleaning up the storage area. I figured, between the two of us, we could get it done in about four hours.

When I rang the doorbell, Ches shouted, "C'mon in, the door's open."

I went in as Ches was walking down the stairs from the second floor. "C'mon into the kitchen," she said.

I followed her. On the table was a huge turkey club sandwich, chips, and a large glass of milk.

"I'm guessing you're hungry after school, so I thought a snack would be in order before we tackle the storage room again."

I was hungry and happy to attack that sandwich. "Thanks," I said as I started stuffing down the sandwich.

She smiled as she squeezed my arm and said, "No need to rush. Enjoy it."

I did. I could see that Ches was pleased that her efforts made me so happy. After that, there was always food waiting for me whenever I came to work.

Once we were finished cleaning up the storage area, she said, "I hope we have better weather next week. I'm anxious to start on the yard. I'm not quite ready to tackle Rob's office and the rest just yet." Then she got her purse and took out some money. "Payday." She smiled and continued, "I'm happy with what we've accomplished this week. You've done a great job, Eddie."

She handed me twenty-five dollars. "I know you give all your money to your mom, so the extra five is just for you." Once again, she smiled and squeezed my arm.

Embarrassed, I could feel my face getting hot. I really didn't know how to thank this gorgeous woman. Hell, I would've worked for her for nothing just to be able to be near her. Instead, I mumbled a garbled thank you and said, "I hope you have a nice weekend, I'll see ya Monday."

"Okay, Eddie, bye now."

==

WHEN I CAME IN TO work on Saturday morning, the first thing Mr. G said was, "So, sonny boy, how's the new job going? Is it going to work out for you?"

I told him I thought it was going to work out fine.

"Good, I'm glad to hear it. Now there's lots to do, so get busy."

We worked steadily all day and by the time I got home, I was bushed, so I just opened a can of soup, ate it, fell asleep, and didn't wake up until morning.

Mom was still asleep when I got up. I decided to let her sleep in. I did my homework, and when she got up, we talked about how our life had improved. "I hope this means we have nowhere to go but up," she said.

"Amen." I didn't know then that my life, at least, would improve greatly within a very short time.

==

I'D BEEN WORKING FOR CHES for a month now. She seemed much lighter somehow. She smiled more, and as we worked in the yard, she was humming. The yard had been neglected for so long it seemed as though we faced an impossible task. Between Monday and Wednesday, we must have raked thirty bags of leaves, pine needles, and debris. By Friday, we started clearing some of the flowerbeds. They were muddy, and I ended up getting pretty dirty.

"Eddie, come in the house and take off those dirty clothes. I'll wash them while you take a shower."

I didn't know what to say. I felt embarrassed at her sugges-
tion, but I followed her into the house and up the stairs into her
bedroom. She went to a closet and took out a terry cloth robe.

"This belonged to Rob."

Without a word, I followed her directions. When she left
the room, I looked around as I removed my dirty clothes and
put on the robe. This was the first time I had been upstairs. The
bedroom looked like it came right out of the pages of a magazine. Just like on the main floor, the furniture was black. I'd
learned in the last week that this style of furniture was called art
deco, which was making a comeback in the 1970s, and I found
that I really liked it. The colors in the room were black, yellow,
and white.

The bathroom looked huge to me. Probably half the size of
our whole apartment. Like the bedroom, it had the same colors.
I quickly took off the robe and jumped into the walk-in shower.
The water was steaming; the soap smelled wonderful and lath-
ered up into huge bubbles. I found shampoo on the shelf and
scrubbed my scalp until it tingled. I had no idea how long I
stayed in there.

When I got out, as I grabbed a bath towel, I saw myself in
the full-length mirror. This was the first time I really saw my full
body. In our apartment, the only mirror we had was a small mirror nailed up by the kitchen sink so I could see my face to shave
and Mom could put on her makeup. At school, the mirrors were
old, scarred, blackened, and cracked. The best you could do was
see enough of your hair to get it combed.

Since we had so little privacy in our small one-room apartment, I mostly got dressed under the covers. I had nailed some

hooks from the ceiling and hung a sheet when Mom needed to get dressed.

What I saw when I looked into that full-length mirror was a young man with black wavy hair, my dad's square chin and long nose, and my mom's brown eyes and forehead. My lips looked more like my mom's fuller lips than my dad's thin lips. I never realized how muscular I had become. All that work lifting and moving barrels up and down the ladder at Mr. G's had developed my arms and legs. For some reason, it embarrassed me, so I quickly put on the robe.

When I came out of the bathroom, Ches was lying on the bed wearing a robe. I jumped back, almost tripping.

"It's okay, Eddie, come here and sit down."

I could feel the shivers running down my back and the hairs on my arms stand up. *What does she want?*

"Tell me, Eddie, what do you know about sex?"

What do I know about sex? Shit, what am I supposed to say? I know what most boys my age know, I guess, and I've heard a few things around the gym and in the showers. Other than that, not much. I finally choked out a "Not very much."

"Have you ever kissed a girl?"

"No," I mumbled.

"Look at me, Eddie. It's okay. Don't be ashamed. Having sex is perfectly natural. It's a way of showing love for each other and a way of giving each other pleasure in that love. Would you like to kiss me?"

Is she kidding me? Omigod, yes. Ever since I first set eyes on those delicious pink lips, I imagined kissing them. "Yes," I said.

"Come here and lie next to me. Now gently kiss me."

I did what she told me. I couldn't believe how soft and warm her lips were. My whole body began to tingle and made my body flush with heat.

"Oh, Eddie, it just feels so good to have a man around again. To have him put his arms around me. I hope I'm not making you feel too uncomfortable."

Blushing, not knowing what to say, I said, "Um."

"It's okay, Eddie," she said. "Now, it's time for you to get dressed and go home. I'll go get your clothes from the dryer."

I closed my eyes so I could relive that moment and must have instantly fallen asleep on her bed. When I woke up, Ches was standing over me, smiling. "Here's your clothes, Eddie. Go ahead and get dressed," she said gently before leaving the room.

After I got dressed, I went down to the kitchen where Ches was making some dinner. I didn't know what to say, so I just said, "Thanks."

"You're welcome. I'll see you next time." Then she led me to the door, kissed me, and let me out.

The realization that I'd just kissed a woman for the first time, and a totally gorgeous one, left me feeling exhilarated and a little lightheaded. I smiled all the way home.

I looked forward to kissing Ches again the next time I came to work. The next time, however, turned out differently after I lay on the bed with her.

This time when I kissed her, she stuck her tongue in my mouth and set off sensations that made my body flush with heat. She put my hand on her breast and slowly moved it around. Then she guided my hand down her body and I felt myself stiffen. Ches obviously felt it too, and somehow, she slowly guided me into her. Oh. My. God. Holy shit. It took me less than two minutes. Mortified, I choked.

"It's okay, Eddie. That's to be expected the first time. You'll learn to control it."

==

OVER THE COURSE OF THE next couple of months, Ches taught me all the ways of making love. She taught me the things women like to hear. She taught me the things that gave her pleasure. She did things to me that made me feel fantastic.

After she discovered that Rob and I were approximately the same height and build, she went through his clothes and found shirts and slacks that she thought would be suitable for me with a few alterations. We had fun dressing me up in Rob's clothes. She showed me how to look good.

"How will I explain all these clothes to my mom?" I asked.

"Truthfully. Just tell her they belonged to my husband and I would rather have someone I know have them than give them away."

I was so touched by her kindness and generosity that I put my arms around her, squeezed her, and said, "I will never be able to thank you for all you've done for me."

When Mom came home and saw all the clothes hanging on the rod in the hole we called a closet, it was obvious that she was alarmed.

"Eddie, where did all those clothes come from? You didn't steal them, did you?" She began going through the clothes, checking the pockets.

I explained to her that they were Mr. VanMaster's clothes and that Mrs. VanMaster had given them to me rather than give them away.

"What a kind thing to do. She must be a really special woman."

"Yes she is, Mom, she definitely is," I said with a grin that I knew had to look goofy.

⸻

ALONG WITH THE CHANGES AT home, it amazed me how quickly things began to change at school as well. The new confidence I felt must have shown. Many of the guys began saying, "Hi, how's it goin' Eddie?" Some of the girls who'd never said anything to me stopped to talk.

Then I realized what was happening. It wasn't them—it was me who was responsible for not having made any friends before. I was the one who always walked around with my head down, making myself invisible. Suddenly, without any effort, I was now walking around smiling all the time.

SIX

ONCE SUMMER CAME AND SCHOOL was out, I was able to spend more time with Ches. One day she said to me, "All work and no play will make Eddie a dull boy. Tell me some things you'd like to do and we'll have a little fun."

Other than go to an occasional movie and to some of the parks, I'd never done much in the city. Ches decided it was time for me to expand my education. First, we went to the museum. I loved the dinosaurs and the dioramas.

Then we went to the zoo. I behaved like a little kid. I made faces at the monkeys and roared at the lions and giggled with glee. We ate ice cream and drank pop. I don't remember ever having such a wonderful day.

We also worked hard getting the outside of the house fixed up. I repaired the fence, and Ches and I painted it. Oh, how I loved watching her bend over in her little shorts. I worked extremely hard to finish so we could shower and have time to make love.

My next task involved repairing and painting the front porch. Again I worked like a dog so that Ches and I could play after we finished working. This was turning out to be the best summer I'd ever had—probably better than that of any other guy in the entire school.

Since I had no school, I was working Tuesday, Thursday, and Saturday for Mr. G. Until now, I had always given Mom every cent I earned. For the first time in my memory, I was able to save a little for me and a little bit for the future.

One day as Mr. G and I were having lunch, he said to me, "So, sonny boy, it looks like things are going better. I notice you're smiling a lot these days. Um, something going on I should know?"

I could feel my face get hot, but I tried to keep it neutral as I answered, "Yes, I'm having a good summer. With two jobs, I'm able to help my mom more. I hope that as soon as I graduate next year, I'll be able to get a full-time job, and we'll be able to move to a better place." I ignored the second part of his question.

"A noble ambition. I wish you the best. You maybe have a girlfriend, sonny boy?"

"Maybe," I said, and left it at that.

Mr. G just smiled, clamped on his pipe, and said, "Uh, huh."

═ ═

WE'D BEEN WORKING HARD AT getting the outside of the house cleaned up. So far, Ches and I had the yard in fairly good shape.

The flowers were blooming and gave the yard a very cheerful look. The trees were trimmed and the grass looked much better.

It was Monday, and I had to mow the lawn, weed, and do general yard maintenance. Ches was in the kitchen where she seemed to be doing mysterious things. She had kicked me out first thing in the morning and told me not to come back in until lunchtime.

I had just about finished when she stuck her head out the door and said, "Okay, time to come in and clean up. Lunch is ready."

After I signaled my okay, I put away the mower and all the tools. Going through the back door, a wave of wonderful smells greeted me. I couldn't tell what they were, but they sure smelled good. "Wow," I said, as I came in the door. "You've made something special today and it's already making my mouth water."

Ches gave me a big toothy smile and said, "A new lesson in sensuality today."

What the hell was she talking about? *Sexy food? Whatever, I'm up for it. I'm starving.* "I'll wash up and be right down," I said.

When I came back, I noticed she had set the table with a real tablecloth and real napkins. She'd also used the fancy dishes and stuff I'd seen in her china closet. "Is this some kinda party?" I asked.

"Yup, some kinda party. Now sit down. Food, Eddie," she said, "can be very sensual. The taste, the texture, the underlying flavors can be exciting to your senses. So, today I'm going to teach you to develop your sense of taste. First, we have some wonderful soup." She turned and went to the stove and dished out two bowls of soup that looked orange.

I hoped she knew what she was doing. It looked a little weird. I watched as she put a spoonful of what looked like sour cream in the center of the soup and sprinkled some green things on top of that.

She set a bowl in front of me. "Now swirl the cream into the bowl and then take a spoonful. Feel it going down your throat. Check the texture with your tongue. Taste the different flavors as you swallow it."

This was crazy, but I followed her directions. As the soup slid down my throat I noticed that it felt silky, and she was right, there were different flavors—sweet and spicy and hot. *Whoa.* "That is really different. You're right. I never realized there could be so many different flavors."

Her eyes sparkled. "I knew you'd be good at this."

After we finished the soup, she served some kind of meat dish with a sauce and some vegetables with stuff in it that I'd never seen before.

"Now close your eyes and open your mouth." She fed me a spoonful.

I let my tongue roll around the food and chewed slowly. I tried to follow her directions so I could feel and taste everything about it. "This is wonderful," I whispered.

She continued to feed me and talk about food. Then she leaned over and kissed me. The shivers ran down my spine. My taste buds were so revved up that I felt I'd never tasted anything like that kiss in my life. It didn't take long for me to pick her up and carry her upstairs where we spent the next two hours enjoying sensual pleasures of another kind.

IT TURNED OUT TO BE a summer full of surprises and learning. A whole world was out there that I knew nothing about. A world where things were constantly happening, and I seemed to be oblivious to it all. Sometimes Ches would turn on the TV news and explain to me what was happening. Since Mom and I didn't have a TV, up to now, my world had consisted of living day-to-day just trying to survive.

We read books and discussed them, and Ches took me around the city. I was living two lives. On Monday, Wednesday, and Friday, I found life exciting and full of new experiences. The rest of the week, I spent in my real life on Stout Street, striving to survive in the dark, depressing room my mom and I called home.

As summer came to an end, Ches decided it was time to pick up the threads of her life. "I think I'll sign up for a couple of classes at DU. I'm not sure what direction I want to go in, so this may be a good way to stick my toe in the water. I'm actually looking forward to getting out of the house."

I knew this meant the end of the long summer days we had spent together, and that made me sad. It occurred to me that this might change our relationship. I loved her so much that I didn't want anything to change. But, on the other hand, I was also looking forward to getting back to school and being a senior. When I graduated, I wanted to get a full-time job and hopefully get us moved out of that shithole of an apartment.

I was happy for Ches and hoped I had some small part in making her life better after losing her husband. "I'm glad you made a decision to do something new," I told her. I picked up the Coke I was drinking and lifted it into the air. "And here's a toast to good times."

She raised her cup of coffee and clicked my can. "To good times." Then, she kissed me on the cheek.

SEVEN

THE FIRST DAY OF SCHOOL, I saw lots of new faces. Bussing brought kids from other neighborhoods to Manual High School. I found some of the guys I'd made friends with toward the end of junior year, and we stood and looked at the new crop of girls.

I found myself having sexual thoughts about some of them. *Should I have sex with one of them? Hell no. Not when I have a beautiful woman like Ches to make love to.* I wasn't crazy, but it was still fun to look.

"Some pretty good lookin' chicks, wouldn't you say?" asked Tony.

"Yeah, I could go for a few of 'em," Joey smirked, as he ogled the girls and made obscene gestures.

Me, I just grinned and looked. "So you guys gonna do anything about it?"

"Working on it," Joey said.

"Definitely, going to make some new friends," Tony quipped.

MY DAYS RESUMED THEIR NORMAL schedule. Monday, Wednesday, and Friday at Ches's. Tuesdays and Saturdays for Mr. G. Some days when Ches was out, she'd leave some food in the fridge and a note detailing what she wanted me to do that day. I hated being alone. I badly missed making love to her on those days, but we made up for it, sometimes doing it twice when she was home.

I spent most of my spare time studying. I wanted to make sure I would graduate. I missed reading for pleasure, but school was more important.

Before I knew it, Thanksgiving was just a week away. Ches had planned to visit some friends for the week, so I wouldn't see her for several days. I helped her pack. We went over the list of things she wanted done while she was gone. Then we made love.

Afterward, Ches said, "If you'd like, bring your mom and your food here for Thanksgiving. I wouldn't mind."

"Thanks. That's nice of you. I'll ask her."

"No problem. Have a good Thanksgiving." We kissed and said goodbye.

I told Mom that Ches had offered to let us have our Thanksgiving dinner at her house.

"Really? That seems strange. It's very nice of her, Eddie, but I wouldn't feel comfortable being in someone else's kitchen."

We ate our dinner in our dreary little apartment and then went to the movies. I was bummed. On the other hand, it felt good to spend a nice day with my mom. We got to see each other so little between school and our jobs. I felt secure knowing that we wouldn't be moving in the middle of the night anytime soon.

══ ══

CHES ANSWERED THE DOOR. I could tell by looking at her that she had had a good time. She seemed to shine. "Eddie, it's good to see you, come in."

As we walked into the kitchen, she started talking nonstop, telling me what an enjoyable week she'd had. "And how was your holiday?"

"The usual. I missed you a lot." I hugged her.

She had a huge roast beef sandwich, chips, and a Coke waiting for me. "Well, I'll try to make it up to you."

I couldn't help the goofy grin on my face. "While you were gone, I took all the mail and put it in the library separated by day. It snowed, so I shoveled. Other than that, I did the other things you had on your list. Is there anything special you want me to do today?"

"Before I left, I started going through Rob's office. I want to get it cleaned out so I can turn it into an office for me. So I thought we'd start down there today."

I'd finished eating my sandwich, eager to start in hopes that we'd have time to have sex before I left.

After we'd spent about two hours sifting through Rob's stuff, Ches declared we were through for the day. "It's time for us to get reacquainted."

I was more than ready, and I could feel the anticipation spread through my crotch. I took her hand and led her up the steps. During the next hour, we definitely got reacquainted. I went home feeling happy and satisfied.

═ ═

AT THE END OF NOVEMBER, Ches studied for her finals that were scheduled for the following week. When she finished them, she announced that the Christmas season had arrived. She began baking and getting ready for the holidays. The house smelled of spices and other mysterious, delicious scents every time I came over.

About ten days before Christmas, Ches announced that she'd been invited to spend the holiday with a group of her friends in Breckenridge at their cabin. She'd be gone for Christmas until after New Year's.

I was devastated. I'd hoped to spend a lot of time with her over the holidays, since we'd both be on vacation. I tried not to show how sad and jealous that made me. I pasted a smile on my face and told her how happy I was for her.

"I'll miss you, too, but I just can't pass up this great opportunity."

"I know. I'm sure you'll have a great time."

The next couple of times I was there, I helped her wrap the gifts she'd purchased for everyone and packed them in a box. The last day, we just spent the time making love, and then she gave me the gifts she'd bought for me.

"I want you to open them now before I leave," she said.

"Okay." The first gift was a soft pullover sweater with a V-neck. "It feels so good," I said.

"Put it on." I slipped it over my head. "Now that's what I call sexy." She grinned. "Could give me ideas."

"I'll remember that and be sure to wear it all the time."

She also gave me three new books, a basket of food, and an afghan. I felt tears well up in my eyes, so I coughed to try and suppress them. I kissed her and thanked her. I clutched the afghan to me as if I'd never let it go. Then I remembered I had a gift for her too.

One day when Ches was all dressed up to go to a luncheon, she had handed me her camera and asked me to take a picture of her. When she showed the picture to me, I'd asked her if I could have it. I'd made and decorated a frame in my shop class. The teacher helped me cut a mat and frame the picture.

"It's not much, but I hope you'll like it."

She unwrapped it, and when she saw the picture, tears welled up in her eyes. "Did you make this frame?" she asked. "Of course, you did. It's the most beautiful frame I've ever seen. Thank you so much."

We hugged. I gathered up my gifts, told her to have a good time, and left. Although I was thrilled that she seemed to really like my gift, I couldn't help but feel jealous. I hated sharing her with her friends. I wanted her all to myself.

＝＝

DURING THE HOLIDAY SEASON, I experienced a deep sense of loneliness. Except for Christmas and New Year's when my mom was off, I spent my time either working for Mr. G or staying at home reading.

I went over to the house to shovel, pick up the mail, and check the furnace. The house seemed lonely and forlorn, too. Empty. No good smells. Anxiously, I waited for the holiday to be over and Ches's return.

I rushed over to the house after school the day Ches was supposed to be home. When she answered the door, I could see she was in high spirits.

"Hi Eddie. Good to see you. C'mon in. We've got lots to do."

I walked in, prepared to hug and kiss her, but she was already flying down the hall to the kitchen. There was a little nagging feeling in my stomach, but I ignored it and followed her.

"I can see that you had a good time," I said.

"Fantastic. We skied, went snowshoeing, played games, ate until we couldn't eat anymore. We slept late, stayed up until the wee hours around the fire drinking hot-buttered rum, laughed, and told stories. I can't remember the last time I had so much fun."

"I'm so happy for you." I hoped my voice sounded happier than I felt.

"And you, how was your holiday?"

"Oh, I worked and slept and read. The afghan is great. Kept me warm. I already finished the books you gave me. Maybe you want to read them?"

"Maybe I will. Now help me get things put away and then we'll work on the office again. I'm anxious to get that finished."

I did as she asked. It seemed we'd been working in the office for a long time. Ches finally thought so too. "Let's call it a day, Eddie. We're almost finished. Let's go upstairs and *visit*."

Boy was I glad to hear that. I thought she'd never get around to it. Somehow I felt she wasn't all there when we were making love, but I decided to just enjoy it and worry later.

＝＝

FEBRUARY FLEW BY. CHES WAS almost never home when I was there. She left food in the fridge and notes saying she was busy doing this or that and to please do this or that. I was unhappy, but I didn't know what to do about it.

March was the end of the quarter. Ches busied herself in the office studying for her finals.

＝＝

I'D BEEN SAVING MONEY EVER since I started working for Ches. Easter would be coming soon, and my graduation not long after. I wanted my mom to look nice for Easter and at my graduation. On the second Saturday of March, I told her, "Okay, Mom, get dressed, we're going shopping."

"What are you talking about? What do we need to go shopping for?"

I grinned. "Don't ask questions. Just get dressed and you'll see." I could see that she was tickled. It made me happy to see her happy for a change.

"I'll be ready in a jiffy."

Ches had taught me a lot about dressing, so I knew what to do and what to look for. We took the car, since I expected to have several packages to bring home. I found a space on the street, and I took Mom into Penney's. I headed straight for the women's dress department. I found a rack with just what I was looking for. The sign said, "Spring Suit Sale."

"Whatever are you doing, Eddie?"

"Mom," I said, "Mrs. VanMaster has been giving me a little extra money each week. I've been saving it all year. Easter and my graduation are coming, and I want my mom seen as the prettiest mom. Now you just let me do what I want. It's my turn to do something for you."

She blinked and teared up. Then she came over and hugged me. "Thanks, you're a wonderful son."

I went through the suits and found three that I liked. "Go try these on and see how they look." In the meantime, I found a saleslady to help us. Mom came out and modeled each of the suits. We settled on a light blue suit with a blouse to match.

I could see that Mom was having a good time now. Her cheeks were flushed with color and she and the saleslady were having conversations about each item. After we paid for the suit, I said, "Now we have to find some nice shoes and a hat to go with the suit."

"Now, Eddie, this is too much. I don't expect you to do all this for me," she protested.

Determined, I said, "Now you just be quiet. I'm the man of the house now and this is what I'm going to do."

Startled, she shut her mouth and then she broke out into the biggest smile I'd seen on her since before my dad abandoned us.

We headed to the shoe department where we found a nice pair of shoes to go with the suit. And, last, we bought a blue hat trimmed in white and a new purse. I now felt satisfied I had accomplished my mission. I gathered up all the packages and said, "Now I'm ready to go home."

One more time, Mom hugged and kissed me and said, "Thank you for a wonderful day."

—==—

IT WAS THE END OF March and finals were over, and Ches was home at last. She said to me, "Poor Eddie, I've really been ignoring you, haven't I?"

I didn't know what to say, so I kinda just shook my head and said, "I know how busy you've been."

"Yes, and April isn't going to get any better. I'm going to be working on my class project, so I'll be gone most of the time. Let's at least enjoy the rest of today."

I wasn't sure if I felt like crying or laughing. Somehow things didn't feel right, though. But, once again, I decided to savor the moment and ignore my feelings.

—==—

THE FOLLOWING SUNDAY WOULD BE Easter. On Saturday, I washed the car. I had taken good care of it all these years, and it still looked nice. I planned to take Mom to Bauer's for Easter dinner.

We lucked out. Easter turned out to be a nice, sunny day. Mom put on her new outfit.

"You look beautiful, Mom."

"Thank you, kind sir. You look handsome yourself."

I'd put on the navy blue suit Ches had given me, along with a white shirt and red tie. I felt grown up taking my mom out for a nice dinner. We both smiled a lot. It turned out to be one of the happiest days we'd had in a long time. Silently, I thanked Ches for all she had taught me.

 ══ ═

CHES WASN'T KIDDING. I DIDN'T see her at all the first two weeks of April. I no longer smiled every day. Most of my time was spent feeling jealous and mad.

As I walked to school on the third Wednesday of April, I realized I felt happy. It must have been because it finally stopped raining and the trees had begun to bud and the grass was green and smelled fresh. I hoped Ches would be home. I knew she didn't have any classes or clubs that week.

After school, I whistled on the way to her house. I rang the doorbell and heard her coming down the hall. I knew this would be my lucky day.

She opened the door and said, "We have to talk. C'mon into the kitchen."

Somehow, I knew this wasn't going to be good. I could feel my gut clench as I sat down at the table. Ches reached across and took my hand.

"Eddie, I'm not sure how to say this, so I'll just spit it out. I've met a wonderful man. We're in love, and we're going to be married."

It seemed as if the blood was draining from my body. I felt cold and sweaty at the same time. I could hear Ches talking, but she sounded as if she were far away. I tried to listen.

"I'm sure you've always known in the bottom of your heart that our relationship wouldn't last forever. You're a young man just starting out. I'm an older woman at a time in my life when I'm ready to experience more of life, like possibly creating a family, a business, and even traveling. You know I'll always have a special place in my heart for you," she added, looking at me as if she expected me to say something. The lump in my throat kept me from saying anything. Tears burned behind my eyes.

Then she continued. "I want you to have this gift for graduation." She took an envelope out of her pocket and put it in my hands. "Don't open it until you get home. I want to thank you for all that you've done. You've not only helped me physically clean up my life, but mentally as well. And, I thank you for that. Now, Eddie, it's time for us to say goodbye and time for you to leave." She got up from the table and guided me toward the front door.

As she opened the door for me, she gave me a kiss on the cheek. "Take care, Eddie. Have a good life. I know you'll do well."

Numb, I somehow walked down the steps and out of the gate.

Abandoned. Again. I cried all the way home.

EIGHT

AS SOON AS I GOT into our apartment, I lay down on my mattress, covered myself with my afghan, and cried and punched my mattress until I was exhausted and had no more tears left.

The envelope was on the floor next to me. I reached over to get it and read the front of the card. When I opened it, a wad of money fell out. After counting it, I realized Ches had given me $500 as a goodbye gift. Omigod, I'd never seen so much money in my life. I wasn't sure how I felt about it.

I needed time to think. What should I tell my mom? Should I tell her about the money? How should I tell her I no longer worked for Ches? Questions, questions. I decided I'd give myself a week to think it over and make a decision. In the meantime, I took the money and hid it in a sock and put it in the bottom of the box where I stored my underwear, socks, and shirts.

Mom was working residential for the week, which meant that she had the day shift and would be home every night for dinner.

I hadn't told her yet that I was no longer working for Ches, so I spent Monday and Wednesday afternoons shooting hoops with Tony and Joey. We ended up at the drugstore. We ordered Cokes, and after they left, I sat at the table and did my homework. I went home at the same time I'd have returned if I were still working. I decided I would tell Mom on Friday—not about the money, just about not working anymore. In the meantime, I asked Mr. G if I could work an extra day each week and he said okay.

After dinner on Friday, I planned to go to the library to return our books and get new ones. "Mom, are you ready to go to the library yet?"

She sat in the rocking chair. "If you don't mind, I think I'll stay home tonight. I'm so tired. I think I'd just like to rest."

Damn, I'd planned to tell her on the ride to the library. "It's okay, Mom. Any special book you want?"

"How about some mysteries, for a change?"

"Sure thing, Mom." I kissed her on the forehead. "See ya later."

On the way home from the library, I planned what I would say. I parked the car and took the stairs two at a time, eager to get my story out. I opened the door to our apartment and saw Mom still in the rocker, apparently asleep.

I walked over to her and gently started to shake her. Suddenly, I realized she wasn't breathing. She looked very pale. I bent down to listen to her heart and couldn't find a heartbeat. I put my mouth to her face to see if I could feel her breath, but there was none.

Oh shit, oh shit, oh shit. She's dead. My mom is dead! I tried to think what I should do. I felt in my pants pockets for some change. I ran to the telephone in the hall and called Mr. G, figuring he'd just be getting ready to leave.

"Greenstein's Cash Grocery. Can I help you?"

"Mr. G. This is Eddie. Mr. G, I think my mom is dead. What should I do?" I started to cry.

"Did you say you think your mom is dead?"

"Yes," I said through my tears.

"Just stay put. I'll be right there. It'll be okay, Eddie. I'm coming. Call the police and ask them to send an ambulance."

After I called the police, I went back into the apartment and once again took my mom's hand and checked her wrist for a pulse. Nothing.

Mr. G came bursting into the apartment, panting from running up the stairs. He came over to my mom and felt for a pulse and listened for a heartbeat. He looked at me and shook his head. "I'm so sorry, Eddie. What happened?"

"I don't know. She said she was tired and wasn't going to go to the library with me. She just wanted to rest, so I went by myself. When I came home this is how I found her."

At that moment, two policemen came rushing in. They ran over to Mom and checked her. "What happened here, son?" the first officer asked.

"I don't know. When I came home this is how I found her. I thought she was sleeping, and I tried to wake her up and I couldn't. So I called Mr. Greenstein."

By this time, the guys from the ambulance came rushing in and ran over to my mom. They examined her and one of them said, "I'm sorry, son."

Officer Bennett, the taller of the two officers, had more questions for me. "What about your father? Where is he?"

"My dad left years ago. I have no idea where he is, or if he's even alive."

"Any other family, son?"

"Nope. It was just me and my mom." I felt dizzy. As I started to fall, Mr. G caught me and eased me down into a chair.

He went to the sink and poured a glass of water. "Here, Eddie, take a drink."

I drank the water and felt a little better. The officers were talking to the ambulance medics. Then Officer Bennett came over to me. "Eddie, we'll have to take your mother to the morgue. The medical examiner will want to do an autopsy."

Confused, I looked to Mr. G for answers.

He said, "Officer Bennett, can you explain to Eddie exactly what's going to happen and how long it will take? And, is there anything he needs to do?"

Officer Bennett told me it might take a few days for the autopsy. Then the body would be released to whatever mortuary I chose. Then she could be buried.

I had no words. I just shook my head. I realized then that Mom had never taken off her wedding band. While the ambulance guys readied their gurney, I picked up her hand and removed the ring, putting it in my pocket. I watched as they put my mom on the gurney, covered her up, and took her away. The second officer went with them. I grabbed Mr. G and wailed. "What should I do?"

Officer Bennett asked, "Eddie, do you have someone else you can stay with? If not, will you be okay here alone?" Then he gestured to Mr. G. "Is it okay to leave him here with you?"

"Fine, Officer. I'll take care of things."

Officer Bennett wrote a few more notes on his pad. "Okay, I'm going to leave now. He handed me a card with his name and telephone number on it. "If you need any information, call me. I'm sorry about your mom." He glanced around the room one last time and departed.

Mr. G and I just sat there without speaking for the next few minutes. Then he broke the silence. "I know this is hard, but we have to talk about a few things. There are decisions that you'll need to make. First, where will your mom be buried and who will perform the service? Do you belong to a church?"

"My mom gave up on religion when my dad left us. I've been going to the Baptist Church off and on for the last couple of years."

"Yes. I know the pastor there, Doug Peterson. He's been a customer for years. If it's okay with you, I'll call him and ask him what we can do."

"Would you? Thanks . . . that would be great." I felt relieved. Mr. G would get me through this.

"Another thing. What's the name of the company your mom worked for and what is her boss's name? I'll have to call him tomorrow, too."

"It's Jackson's Complete Cleaning Service. Her boss is Ted Jackson. I have the number here." I shuffled through my books and pulled out my notebook. I tore out a page and wrote down Ted Jackson's number. "Here, Mr. G, here's the number."

He pocketed it. "Good, I'll make both these calls in the morning. Now, are you going to be okay here alone? Tell me the truth. If not, we'll figure out something. You're welcome to come home with me and stay at our house. If you're okay, then I'll be getting along. Mrs. G will be wondering where I am."

I gulped. *Will I be okay? I have to be. I have no other choice.* "I'll be fine. You go home. Thanks for everything, Mr. G."

He patted me on the back as he got up. "I'll be in touch in the morning. Try to get some rest."

I followed Mr. G to the door and locked it after he left. Then I collapsed on my mattress and let the tears flow that had been building. My mind filled with memories, with questions, with all kinds of thoughts. I guess I fell asleep for a short time.

When I woke up, it was still dark outside and I started to feel really bad. It was my fault my mom died. If only I'd been a better son. I should have quit school and gotten a job so she didn't have to work so hard. Oh, God, what was I going to do now? I felt so alone. I'd never felt so alone in my life. Not when my dad abandoned us, not when Ches said goodbye. And I felt cold. I wrapped the afghan around me as tight as I could, but still my veins seemed to have ice water running through them.

Oh shit, oh shit. What am I going to do?

＝＝

MORNING CAME AND I GOT up. As I stared at the rocking chair, last night's scene replayed itself in my head.

I struggled with the memories as I dressed. I was sitting at the table eating when a knock sounded at the door.

"Eddie, it's me. Mr. Greenstein."

I opened the door and he came in. "I talked to the pastor last night. I explained your situation to him and he said that he would be happy to perform the service and have your mother buried in the Baptist cemetery."

I choked with relief. "How can I ever thank you, Mr. G? But . . . how can I pay for it? Will it cost a lot? I don't have much money."

"Stop right there. Don't worry about it. I also talked to Ted Jackson. He was sorry about your mom. He told me that he would see that you get your mom's last paycheck on Monday. He also told me that your mom had a $1,000 life insurance policy through the company. You can use part of that to pay for the funeral. The rest will help you until you graduate and get a full-time job."

It took a few minutes for this to get through the fog in my brain. Then I embraced Mr. G. "I don't know what to say. I'm just so grateful for everything you've done."

"It's okay, Eddie. No one should have to go through such a thing alone. Now I've got to get to work. Is there anything else I can do for you before I leave? Remember the invitation is still open to stay with us. And as soon as we hear that your mom's body has been released, we'll get the funeral together."

"I'm okay, but I don't think I'll get in to work."

"Of course not. I certainly didn't expect you to work today."

═══

AFTER HE LEFT, I WANDERED around the room, trying to decide what to do. I had put the ring on my little finger, so first I took it off and put it in the envelope with the money. I went to the rack where Mom's clothes hung and removed them and laid them on her bed. I set aside her blue suit. Then I took her things out of the boxes that she used for a dresser and picked out the matching blouse that I had bought for her. Then I found her best underwear and some stockings and her new shoes. Carefully, I packed them into a box. I had made the decision that this outfit was what she should be buried in.

Then I took the rest of the clothes and packed them in a separate box. I wasn't sure what I was going to do with those things, but until I decided, they wouldn't be staring me in the face as a reminder. Right now, it hurt too much to think about it.

I spent the rest of the afternoon in a haze. Some people from the building stopped by, and a couple of them brought food. I felt bad taking it, because I knew they were all having a hard time getting by.

Later, Mrs. Greenstein came over with a huge basket of food. "If you need anything, you be sure and let me know." She unpacked the basket and put the food away as best she could. "I'm so sorry about your mom. Such a tragedy, such a terrible waste. She was much too young . . ." Her voice trailed off for a moment, then she spoke again, trying to sound optimistic. "But you're a strong young man, Eddie. You'll get along. And don't you forget you can always call on us for help and a place to stay if you need it."

I thanked her for the food and promised to call. I realized I hadn't eaten anything since breakfast, so I made some dinner. Funny, all the food looked and smelled delicious, but for some reason, it tasted like sawdust.

By the time I finished cleaning up, I was exhausted. I lay down on my mattress in hopes of getting some sleep. I couldn't help but think about both Ches and my mom and the feeling of being totally alone. No one to talk to, no one to care about. Once again, I thought about my dad and how angry I was that he did this to us. I slept in fits and starts. In the morning, I felt as tired as when I went to bed.

As I ate breakfast, I tried to figure out what to do. Since it was Sunday, perhaps I would find some peace by going to church. At least I would be among other people and wouldn't have to spend the whole day alone.

━ ━

PASTOR PETERSON STOOD AT THE front door welcoming people as they came in. When he saw me, he came over and clasped my hands in his. "I'm so sorry for your loss, Eddie. I will do what I can to help you out. God will give you strength to go on."

Struggling for words, I finally managed to say, "Thank you."

I found a measure of peace and comfort in the service, but I didn't stop to talk to anyone afterward. Even among all these people, I had this terrible feeling of loneliness. It just seemed too difficult to try and have any conversations.

Back at the apartment, the knowledge overwhelmed me that now I really was alone. An orphan. I was an orphan. I had no one to care about me.

I wept until I had no more tears left. *Stop it, Eddie. Pull yourself together. You must make a plan.* I remembered the money that Ches had given me. *Okay, I have some money to get by for now. I'll have Mom's last paycheck, and I'll have her life insurance. I'll have some money from Mr. G too. I've got to finish school. It's only a little over four weeks until graduation. I can do it. Then I'll find a full-time job and get the hell outta this shithole.* With these thoughts, I felt better.

Someone knocked on the door. "Who's there?"

"It's Officer Bennett."

I opened the door. "C'mon in."

"Thanks, Eddie. How are you doing, today?" He peered at me.

"I'm okay. Everybody's been very nice."

"Glad to hear it. Just wanted to let you know that your mom's body will be released tomorrow. The medic and I talked with the coroner about your situation and what happened. He was able to do the autopsy yesterday and found that your mom died of a heart attack. No need to do anything further."

"Thanks a lot, Officer Bennett. I appreciate everything you've done."

"You're welcome, Eddie. Take care." He left.

I found some change and went down the hallway to call Mr. G. He was pleased that Officer Bennett had expedited the autopsy. He promised to call the pastor.

"I think we should have the funeral on Tuesday. Would that be okay?"

"Fine, I have the clothes picked out that I want my mom buried in. What should I do with them?"

"I'll let you know after I talk to Pastor Peterson."

A short while later, he called me back. "It's all set. The funeral will be on Tuesday. Tomorrow you can take the clothes to the mortuary. Pastor Peterson will meet us there and we can complete the arrangements."

FIRST THING ON MONDAY, I called school and let them know what had happened. I told them I'd try to be back in school on Wednesday.

"Don't worry. Do what you must do. Come back as soon as you can." The principal, Mr. Jordan, seemed pleased that I had called. "Please accept my condolences, Eddie. I'm deeply sorry for your loss."

"Thanks, Mr. Jordan." I said goodbye and hung up.

That afternoon, Mr. G and I went to the mortuary. He helped me pick out a simple casket. I promised to pay for it as soon as I got the insurance check. The director told me that would be fine. I didn't know it at the time, but Mr. G had arranged to pay the major portion of the expenses, and the church was also picking up some of the tab. Since I had no idea what a funeral cost, I was happy that I was able to pay the $200.

I'D NEVER BEEN TO A funeral before, and I didn't know what to expect. First, there were more people than I expected. Besides Mr. and Mrs. G, there were several people from work, including Mom's boss, Mr. Jackson. Some church members that I had met over the last couple of years also attended, and some people from our apartment building came. The Greensteins sat with me. Mrs. G placed her hand over mine during the service.

I liked the way the pastor spoke about my mom. *But where did he get all this information about her?* I wondered. He told everyone what a good mother she had been, doing her best to take care of me all these years. He told the group what a good worker she had been and how much her coworkers liked her.

After the service, we went to the cemetery. When they lowered the casket into the ground, I lost it for a few minutes. I pulled myself together and tried to remain stone-faced until they finished. Pastor Peterson invited everyone to join me in the social hall for refreshments.

This surprised me, too. I didn't know that the church ladies had prepared food for after the service. Several of my mother's coworkers sat with me at lunch and talked to me about my mom. I learned more about how much they all had loved her. After everyone left, Mrs. Greenstein drove me back home. Mr. G had left after the service. He didn't like to be away from the store for too long.

As promised, before he left the service, Mr. Jackson had given me the cash for my mom's last paycheck. I put it with the money Ches had given me until I figured out exactly what to do. *Shit, should I have called Ches and let her know? Damn, I haven't even thanked her for the money.* I put those thoughts out of my mind. Right now I was too exhausted from the events of the day and needed to lie down.

As I lay there, I realized that now I was a man, responsible for my own life. Me, no one else. No one else to care about me or worry about me. The realization made me shudder, and the sense of aloneness threatened to overtake me. I understood I needed to take charge and figure out how I would manage my life. Ches had taught me that there was a whole big world out there. I knew I must finish school, get a job, and get away from here as soon as possible.

I tore a piece of paper out of my notebook and listed the expenses that I would have during the next few weeks until I graduated. I also had to plan for time to look for a full-time job and wait for my first full-time paycheck. I estimated that I would need money for a few months to supplement what I would make working part-time for Mr. G.

I chewed on my pencil. *Um . . . rent, utilities, car insurance, gas, food . . . what else?* My brain felt fuzzy. *Hmm . . . keep the list and add to it anything else that needs to be paid.*

Then I counted my money. I wasn't quite sure what the final funeral expenses would be. At least the $200. When all was said and done, I should still end up with around $1,300 set aside. A huge sum of money, in my mind. *I should be able to live on that for quite some time with my earnings from Mr. Greenstein.*

Satisfied that I had done everything I could for the moment, I let loose the tears that I'd been swallowing and thought about how much I missed my mom.

NINE

THE NEXT MORNING, I GOT dressed and went to school. Mrs. Mason, the secretary, told me that the principal wanted to see me. As I entered his office, Mr. Jordan stood and came around his desk. He shook my hand and said, "Eddie, I'm so sorry about your mom. Let me know if there's anything we can do to help. I want to make sure that you graduate."

"Thanks. I'm okay. I absolutely plan to graduate."

He patted me on the shoulder. "Okay, Eddie, better get to class now. Don't forget, anything you need."

He ushered me out of his office, and I quickly headed to my first class. I felt out of it. All the teachers were nice and gave me a minimum amount of homework to catch up on from the previous week. My friends, Tony and Joey, hung around with me all day helping me get through it.

THE NEXT COUPLE OF DAYS passed by in a blur. I was happy when the weekend came. It helped that I had to go to work on Saturday. I wouldn't have time to sit and think about my future. Mr. G kept me busy, and my whole body burned with exhaustion when I got home. I fixed a couple of eggs, some bacon, and toast. I sat down to eat when someone knocked on the door.

"Who's there?" I shouted as I got up from the table.

"It's L.T."

Oh shit! L.T. lived upstairs. His real name was Lawrence Thomas Sanders, but everyone called him L.T. He was a mean son-of-a-bitch who weighed about 300 pounds. If he wore a pullover shirt, it crawled up over his fat, hairy belly. Gross. His black hair always looked greasy, and he had slits for eyes and a big ugly nose with hair growing out of it.

Funny, though. L.T. had always been nice to my mom. He always greeted her politely, and if she was carrying groceries or something, he helped her. He usually just grunted at me.

I went over to the door and opened it a crack.

"Eddie, just stopped by to say I'm sorry about your mom."

"Thanks. That's nice of you." I wanted to shut the door on him so he'd go away.

"Okay if I come in?" he said.

"Um . . . I guess so." I was scared to say no. I opened the door wide enough for him to enter. He lumbered in and sat down in my mom's rocking chair. I hoped he wouldn't break it.

"Eddie, what are your plans now?"

I wanted to say, "None of your fucking business!" Instead I said, "To finish school and work."

"Smart kid. I always thought you were a smart kid. So I have a little job I want you to do for me. I'll pay you twenty-five bucks." He eyed me to see if he could tell what I was thinking.

Damn. Everyone knew that L.T. was a big-time gambler. Rumor had it that he paid for his gambling by dealing drugs. I didn't want any part of L.T. and his business. I didn't know what to say.

"What did you have in mind?"

"Simple. I have this package. You walk around the block. A guy will come up and hand you an envelope. You take the envelope and give him the package. Then bring the envelope back to me."

I'd lived on Stout Street long enough to know that this was a drug delivery. I didn't want to do it, but I feared what L.T. might do if I said no.

"I'm not sure, L.T.," I said. "I need to go to work, catch up on my studies—"

"It'll only take a few minutes. Tomorrow morning, kid. I'll come down and get you." He punched me in the arm and got up to leave. "See ya in the morning."

"Yeah, right." I closed the door and collapsed on the bed. *Fuck! What am I getting myself into?* I managed to swallow my dinner and then went to bed, hoping that I'd fall asleep fast so I wouldn't have to think about what was going down the next day.

==

I DIDN'T SLEEP WELL, WORRYING about L.T., and I woke up with a wicked headache. I found an aspirin and drank some orange juice. Then I decided I'd better eat a real breakfast, hoping it would make me feel better.

Then I waited. The time dragged. About ten-thirty, there was a knock on the door. "Hey kid, it's me, L.T."

I went to the door and motioned him to come in.

"Here's the package. Walk around the block, Stout to Champa. The guy should find you in a few minutes. I'll wait here for you."

I wasn't thrilled about having him wait in my apartment for me, but I didn't know what else to do.

"I'm on my way," I said.

Everything went as planned. The transaction took all of five minutes, and I was back at the apartment within ten minutes.

L.T. waited at the window, watching. As soon as he spotted me, he came out of the apartment and met me at the top of the stairs. He took the envelope and turned his back to me while he opened it. Then he grunted, turned to me, and said, "Good job, kid." Then he handed me twenty-five dollars and waddled down the hall to the stairs and up to his apartment.

I ran into my place, slammed the door, and ran to the box where my money was hidden. Nothing had been disturbed. The money was still there. I counted it to make sure nothing had been taken. Relieved, I hoped that L.T. wouldn't bother me again, but I knew it was foolish on my part to think he'd leave me alone. *Just let me graduate and get the hell outta here.*

The next week passed uneventfully. I caught up on my homework and did my best to keep up on my studies, and I worked at the grocery store. The insurance check came on Friday. I hid it with the rest of my money.

Mr. Greenstein had promised to help me open a checking account when the money came. Mom and I never had a checking account. She was paid in cash, and we paid for everything that way.

I breathed a sigh of relief. I hadn't seen L.T. all week.

＝＝

AFTER DINNER ON SATURDAY NIGHT, I was listening to the radio when there was a banging on my door.

"It's me, L.T. Answer the door, kid."

I didn't want to see L.T., but I didn't know what to do. I opened the door a crack, and L.T. came bursting through. He grabbed me by the arm and dragged me out into the hall.

"We're having a party, kid. You're invited."

I tried to escape, but that son-of-a bitch was too damn strong. I screamed, but to no avail. For sure nobody would try to interfere with L.T. He continued dragging me upstairs to his apartment.

"Open up," he shouted. The door opened, and he pushed me in.

The stench of sweat, urine, and marijuana gagged me. L.T. threw me in a chair. Two other guys were in the room. I'd seen them around here, but I didn't know who they were. They were smoking shit and laughing it up.

"So, it's party time for the kid, huh?" the one with the glasses said.

"Yeah, party time, alright." He gestured to both of them. "Hold him down while I get his party favors ready."

The two guys grabbed me and held me down. Horrified, I watched L.T. get a needle ready. Oh shit, he wanted to make me an addict so I'd come work for him. I tried to kick and get away, but it didn't do any good.

"Calm down, kid. Relax, you'll love it." He stuck the needle in my arm.

Things got crazy. I thought I could fly. Man, I never felt like this in my life. I remember laughing so hard my belly hurt, and then it was like a nightmare. I must have passed out.

— —

I WOKE UP IN MY apartment on the floor feeling like shit. My head ached. So did every bone in my body. I had no idea what time it was; I only saw that it was still dark. Suddenly, I became cold sober. *I have to get away from here. Now!* I picked myself up off the floor and got the box where my underwear, money, and mom's ring were hidden and put it on the bed. Took a couple hundred out and stuffed it into my wallet.

As quickly and quietly as I could, I got things together. On the bottom of the box, I packed the afghan and sweater from Ches, my clothes, toiletries, and the envelope with the money. I placed my books and shoes on the top. Then I noticed the angel figurine that Mom kept by her bed. I grabbed it and put it in one of the shoes. Quietly opening the door, I peered out into the hall. Everything was quiet. With my pulse racing and heart pounding, I opened the door wider, picked up the box, and crept into the hall in my stocking feet.

Melting into the wall, I waited. Silence. I sneaked down the hall to the back stairs and stared into the dark stairwell.

Nothing. Balancing the box carefully, I slowly walked down the stairs to the back door.

I looked out. Again everything was quiet. No one was in the parking lot. Silently, I stepped outside, took a deep breath, and slithered over to the car. Opening the door slowly, I shoved the box in and got into the car and shut the door.

Holding my breath, I turned on the ignition, backed out into the alley, and drove slowly down to Park Avenue. Then I sped up and drove as fast as possible to East Colfax. After turning onto Colfax, I began looking right and left for a place to stop. All the while I thanked my dad, bum that he was, that he taught me early on to take care of the car and always make sure it was ready for any emergency. Once more, it was providing me with a means of escape.

The few motels I passed seemed too close by, so I kept driving. I tried to formulate a plan. Finally, I spotted a motel that seemed like it might work. The front office took up most of the space on Colfax. It looked like the bulk of the rooms were in the rear. I found the alley and drove to the back. Perfect. There were some rooms close to the alley that couldn't be seen from the street. I then drove back to the front of the motel. The sign said "Sleep Inn." Underneath it said, "$5.00 a night." The vacancy sign was still on.

I parked, put my shoes on, got out, and locked the door. I checked the street and sidewalk. Nobody was looking for me or watching me. Everything seemed quiet. A bell tinkled as I opened the door. A middle-aged man, startled by the noise, jumped up from the chair where he sat watching TV. He came over to the counter.

"Can I help you?"

I'd had a plan, but I wasn't sure how to start, so I just plunged in. "Hello. My name is Eddie Anderson, and I want to rent a room for several weeks."

He gave me a surprised look. I launched into how my mom died and I was alone. "I need a place to stay until I graduate high school and get a job. I'd be willing to pay twenty-five dollars a week in advance for six weeks." I took a breath and waited for him to answer.

He had listened intently during my recital and kept watching me. Finally, he spoke. "Well now, I don't have the authority to do what you want. What I can do is rent you a room for tonight. I'll tell the owner your story and you can come in and talk to him tomorrow."

"Thanks, I'd appreciate anything you can do. I'll take a room for tonight. A room in the back, if possible. I need a quiet spot away from the street so I can study."

"Done," he said. "My name is Al and I'm here almost every night." He took a key from the rack behind him and handed it to me. "This is for Room 130 and it is in the back."

Taking the key, I thanked him, got in the car, and drove around to the room. Inside the room, I took my box of stuff and put it in the closet opening. Then I surveyed the room.

The furniture and carpet were old and somewhat worn but exceptionally clean. The drapes and spread looked fairly new. The room appeared to be sparkling clean, but somehow it struck me as odd, and I didn't know why.

The same in the bathroom. The fixtures were old but shiny clean. White, fluffy towels hung from the towel bar, with extras on a shelf above. The room reminded me of the first time I took a shower at Ches's. *Forget it, Eddie. But shit, why didn't I do this before? This beats Stout Street all to hell. A real bathroom.*

The adrenalin of the last couple of hours drained from my body. Exhaustion took over. I shook as though I was experiencing an earthquake. Then I collapsed on the bed and passed out.

= =

THE ROOM WAS LIGHT WHEN I woke up. The clock on the nightstand said eleven o'clock. When was the last time I slept that late? My body still ached and I was ravenous. I got out of bed and took a shower. The hot water streaming over my body took away most of the aches and pains.

My mouth still tasted like shit, so I brushed my teeth. I dressed in clean clothes. Still starving, I decided to find a place to have breakfast. I would go to the office later and talk to the owner about staying here for the next few weeks.

I opened the door and checked to see if anyone was around. The coast was clear, so I strolled through the alley to Colfax. After about a block, I spied a small coffee shop.

The smell of fresh coffee, cinnamon rolls, and bacon greeted me as I entered. A waitress who was walking by with a pot of coffee motioned me to the back of the room. I followed her pointing finger and found a small table for two in the back.

In a few minutes, the waitress returned, took my order, and poured a cup of coffee. I settled back in my chair and observed the crowd. There were young couples, families, single guys like me, and a few groups of elderly people enjoying a Sunday breakfast together. I relaxed as I breathed in the delicious smells of bacon, eggs, and pancakes.

After such a gigantic meal, I knew I needed some exercise, so I jogged back to the motel. I went into the office and saw a young-ish looking man on a ladder painting over a repair on the wall.

Suddenly, I knew what struck me as odd in the room: the precise way that the furniture was placed, about four inches from the wall and four inches from the edge. Same with the floor lamps. They all looked to be the same distance from the wall. *Obviously military.*

The man had a standard military haircut. His shirt was precisely starched and buttoned. The crease in his pants, knife sharp. Shoes polished until they shone. No wonder everything was so clean.

"Good morning," he said. "Have a cup of coffee. I'll be through here in a minute." He pointed to a table in the corner.

"Thanks, I will."

I fixed myself a cup and sat down to wait. Within a few minutes, he was finished, and as he stepped down the ladder, I could see the tattoo on his arm: Semper Fi. He closed the paint can, put the brush in a pail, folded up the ladder, and came over to me.

"I'm Jeff Stevens, the owner," he said as he extended his hand. "How can I help you?"

I took his hand. *Firm grip.* "I'm Eddie Anderson. I checked in last night. I spoke with Al and told him that I'd like to stay for the next few weeks. He told me to talk to you in the morning."

"Yes. Al told me." He walked behind the counter and picked up some papers. "I'd like to hear your story from you." He focused his gray eyes on mine.

I recounted the story I'd told Al. Jeff listened until I finished. "I'm sorry for your loss. I understand how tough things are for you right now. Here's what I'll do. You can stay for two weeks. If at the end of that time, there's been no problems, then you can stay until you find a job and get settled. So right now, I'll accept your advance for the two weeks."

I breathed a sigh of relief and held out my hand. "Thanks, Mr. Stevens. I really appreciate it." I took out my wallet and handed him fifty dollars.

"You're welcome. You can call me Jeff, Eddie. Just a couple of ground rules. Since you'll be here by the week, the maid will only clean your room and change the linens and towels twice a week. No loud noise or guests after ten. Okay?"

"No problem. I'm not familiar with the area. Could you tell me if there's a grocery store around? Also, can you tell me about the bus so I can figure out how to get to school?"

"Of course. There's a neighborhood grocery store about three blocks from here." Jeff took a piece of paper and drew a map for me. "Carbone's is the name. There's also a small produce store and a tea and spice shop."

Then he took a bus schedule from the rack on the wall and circled the right bus and times for me. "Anything else just let me know. I hope everything is going to work out okay for you."

I picked up the map and bus schedule, said goodbye, and went back to my room. Time to unpack, get some groceries, study, and make a plan. I took the little angel figurine out of my shoe and looked around the room. Then I put it on the nightstand next to the bed. *God, I miss you so much, Mom.*

After I put away my clothes, I checked out the small kitchenette. As with everything else, the fridge, stove, and sink were sparkling clean. The cupboards and drawers were well stocked with the usual kitchen stuff. Good. I can easily cook and eat right here in my room. Checking the time, I decided I'd better get to the store right away so I'd have some food for dinner and breakfast.

I followed the map to Carbone's. It reminded me of Mr. G's, only bigger. I took a basket and picked up some cereal, eggs, milk, and bread. Then I walked over to the case and looked in to see if there might be something I could buy for dinner.

The woman behind the case looked up at me and said, "Yes, young man, what can I get for you?" She was an ample woman with jet black hair. Her cheeks were rosy. A bead of sweat trickled down the side of her face. She swiped at the sweat and said, "Whew, it's very warm in here today."

I nodded my head and surveyed the goods in the case. I saw spaghetti and meatballs, lasagna, various salads, and other things that I couldn't quite make out. "The meatballs and spaghetti look good."

"Good choice. And a good helping of salad. I'll throw in some garlic bread. You'll have a good meal, I guarantee."

I gave her a big grin. "Thanks, sounds just right."

She loaded up everything in a brown shopping bag. "Anything else?"

"No, thanks." I took the bag and the rest of my groceries and headed toward the front counter. I spied the produce bin and stopped to pick up a couple of oranges. As I stood in line waiting to pay, I looked around just to be sure that nobody was watching me.

After I paid, I strolled back to the motel. L.T. didn't know it, but he did me a big favor by getting me out of Stout Street. This was the kick in the butt I needed.

When I got back to my room, I checked again to make sure nobody was following me before I opened the door. Then I put away the food and decided to watch TV for a while. Another luxury. I used to watch with Ches. God, how I missed her. I thought about all the things she taught me and the good times we had. How could she have dumped me like she did? Would the wound in my heart ever heal?

Following the evening news, I ate my dinner, did my homework, and went to bed. I was still exhausted from the events of Saturday. Even though the day had gone well, it was stressful getting approval to stay from Jeff, checking out the neighborhood, and trying to get a little organized. At least I was safe.

TEN

SEVERAL TIMES DURING THE NIGHT, I woke up in a cold sweat from nightmares. L.T. chasing me with a giant needle, wild animals chasing me and trying to eat me. I woke up terrified at the thought of going to school and perhaps finding L.T. waiting for me.

Finally, I forced myself to get out of bed, shower, shave, and have breakfast. With a great deal of trepidation, I left the motel, checking to make sure no one was there.

It turned out that I had no problem getting to school. There didn't seem to be anyone suspicious on the bus, and when I got near the school, I didn't see anyone waiting for me. Just to be safe, though, I ducked into the library until school began.

After school, I decided to walk home so I could clear my head. Remembering that I needed to call Mr. G and let him know what had happened, I started jogging, then slowed to a brisk walk, and finally ran until I got back to the motel.

I stopped in the office before heading to my room. Jeff was sitting at the desk, doing paperwork. "Hey, Eddie. Home from school?" he asked, looking up from his work.

"Yeah. I just came in to find out how to use the phone in my room."

"Sure. Just pick it up and dial nine. You'll get a dial tone, and then you can make your call. It will register to your room and you can pay at the end of the week."

"Thanks." I waved and left.

When I got into the room, I threw down my books and sat at the desk to call Mr. G. As soon as he answered, the story of the weekend poured out of me so fast that Mr. G kept telling me to slow down so he could digest what had happened.

"That's some story, sonny boy," he said when I finished. "I'm so sorry. First things first. Are you okay, and is there anything you need?"

"I'm fine." I told him where I was and gave him the address. "I don't want you to let anyone know that you know where I am. That would be dangerous. I won't be able to work for you anymore. I have to stay out of the neighborhood. But I still want you to go with me to open an account at the bank, if you would. I have the insurance check and I need to pay for Mom's funeral."

"Of course. Let me think for a minute." He paused. "Tell you what. Call me back in an hour or so and I'll make arrangements for tomorrow after school. Okay?"

"Sure." I hung up and sat there for a minute to collect my thoughts. Then I took out a piece of paper and wrote down some ideas.

Final grades will be in next week.

*Talk to the principal and see if I can get my diploma and skip
  the graduation ceremony.*

I'd wanted to go to graduation, I'd worked so hard, but no
one would be there except maybe someone I didn't want, like
L.T. Best not to be visible.

I contemplated my immediate future. *What kind of job do I
want to look for? The only thing I know is the grocery business. Do I
have any special talent or burning ambition? No. I have no idea what
I want to do. Perhaps I should just walk Colfax and check out the different businesses. Look around the neighborhood. See what's going on.
Yes, that's it. I'll start doing that tomorrow. Maybe I'll talk to Mr. G
about it when I see him tomorrow.*

I continued my list:

Look for a new job.

*Check the neighborhood to see what kinds of apartments or
  places there are where I can live.*

I knew I couldn't stay at the motel forever. Although it
would be nice, and it sure was a step up from where I'd lived up
to now, it was too expensive.

I sat there a few more minutes and couldn't think of anything else, so I went into the kitchen and poured myself a glass
of milk. Then I remembered that I hadn't checked to make sure
my money was still where I had hid it. It was still there—all of it.
I turned on the TV, anxious for the time to pass so I could call
Mr. G back.

When I called, he said he would pick me up at three-thirty.
"I found a nice bank for you on East Colfax that I think will
work for you."

"Sounds good to me. I'll see you tomorrow. Come down the alley and pick me up in back. You'll see my car parked in front of my room."

Relieved that I would have a place to put my money, I heated up the leftover spaghetti, had dinner, did my homework, and went to bed.

⌐⌐

AFTER HAVING SLEPT BETTER, I felt reasonably good. I wanted to see the principal before classes started, so I quickly got ready and left early. As with the day before, all seemed safe as I made my way to school. Maybe L.T. had moved on. I sure hoped so.

When I arrived at school, I immediately went to the office. I told Mrs. Mason that I wanted to see Mr. Jordan.

"Have a seat, Eddie, and I'll let him know you're here," she instructed as she got up from her desk and went into his office. When she came back, she gestured for me to enter.

Mr. Jordan looked up from his papers. "Eddie, everything okay? What can I do for you?"

"I'm fine, Mr. Jordan. I just wanted to talk to you about graduation."

"Go on."

"I'd like to be able to get my diploma and leave school early. It's important for me to get a job so I can support myself. Since my mom died, there's no reason for me to attend the graduation ceremony. I have no other family."

He sat there silently for a moment. I held my breath.

"I understand. As soon as final grades are in, if you have passed, I will give you your diploma and you may leave school."

"Thank you." Breathing a sigh of relief, I hurried from his office just as the first bell rang.

Elated that I had accomplished the first item on my list, I was able to relax and concentrate on my schoolwork. I rushed back to the motel after classes so I'd be ready when Mr. G arrived.

I'd barely put my books down and gotten the insurance check out of hiding when I heard Mr. G pull up outside my door in his big black Buick. I opened the door and asked him to come in.

He reached over and then got out of the car, carrying a huge basket.

"Mrs. G sent food. You know how she worries you won't get enough to eat," he added with a smile. He set the basket on the kitchenette counter and unloaded it. "Some of this needs to be in the fridge."

I saw a couple of Mrs. G's famous brisket sandwiches, a chicken, a noodle casserole, and a dish of roasted potatoes. Mrs. G had also included an apple pie, a bag of cookies, one of her wonderful fresh-baked breads, and cinnamon rolls.

"Wow! She didn't have to do all this. Thank her so much for me. There's enough food for at least a week."

"You're welcome. Now let's get going. We have business to take care of. Do you have the check?"

"Yes." I held it up for him to see. Then we discussed how much I wanted to deposit.

The bank was located in a small corner building just a couple of blocks from Colorado Boulevard. We pulled into the small parking lot in back and went in. A receptionist greeted us.

Mr. G pulled a card out of his pocket, looked at it, and told the receptionist that we were here to see Mr. Walter Hammond.

Mr. Hammond reminded me of a stiff bean pole—he was a tall, thin man with thinning hair, thin glasses, and thin lips. He greeted us with a thin smile. Mr. G introduced us and mentioned his banker who had referred us.

"Yes, Harry called me and said you'd be over. We've been good friends for years."

Despite his cold appearance, once we sat down and began to talk, I found Mr. Hammond to be a warm, genuine person. He explained the different types of accounts and helped me decide on my best option.

"Anything else I can do for you, Eddie?"

"I don't think so." We shook hands, and I thanked him for his help. Then Mr. G and I left. For the first time since my mom died, I felt like a man. It was a good feeling.

When we reached the car, I turned to Mr. G. "The first check I need to write is to the mortuary to pay for my mom's funeral. How can I find out how much it is?"

"Just write the check to me, Eddie. I took care of the mortuary."

Surprised, I thanked him. "So how much should I write the check for?"

"Make it for $250, Eddie, and you'll be all squared away."

Using my lap, and feeling proud to be able to write a check, I wrote it and handed it to Mr. G. Then we discussed the situation regarding L.T.

"You're right. You shouldn't be seen around the neighborhood. But, is there anything you want me to get from the apartment?"

"No. Just stay away from it. Let the owner find out I've left and let him do what he wants with the stuff. I didn't leave anything behind that was worth keeping."

"Okay, but just remember, if you need anything call me."

By now we'd reached the motel. I thanked him again and reminded him to thank his wife for the food.

ELEVEN

I CHECKED THE TIME. *Too late to start walking the neighborhood.*
Instead, I decided to go to the office and talk with Jeff. It would
be good to have him as a friend in case L.T. showed up. The fact
that he was an ex-Marine reassured me. I guessed that he could
lay that fat, sloppy L.T. flat in a second.

This time I leveled with Jeff. I told him all about L.T. and
how I hoped Jeff would help me.

"I knew there had to be more to the story than what you first
told me. I've met a few L.T.s in my life and I know how to take
care of them, so don't you worry," he told me.

"Thanks, Jeff," I said, relieved and glad I'd decided to tell Jeff
everything. "L.T. drives a big, white Caddy, four-door with red
leather interior." I described L.T. and the guys who had been in
his apartment that night. "I'd really appreciate it if you kept an
eye out for him."

"You can count on me, Eddie."

THE NEXT DAY AFTER SCHOOL, I walked part of the neighbor-hood to get a sense of what jobs might be available. I found the area to be a diverse mixture of small businesses, lots of apart-ment buildings, and houses. *With all the businesses around, I should be able to find someone that needs help.*

The following day, I walked down to Broadway and started working my way back toward the motel. As I strolled down Lo-gan, I spotted what looked like a large apartment building in the middle of the block. It turned out to be a hotel. The sign in front said "The Montgomery." Another sign said: HELP WANTED-BELLMAN-APPLY WITHIN.

This seemed to be a perfect immediate solution for me. The job would give me an opportunity to meet lots of people, and perhaps by meeting a lot of people, I would discover what I re-ally wanted to do.

A bellman greeted me at the front door. I asked him where I could apply for the job.

"Turn right in front of the reception desk. At the end of the hall you'll find an office marked Personnel."

I went in and got an application from the receptionist. "When you finish, bring it back to me and then Mr. Sloan will interview you." She directed me to a small waiting area where I could fill out the form.

After I returned it, I waited for Mr. Sloan. In a few minutes, he came out of his office, greeted me, and invited me into his office.

He had my application on his desk. "I've looked over your application, Mr. Anderson. I see that you've had some experience in the grocery business. Tell me why you think you'd like to be a bellman."

What is he looking for? I wondered. I noticed that his desk was clear except for my application. Neat and organized. His graying brown hair was neatly parted on the side, with brown eyes that looked directly at me. His suit, shirt, and tie looked fresh like he had just dressed five minutes ago.

I thought about his question for a moment. "I'm used to doing a lot of heavy lifting, so I know I can handle that part of the job. To be completely honest, I'm not sure yet what I really want to do with my life. I thought this would give me an opportunity to meet lots of different kinds of people."

I went on to tell him about my mom's recent death and the necessity to get a job soon so I could support myself. I told him I would be graduating in the coming weeks and could start right away.

"That's all fine and good, Eddie. But it doesn't tell me enough. What else can you tell me?"

Shit, what can I say that will convince him? A trickle of sweat ran down my back. I cleared my throat. "I want this job because I know that I can do it well. I'm reliable and honest, and I will always give you my best."

He stared at me as if trying to figure out if I would do what I said. "I like your attitude, so I'm willing to give you a try." Then he explained the shifts, the rotation schedule, and the pay. "So, if you're interested, I'll have you start this weekend. Be here at nine o'clock sharp."

Realizing I'd been holding my breath, I let it out. "Gee, thanks, Mr. Sloan."

"Before you leave, stop into the cleaning office and they'll get your measurements for a uniform. On Saturday, you'll get your uniform and start your training with Mike, our bell captain."

As I left the building, the bellman at the door stopped me. "I see by the look on your face you got the job."

"Yeah. I'm Eddie Anderson and I'm starting on Saturday."

"Welcome aboard," he said as he extended his arm to shake hands. "I'll see you then. I'm Hank Fremont, by the way," he added with a smile.

Elated, I ran back to the motel. I stopped short, within a few feet of the front door of the office. A big, white Caddy with a red leather interior was parked in front. I stepped back as I tried to see if anyone was in the car. It looked empty.

Fuck! I had convinced myself that I was safe now. How in the hell had L.T. found me? Slowly, I crept up to the side of the front door and listened.

I could hear shouting inside, but I couldn't tell what they were saying. My heart was pounding so hard it sounded like the ocean in my ears. Shaking, I tried to decide what to do next. Now or never. Running at full speed, I pushed in the door.

L.T. was lying on the floor; blood was running from his nose. Large red welts covered his fat, ugly belly where Jeff now had his foot.

"You're just in time, Eddie," Jeff said with a satisfied expression. "Go behind the counter. In the bottom cupboard you'll find some rope. Bring it here and tie this fucker up."

As I bent down to tie his hands, L.T. raised his hands and hit me in the nose. At the same time, he kicked up his feet and kicked Jeff in the leg. Without thinking, I hit back, punching him in the face as hard as I could. At the same time, Jeff grabbed his legs and delivered a couple of chops to his knees, which left L.T. screaming.

"Finish the job, Eddie," Jeff said, and rolled L.T. on his stomach.

After I tied L.T.'s hands behind his back, Jeff instructed, "Now go call the police. Tell them an assault with intent to harm has taken place here."

"Are you sure?"

"Just do what I tell you, Eddie. I know how to handle this."

After I made the call, Jeff told me to let him do the talking when the police arrived. Within a few minutes, they showed up and came bursting through the front door with guns drawn.

They holstered their guns when they saw L.T. tied up on the floor. Jeff explained that L.T. had come looking for me and then threatened to harm him if Jeff didn't reveal where I was. The police looked to me for an explanation. I told them the truth about L.T. being a drug dealer who was after me to work for him.

I pulled my wallet out of my pocket and dug out Officer Bennett's card. "You can call Officer Bennett. He knows me and I'm sure he'll let you know that I'm telling the truth."

The first officer, a tall, burly guy, said to Jeff, "Are you willing to press charges?"

"Absolutely," Jeff responded. "I want to see this turkey trussed and thrown into jail." He pulled out one of his cards from his wallet and handed it to the officer. "Call me anytime."

The officer pocketed the card, and then he and the other officer hauled L.T. up from the ground and led him out to their car. Once they were gone, I started shaking.

"Close call. Thanks Jeff. I'd probably be in deep shit right now without your help."

"You're welcome. You look awful. Why don't you go to your room now and get some rest."

I nodded, saluted, and went to my room. Once inside, I fell on the bed and tried to calm myself. Then relief swelled up inside me as I considered my situation. *I'm finally rid of that bastard, rid of Stout Street, and on my way to a new life.* Exhausted, I fell asleep.

TWELVE

THE NEXT MORNING, I WOKE with the sunlight streaming through the window. The sun's rays hit me right in the eyes when I opened them. I lay there for a moment, thinking about all that had happened the previous day. Then I laughed, a big raucous belly laugh, before I jumped out of bed.

I felt lightheaded and free. *No wonder I'm dizzy. I missed dinner last night.* Starving, I made myself a quick cold breakfast. I needed to hurry since I'd obviously overslept. Gathering my books, I sprinted out the door and practically flew to school.

That afternoon, Mr. Jordan flagged me down and said that I could have my diploma on Friday. Since I'd completed everything necessary to graduate, I wouldn't have to come to school anymore. At the end of the day, I hung around for a while so I could say goodbye to my friends. Then, feeling somewhat let down, I decided to take my time and slowly walk back to the motel.

By the time I got there, I was feeling exhilarated. A new life awaited me. I stopped in the office to tell Jeff my good news. I had forgotten to tell him about my job.

"Congratulations. You're on your way now."

Once again, I expressed my appreciation to Jeff and then went to my room for the first time without checking the street and the alley for L.T.

When I called Mr. G and brought him up to date, I knew he was relieved for me. "Congratulations. I'd heard that L.T. was in jail. Good riddance." He wished me well and reminded me to keep in touch.

As the principal promised, my diploma was waiting for me when I went to school on Friday. Back in the safety of my motel room, I carefully unwrapped it and admired the gold-and-black print stating that I, Edward Allan Anderson, had graduated high school. Yes, I had done it. Damn right. I was now a high school graduate. I vowed that I would do something with it to make my mother, the Greensteins, and Jeff proud of me one day soon.

On Saturday, I arrived at the hotel early and was greeted by Mike, the bell captain. I was excited to begin my first day as a full-time employee. Mike and I chatted about the day's activities. Then I reported to the cleaning department.

Frank had my uniform ready. "Try one on to make sure it fits properly. Old man Montgomery insists that his bellmen look well-tailored and professional," he told me as he handed me one of the uniforms from the garment bag he was holding.

Admiring the simple yet well-cut uniform, I tried it on. The pants were dark black with a gold stripe on the side. The matching jacket had gold buttons and a stripe on the sleeve.

To complete the look, the black hat was finished off with a gold-braid-trimmed visor. I checked myself out in the mirror. "Looks good to me," I said, secretly feeling proud of the image reflected back.

"Yeah, it'll work. You'll pay for your uniforms out of your first paycheck. Cleaning is free. Usually the guys bring them in every other day, except when it's hot . . . then they change every day. You'll get your winter uniforms at the end of the summer when we're sure you're still going to be here."

"Thanks, Frank."

I took the garment bag that held my second uniform and ran up the stairs to Mr. Sloan's office. He came out of his office to give me the once-over.

"You look good, Eddie. Leave your clothes here until you get your locker. Mike will help you with that shortly. First, I'm going to take you on a tour of the hotel and give you a little history."

As we walked down the hall to the front lobby, Mr. Sloan began with the history of the hotel. "The Montgomery began as a general store with rooms above it that they rented to new arrivals either by the day or week. This hotel was originally built in the late forties. A lot of the hotel was destroyed in a fire in the early sixties, so much of it has been rebuilt. The Montgomerys have three sons: Peter, James, and Matthew. They also have one daughter, Annie. Mr. Montgomery comes in occasionally but is basically retired, so now the three boys run the hotel. Peter is the president, James manages all the financial aspects, and Matt runs our newsstand. We'll meet him now."

Although it was referred to as the "newsstand," they also sold candy, cigarettes, cigars, and small gift items. Additionally, they sold things that people often forget to pack, like toothpaste, shaving cream, and razors. Mr. Sloan introduced me to Matt, who welcomed me warmly and wished me well.

Mr. Sloan then took me across to the other side of the lobby where the coffee shop was located. "The restaurant is run by Mr. Montgomery's daughter, Annie, and her husband, Walt McLaughlin. We'll do a quick hello. You'll have a chance to get better acquainted later."

We found Annie busy serving customers and moving from one table to another. She paused when she saw Mr. Sloan and then came over to us. "This must be our new bellman. I know the boys will be happy to have you aboard."

"Eddie, this is Annie." We both acknowledged the introductions. "I know you're busy, Annie, so we'll move along now."

"Come back later for lunch, Eddie, and we'll become acquainted then." She moved back to the last table she'd been serving as we left the shop.

Mr. Sloan pointed to the hallway on the left of the reception desk. "Down that hallway are some small meeting rooms and a couple of larger rooms. Unlike most big hotels, we don't have a ballroom, but we can put several rooms together to accommodate a reasonably large crowd. Now we'll go look at a couple of the rooms." He took keys from the reception desk and we headed to the elevators.

I had never been in a classy hotel before, so I was looking forward to seeing what hotel rooms really looked like. First, we stopped in a room with two double beds. Mr. Sloan pointed out all the amenities, and I worked on memorizing everything he told me. We also visited a suite and a room with single beds. I was impressed with the hotel itself and the people I met, but realized there was a lot to remember.

We strolled back to the elevators. "On the top floor we have our restaurant. It's open evenings-only during the week. On Friday and Saturday nights, we have a band. It's quite a favorite place with the local people who come for cocktails, dinner, and dancing on the weekends. On Saturday and Sunday mornings, we serve brunch as well."

We walked into the dining room. This was the first time I'd ever seen the city from above. The view was spectacular. Suddenly, though, I felt small and insignificant. *Will I, Eddie Anderson, ever amount to anything?*

"Quite impressive, isn't it?" Mr. Sloan said.

"Yes, it really is. I've never seen such a view before."

I followed him back into the hallway. Mr. Sloan pointed to a set of double doors. "Behind those doors are the executive offices. No one is in today, but on Monday I'll introduce you to Peter and James. Now we'll go back downstairs, and I'll turn you over to Mike so he can start explaining your duties and assign you a locker."

I knew now that I had made the right decision. I was going to like my job here. When we got back to the front lobby, Mr. Sloan retrieved my clothes from his office, shook my hand, wished me well, and turned me over to Mike.

Mike then introduced me to Hank and Bill who were working the day shift. I recognized Hank as the bellman who'd greeted me the day I applied for the job.

"Glad to have you aboard," Hank said. "We've been working our tails off because we've been short-handed."

"I'll do my best," I replied, knowing I had a steep learning curve ahead of me.

As we walked down to the locker room, I checked out Mike. I thought I was tall, but Mike was at least three inches taller than me. His hair was curly and some of the curls peeked out from under his cap. Even though his uniform hung smoothly from his body, I could tell that he was muscular underneath. He looked impressive—just like a bell captain should.

I put my clothes away, and we went back upstairs where Mike spent much of the rest of the day explaining how the shift rotation worked and teaching me how to do my job.

"Often when you deliver the bags to the room, guests will also ask you about places to eat, entertainment, etc. It's always a good idea to have a list of several of those places. Sometimes they'll even give you a tip. You'll find your own ways of earning a little extra, I'm sure."

At the end of the day, I was allowed to greet some new guests and take their luggage to their room. This also turned out to be my initiation by the guys.

I thought I'd figured out how to load luggage pretty well. Apparently, this was not the case. This particular family had a ton of luggage, and I tried to put it all on one rack. I hadn't gone five feet when everything started falling off one after the other. Horrified, I tried to stop the "domino effect," but failed miserably. The guys just stood there and laughed for a second before they came to my aid.

"Guess we forgot to teach Eddie that sometimes you need to use two racks," Hank cackled.

"Thanks a lot, guys."

Mike patted me on the back. "It's okay. We've all done it. We'll help you pick it all up."

As Bill and Hank retrieved the luggage, Mike instructed me on how to load and use more than one rack for a lot of luggage. "Now get this up to the room before they think you lost their bags."

I couldn't believe how fast the day passed and how tired I was at the end of it. When the night shift came on, I was introduced to Fred and Art. After I changed, I walked slowly back to the motel, grabbed a bite to eat, and fell into bed. I never realized how much there was to learn just to be a bellman.

＝ ＝

AFTER THAT FIRST DAY, THINGS fell into a routine, and I enjoyed meeting the many guests, horsing around with the guys, eating lunch, and talking to Annie. Best of all, the tips were adding up. I felt certain that by the end of the month, I would be able to move into an apartment of my own.

On my days off, I went out apartment hunting. I needed a furnished place, since I left what few possessions I had at the place on Stout Street. There were a lot of nice places in the area near the hotel, but so far nothing I could afford.

Having spent several days perusing the ads in the paper, I noticed several vacancies were near the hospitals in the Colorado Boulevard vicinity. On my next day off, I took the car and began looking around. I found several nice apartments, but again, nothing affordable. The rents did seem more reasonable, since they catered to the hospital workers. I figured that if I kept looking, I'd find something.

In the meantime, I learned that many guests had the same questions that Mike had informed me about. *Where's a good place to eat? What movies are in town? What places should we visit? Are there any good places to go hear music?* Every morning as I visited with Matt at the newsstand, I checked the papers for what was going on in town.

I began investigating local restaurants by visiting with the owners, checking their menus, and asking what their specialties were so that I could compile my own list for hotel guests.

Several of the owners promised to give me tips for recommending their restaurant. *Interesting.* Another way to earn money that I hadn't thought about. I made sure those restaurants got a star on my list and that those owners had my name and where I worked. I would make good on those promises.

I'd also discovered that a hotel was a place where niche businesses flourished. Jake, the shoeshine man, took bets on the side, mostly on the horses, but during football season he also took bets.

Sue, who worked at the newsstand, sold souvenir keychains that she made at home. She had a separate little box where she kept her supplies and money.

Like me, all the bellmen provided additional services for the guests, like going to the liquor store or local market. Anything to earn a little extra.

≈≈

SOME OF MY SPARE TIME was spent shooting the breeze with Jeff and bouncing my ideas off him. Jeff never really offered advice. He asked questions instead. How do you feel about that?

What do you think about it? In the long-term, would that be a good move? Questions, questions.

"What?" I would ask him. "Are we playing twenty questions?"

He'd joke back. "With you being such a dimwit, it's more like forty questions."

We'd go on like that, and I had to admit that I found his probing valuable. He'd become a good friend to me. So had Al, the night man. I'd often stop by the office after my night shift and watch TV and chat with Al. As an older man, he had some different perspectives.

THIRTEEN

AFTER WORKING FOR A MONTH, I began to think I was a real hotshot bellman, ready to answer any question. I was about to find out that I didn't know it all after all.

I was giving a guest my list of where to eat and what to do in Denver. As I was preparing to leave, I asked, "Is there anything else I can do for you, sir?"

"Yeah, I'd like a girl for tonight. Can you help me?"

Momentarily stunned, I didn't know what to answer. I knew this kind of thing went on in hotels, but this was the first time I'd come face to face with it. After pausing, I said, "Sure, I'll see what I can do."

I fled the room and raced toward the elevator, eager to talk to Mike. When the elevator came, Hank happened to be in it. I related the request to him.

"Gee, Eddie, I don't know how we all forgot to tell you about that. We have an arrangement with the pimp who has this territory. He has a stable of girls who work the streets around Colfax and Broadway, but he also has a few upper-class broads, as he puts it, that service the hotels in the area. His moniker is "Double T" for his name, Terry Thompson, though his girls refer to him as Tomcat cause he's always on the prowl and does every girl around. So, just tell Mike and he'll set it up."

"Sure thing," I said as I tried to keep the shock off my face.

As soon as I got off the elevator, I hastened over to see Mike. I told him about the request.

"Sure thing, Eddie. What time did he want and for how long?"

"Geez, I didn't think to ask. Sorry."

"No problem. What's his room number? I'll give him a call."

I had to stop and think for a second. "Room 505, and his name is Jim."

Mike dialed the number. "Hello, Jim, this is Mike the bell captain. What time did you require that service and for how long?" Mike listened and then he said, "No problem, I'll take care of it." He hung up and turned to me, "I'll take it from here, Eddie."

Relieved that I didn't have to do anything else, I headed over to the coffee shop to grab a cup. I sat down and tried to gather my wits. It's not like I didn't know about prostitutes. I used to see them all the time around Stout Street. It's just that I'd never had any firsthand experience with this kind of thing.

After that, I probably had requests for "services" at least once or twice a week. At the end of the month, Mike got us all together in the locker room and handed us each an envelope.

"What's this for?" I asked.

"That's for our arrangement with Double T. We give him our referrals and he gives us finder fees at the end of the month. We split it up among all of us."

"Hey, thanks," I said as I pocketed the envelope. *Hmm, another source of income. I may be able to afford a better place sooner than I was thinking.*

When I got back to the motel, I opened the envelope and found ten bucks. Not bad, considering the usual tip from a guest was anywhere from two bits to fifty cents a shot. My finances were definitely looking up.

═ ═

THE SEARCH FOR AN APARTMENT had continued—so far it had been a never-ending and disappointing waste of time. However, on my next day off, everything changed. The day turned out to be *my day*.

The very first place I looked at was perfect. A furnished, buffet apartment just a couple blocks off Colorado Boulevard on 11th Avenue. The bus stopped at the corner, so I could take the bus to work.

One of the things I liked best was that the living room and tiny kitchenette had big windows with Venetian blinds so I could look outside. The living room had a gray sofa bed, blonde coffee table, and tables on each side of the sofa with matching lamps. Over the sofa was a pastel painting of the sea. A dark gray lounge chair completed the furnishings.

The kitchen had a small gray Formica-topped table with two chairs. A bank of white cupboards, sink, an apartment-sized stove and refrigerator completed it.

Off the living room, there was a little dressing area with a chest and hanging space for clothes. Off the dressing area was the bathroom. The fixtures were also gray and the tile was a soft creamy gray.

Man, it looked so cool to me after that dump on Stout Street. So clean. No peeling wallpaper or stinking cabbage.

"Does this apartment work for you?" the landlady, Mrs. Monroe, inquired. "There's also covered parking in the rear of the building. If you have a car and want a space, that would be an extra five dollars per month." She waited for my answer.

"Yes. I want the apartment and a parking space."

We went to her office and I signed the rental contract for one year. I was so excited I could barely sign my name. I didn't bother to read the contract, but I didn't even care. A place of my own. And by my standards, luxurious. I would be working the day shift the following week, so I asked if I could move in the week after that. Mrs. Monroe agreed. I wrote a check for a month's rent and the required deposit.

Before I got back into my car, I looked up to the sky. In almost a whisper, I spoke, "Things are really beginning to look up, Mom. I hope you're feeling proud of me. I just wish we'd been able to do it together."

━ ━ ━

BEFORE I EVEN WENT TO my room in the motel, I ran into the office to tell Jeff about my new apartment. He congratulated me and asked when I planned to make the move.

"Week after next." I told him everything I could remember about the place. I went to my room to make a list of what

I would need. With the list in my pocket, I drove downtown to Woolworth's to buy some necessities.

I grabbed a bunch of kitchen stuff, as well as pillows, sheets, and a blanket, then checked those items off my list. I chose some gray-colored towels and washcloths and a rug for the bathroom floor. It took me three trips to the car to get everything loaded in.

Wait till the guys at work hear that I've found an apartment! I knew they'd be happy for me.

In some ways, it saddened me to leave the motel, as it had been my home for well over a month, during which time I had become good friends with Jeff and Al. I would miss my conversations with them. Not to mention that Jeff had saved my life by taking down L.T.

On the other hand, I was excited to be moving to my own home. Since I didn't have much stuff, I accomplished the move in one day with everything put away and in place by the time I had to leave for work. The only item I added from my past was the little angel figurine of Mom's that I set on the coffee table.

===

THE REST OF THE SUMMER passed uneventfully. Since the only friends I had were the guys at work, I did what I'd always done. I went to the library at least once a week and loaded up on books, spent a lot of time walking around the neighborhood, and started taking a judo class at the Y. I talked to Mr. G and stopped to shoot the breeze with Jeff whenever I could.

Occasionally Hank and I grabbed a burger together and went to the movies. The other guys were all married or engaged, so they rarely wanted to spend an evening with me. I was lonely.

And horny. I hadn't had sex since that night Ches sent me on my way.

During the Labor Day sales, I finally bought a small black-and-white TV. Although I had watched TV when I worked for Ches and at the motel, it was still a novelty for me, and it helped make the time seem less lonely.

FOURTEEN

IT WAS A WEDNESDAY EVENING late in September. As I saun-
tered toward the bus stop after work, I saw a young girl sitting on
the bench. Beside her on the ground was a large shopping bag. I
could see that she was crying. Her appearance made me pause:
short skirt, skimpy midriff top, fishnet stockings, heavy makeup.
She was obviously a hooker.

I sat down at the other end of the bench. "Not having a very
good day, huh?" I said to her in a quiet voice.

She sniffed. "No."

I reached into my pocket and handed her a handkerchief.
She took it and cried even harder. I guessed by the looks of
things that she was in trouble with her pimp.

"There's a café across the street. C'mon, I'll buy you a cup of
coffee. It'll make you feel better."

She peered up at me from under her eyelashes. "Are
you sure?"

"Sure I'm sure. This your bag?"

"Yes."

I picked it up, took her by the hand, and led her across the street. The café was quiet, and I found a table in the rear and directed her to it. We sat down.

"My name is Eddie," I said. "What's your name?"

"Abbey," she answered.

"That's a nice name. Since it's almost dinnertime, how about something to eat?"

She nodded her head.

"Anything special you like or do you just want me to order?"

"You order."

Hmm, a woman of few words. Difficult to know what she was thinking. I ordered some chicken and mashed potatoes. As we waited for our dinner, I told her a little about myself. When she seemed to relax some, I asked her to tell me about herself.

"I'm from Nebraska," she said. "My father used to beat me, so when I graduated high school I ran away and came to Denver, thinking it would be easy to find a job and start a new life here." She sighed. "I didn't know anyone and couldn't find a job, so I was out on the streets and this guy named Tomcat found me and offered me a job as one of his girls. Then this morning he told me I was a worthless piece of trash and he kicked me out." She started to cry again.

So, she was one of Tomcat's street girls. I didn't know that any pimp would ever throw anyone out. Apparently he did, which surprised me.

"So do you have some place to stay? Or someone to stay with?"

"No. I was just sitting on the bench trying to figure out what to do."

I thought about it and then said, "Look, why don't you come home with me? Tomorrow you can try to get yourself together. When I come home from work, we'll talk about it and see what we can do."

"Do you mean it? You'd really let me come home with you?"

"Yes, I mean it." I stood up and picked up the check. "Is this all your stuff?" I pointed to her bag.

She nodded.

"Let's go. We have to catch the bus."

On the bus, I told her that my landlady was pretty much a snoop and extremely strict. I instructed Abbey that if she ran into her, or anyone else for that matter who started asking questions, she should say she's my sister and would be staying with me for a while.

Abbey seemed worried. "Are you sure it's going to be okay?"

I assured her it would be. When we got off the bus, we made our way down the street. Fortunately, we didn't run into anyone as we approached my apartment.

Things got a little awkward once we were in my apartment. Neither of us quite knew what to say. After a few minutes, I suggested, "Why don't you go take a shower? I'm sure you'll feel better once you get cleaned up."

"Thanks, I think I will."

While Abbey showered, I opened the bed and changed the sheets. Then I closed it up, turned on the TV, and sat down to watch. When she came out, she had on an oversized T-shirt that I assumed she slept in. With her face scrubbed clean and

divested of her sleazy clothes, she really wasn't so bad looking. She had powder-blue eyes and light brown hair that she
had tied back in a ponytail. She had a beautiful creamy com-
plexion. I imagined with the right makeup she could be quite
attractive.

"So would you like to sit down and watch a little TV?"

"Excuse me," she said as she took a perplexed look around
the room, "but where do you sleep?"

"Oh, this sofa turns into a bed."

"Oh," she said.

I could feel my face get hot. "Don't worry. You can sleep in
the bed. I'll sleep in this chair."

"Oh you don't have to do that. We can both sleep in the bed."

We watched TV for a little longer. "I've got an early shift
tomorrow, so if it's okay with you let's go to bed."

That was fine with her. Usually I slept naked, but decided I'd
leave my shorts on.

After a while, she said, "We can have sex if you like."

Is she kidding? Ever since she went to take a shower, the bulge
had grown in my pants. I hadn't had sex in so long, just the
thought of it made me hard. I mumbled a yes.

Having sex with Abbey was like jerking off with a *Play-
boy* centerfold. It did the job, but it just wasn't the same as having a warm body beneath you, moving with you and urging you
on to climax. Not the hot, exciting, heart-pounding, fireworks
sex that I'd had with Ches. No matter, it still felt good. But no
wonder her pimp had thrown her out. She really wasn't very
good. She was a street hooker—in, out, and on to the next guy.
But then who was I to complain?

When I got up the next morning, Abbey was still asleep. She looked so young and innocent, and it made me sad to think of what she'd gone through so far.

I got ready as quietly as I could so I wouldn't wake her up. I left a note telling her where the washer and dryer coins were in case she wanted to wash her clothes. Lastly, I wrote that I would be home sometime between six and six-thirty, and we could talk about what she was going to do after that. Then I slipped out and went to work.

⌐ ⌐

THE SMELL OF MAC AND cheese greeted me as I opened the door. "Mmm, that smells good," I hummed.

Abbey stuck her head around the corner. "I hope you don't mind that I looked through your cupboards and fridge. I thought maybe you'd like dinner ready when you got home." She beamed at me.

As I walked into the kitchen, a warm feeling enveloped me. The table was set with a small salad beside each plate. Abbey had even put some flowers in a glass of water in the center of the table. It all looked so homey; I felt my eyes tear up a bit.

"Looks and smells delicious. This was so nice of you."

"Golly, it's the least I could do. Now sit and we'll eat."

As we ate, I asked her if she would mind telling me how long she'd worked for Tomcat and why she thought he threw her out. I was curious to know what had happened.

"I've worked for him for about five months."

That explains a lot. Inexperience. Not enough time to even become a hardened prostitute.

"And?" I prompted.

She said that he got mad because she didn't work enough and bring in enough money. "He complained that I always either had my period or was running to the clinic."

"Running to the clinic?"

"I wanted to make sure I hadn't gotten anything like, you know, syph or other VD."

With that comment, my mind started racing. *Oh shit. I was so anxious to have sex I didn't use a rubber last night. Fuck, I hope she isn't going to tell me she has something.*

She must have seen the horror on my face because she quickly said, "Don't worry, I'm clean."

Thank God. I've got to remember from now on to always be like a boy scout, prepared. I breathed a sigh of relief. "So what do you think you might want to do?"

She shrugged. "I really don't know. I don't have any special skills. I ran away right after I graduated."

Wow, did that sound familiar. "Tell you what. I have this weekend off and the night shift next week. That means I'll be off until Monday evening. We'll spend the time looking to see what jobs are out there. In the meantime, I'll see if there are any jobs open at the hotel."

We finished dinner, took a walk, watched TV, went to bed, and had sex. I decided I could get used to this.

＝ ＝

ON THE WAY TO WORK the next morning, I had what you would call a lightbulb moment. Why couldn't I be Abbey's agent? I had calls for service. Why not provide the service myself with

Abbey? Why turn it over to Tomcat? My mom always said that when opportunity knocks, answer the door.

Suddenly guilt welled up inside me. *What would my mom think? You know damn well what she'd think. She'd kill you for even thinking about doing this.* On the other hand, I couldn't deny that this would give me an opportunity to make enough money to take care of myself so that I would never have to live on a "Stout Street" ever again. And, if I did it right, Abbey would never have to live on streets like that either. Taking a deep breath, right or wrong, I made the decision to ask Abbey if I could be her pimp.

My mind raced. Of course, I'd have to teach Abbey how to please a guy just like Ches taught me how to please a woman. I'd have to get her hair and makeup fixed. I'd need to get her some decent clothes so she'd look like a high-class call girl. Memories of all the things Ches had taught me flooded my mind.

Abbey would have to pay me back out of what she earned. I knew I had enough money to cover the cost. I had been living frugally since I had nothing better to spend my money on. At the end of the week, I usually took my tip money, deposited some of it into my bank account along with my paycheck, and kept the rest for weekly expenses. Generally at the end of the week, I still had a little left over. I'd been saving that extra money in a box I kept hidden in my closet with the money still left from what Ches gave me for graduation. Yes, this could work. It would be a step up for Abbey and more money for me.

My mind churned all day with thoughts and ideas of what needed to happen next—if Abbey agreed. I went into the coffee shop and talked to Annie.

"I have a friend in from out of town and she wants to get her hair done. Do you know of a good shop I can take her to?" I asked.

"Sure, Eddie. I know a couple of good shops. Hold on a minute and I'll get the names and telephone numbers." She went to the cashier counter and pulled out a phonebook and pad of paper. She found what she was looking for and brought the paper over to me.

"Here you are. I'm sure your friend will find either one of these okay." She stared at me. "Is this perchance a girlfriend?"

"Oh, no. Just an acquaintance. Thanks for your help, Annie."

Feeling embarrassed, I fled the coffee shop. So now I had the name of a beauty shop. I'd been to some of the makeup counters with Ches, so that wouldn't be a problem. I could handle shopping for clothes, too. Now all I had to do was tell Abbey about it.

⇌ ⇀

DELICIOUS SMELLS GREETED ME AS I let myself into my apartment.

"Something smells good," I yelled.

"I hope you like meatloaf, 'cause that's what you're getting," she called back.

"I love meatloaf," I said as I walked into the dressing area to put away my stuff. Funny how a little thing like meatloaf could make me feel so happy.

At dinner, I asked Abbey about her day. I could hardly wait to tell her my idea, but I thought I'd better get around to it slowly. Have dinner, do the dishes, then sit down and have a little talk.

We settled into the couch. "So I had an idea today that I thought we might talk about."

"Sure. What's your idea?"

"Well, I thought that I might be your agent. You know, at the hotel. I get a lot of requests for services."

Abbey frowned and gave me a puzzled look. She seemed to process what I said and then she burst out laughing.

"You mean you want to be my pimp. Is that it?"

Fool. Of course, that's what I meant. Why couldn't I say the word? Did I think I was some high-falutin' Hollywood agent? Yeah, they're pimps, but of a different kind. I coughed.

"Yeah, I guess that's what I meant."

"It's okay. I know you're just trying to help me. Go ahead, tell me your ideas."

Um, how could I say this without making her mad? "Okay. Here's what I'm thinking. Tomcat has these girls . . . call girls . . . that look real classy. When we have a guy that wants a girl, we call Tomcat and he provides one. So, why couldn't you be one of those girls? Except I'd get you the jobs. What do you think?"

"O . . . kay. Go on."

"Well, now don't get mad. Just listen to what I have to say. Uh, first I'd need to teach you some things about having sex. Ya know, how to make a guy feel like he's got his money's worth. Uh, some techniques, that's it." I couldn't tell by her expression what she was thinking, so I went on. "We'd have to fix you up nice. Some different makeup. Some nice clothes, you know, so you'd look high class."

She gave me a funny look, and then she said, "Go on."

"Well, I'd be willing to spend the money to do all this. You could pay me back with the money you earn."

Abbey snorted. "And what money would that be?"

"Well, didn't Tomcat pay you?"

"Are you kidding me? Maybe he'd give us a few bucks a week. He said the money we earned paid the rent, fed us, and took care of us. He always complained he was losing money on us. That we were nothing but worthless trash."

I was shocked. It was not at all fair. "Well, I wouldn't do that Abbey. We'll work out something. Of course, if you stay here and we do this, I will expect you to help pay the rent and food."

"Well, sure. I'd want to do that anyway. And I think it's real sweet of you to want to do this for me. I'm okay with what you said."

Relief spread through my body. She really seemed alright with it. Then my gut clenched. Now that she'd accepted, I couldn't help but feel some reservations. *Is this what I really want to do? Damn right, Eddie. It's a way to do something better. It could give both of us a better life.* "Okay, then it's a deal. We'll start tomorrow. I got the name of a couple of beauty shops. That will be our first stop. Then makeup and shopping for clothes."

Abbey gave me a big, toothy smile. "You have things all figured out, I see. I guess the last thing to do is see about improving my sexual techniques."

Now I smiled. "I guess so."

It could have been awkward, but it turned out just fine. Abbey was now in a playful mood and turned out to be a quick study. We definitely had a good time.

FIFTEEN

I WOKE UP EARLY THE next morning, eager to get started. This wasn't what I'd had in mind to do with my life, but then didn't one have to take the opportunities that came along?

I woke Abbey. "C'mon, let's have breakfast and get started. We have to make a list of things that you'll need."

"Jeez, Eddie, give a girl a chance to wake up." She yawned. "I need a shower, and to clear my head and have breakfast. Then we can make lists."

As I drank my coffee, I made lists while Abbey ate breakfast. "Where's your underwear and stuff? I want to check it out and see what we need to buy."

"My stuff is still in the shopping bag."

I took the list, got the bag, and set all her things out on the bed. There were a couple of bras and panties that would be okay for daytime. And a pair of stockings that would probably work. But everything else was useless for what I had in mind. To the things I already had listed I added underwear and stockings. By this time, Abbey had finished eating and it was time to call the beauty shop.

The first shop on the list had no openings. The receptionist at the second shop said that Brenda could take Abbey at nine-thirty since she'd had a cancellation. "Thanks a lot. We'll be there."

"Okay, we have an appointment at nine-thirty. Get dressed, but don't put on any makeup. We'll get a makeover at one of the department stores after you have your hair done."

"Wow, Eddie," she said. "You really have everything planned, don't you? Are you sure this is what you want to do?"

"I am." I turned on the TV and watched cartoons while Abbey got dressed.

"Ready," she said as she picked up her purse and put on her jacket. "I'm actually excited. I've never had my hair done professionally. We girls did each other's hair."

We arrived at the shop right on time. "This way," the receptionist said. Abbey sat down just as Brenda came around the corner and greeted us.

"Good morning," she said with a smile. Then she stood behind Abbey and ran her hands through Abbey's hair.

"What did you have in mind?" she asked Abbey.

"Ask Eddie," she replied.

Brenda gave me a questioning look.

"Something that makes her look kinda cute 'n sassy and yet a little bit sexy."

Brenda raised her eyebrows. "Okay, I'm no miracle worker, but I'll try." She took a brush and comb and began fiddling with Abbey's hair. "What about the color?"

"What about the color?" I asked.

"Her skin cries out for color. Perhaps a gold chestnut brown." She waited for me to answer.

"You're the pro."

Abbey just sat and watched and waited for the verdict.

"Color it is. Now you just go sit down and read some magazines. I'll call you when I'm ready for you to take a look."

After what seemed like an eternity, Brenda came out and motioned for me to follow her. I could hardly believe my eyes. Even without makeup, Abbey looked adorable. Her hair was kinda short and swingy. It did make her look cute and sassy, and yes, a little bit sexy. And the color did make her skin glow.

Abbey grinned from ear to ear. "Oooh, I think it's just beautiful."

"Me too." I thanked Brenda, paid, and grabbed Abbey's hand. "Let's get going. We still have lots to do."

Our next stop was the May Company. I'd been there with Ches, so I was sort of familiar with the makeup counters. We wandered around looking at the different brands. I didn't remember the prices being so high.

A young woman in a white lab coat approached us. "May I help you?"

I answered. "Yes, this young lady would like some makeup advice."

"Of course." She motioned Abbey to have a seat on one of the stools. Then she eyed me. "Is this for a special event or are you looking for just general advice?"

"I'd like you to show her what kind of makeup to use for daytime and what to use at night." I really couldn't explain it very well because I didn't know all that much about this stuff, but I figured the girl would take the lead and figure it out.

"I can do that." She began to busy herself with an assortment of liquids and colors.

"First, we start with foundation." She applied some to Abbey's wrist, checked the color, and nodded in approval. Then she applied it to Abbey's face. The cosmetician worked on Abbey's eyes, offering instructions as she applied the makeup. When the desired effect was achieved, she moved to lip colors. She picked out an assortment of pink shades and an assortment of oranges and coral tones. "I would suggest that you pick one color from each of these palettes. I wouldn't suggest that you use any of the reds. They wouldn't look good with your coloring."

Abbey gave me a questioning glance. I shrugged. I was out of my element. I had no idea. "Why don't you pick a couple?" I told the clerk.

After she finished, Abbey looked amazingly beautiful. Those flat powder-blue eyes shone like the aqua-blue waters of the Caribbean. Her moist lips begged for a kiss. I beamed at her. "Take a look," I said.

Abbey let out a breath of sheer joy. "Oh, Eddie, I really do look pretty, don't I?"

Nodding, I turned my attention back to the clerk. "Great. Now what would you do for evening? Something that looks a little sexier, I'm thinking."

With a twinkle in her eye, the clerk said, "Can do. You want sexy, I'll give you sexy." She took some different liquids and powders and began working on Abbey, again offering instructions as she went.

When she finished, it was me who gulped. "Whoa," I managed. Was this the same girl I picked up from the street just three days ago? Sexy, sultry, hot, but ladylike and sophisticated. I wanted to kiss the young woman in the lab coat. "Check it out."

Speechless, Abbey could only stare at her reflection in the mirror, not believing that she was seeing herself.

"Is that really me?"

"Yes. It is really you." I turned to the beauty consultant. "We have some more shopping to do. Will you please get everything that she needs together and we'll come back and pick it up after we've finished?"

"Of course. I'll have everything waiting for you."

I checked the time. "C'mon, we still have lots to do."

Next we picked out some lingerie. A couple of black, lacy bras with matching panties and some white ones as well. At the same time, we picked out a couple of garter belts and some stockings.

Then we headed to the dress department. We found several black dresses and then a few of what Ches used to call daytime dresses. "Try these on for starters."

Abbey was skinny. Scrawny probably described her better. She didn't have the curves and roundness that make a woman look sexy, so I tried to pick out stuff that looked soft and offered an illusion of curviness, hoping that it would make her look less like a scarecrow. I chose two black dresses and two daytime dresses. Then I found a soft, cream-colored silk blouse and a swingy skirt that swished when Abbey walked. It made Abbey look incredibly sexy.

While she was trying on what I'd picked out, I hurried over to the coats and picked out a simple black coat that I thought would work for both day and night. As I walked back to see Abbey in the latest outfit she was modeling, I spied a little orange dress on the ten-dollar-or-less sales rack. I grabbed it from the rack and asked Abbey to try it on. Perfect.

"We're done here. Get dressed and we'll get some shoes, a purse, and some jewelry. Then we'll pick up the makeup and go home. I'm pooped."

When Abbey finished dressing, I took all our purchases and paid for them. Time was flying and we didn't have much left. We hurried to the shoe department and settled on two pairs of shoes, one a black pump and the other a dressy high heel sandal.

At the jewelry counter, I picked out two sets of pearls, a single strand and a double strand, plus two pairs of earrings. During the entire day, memories of Ches flooded my mind, telling me what to buy for Abbey. As I paid for the pearls, I remembered Ches telling me that pearls were always right—day or night.

On the way home, Abbey broke into tears. "I don't know how I'm ever going to repay you. You've done so much for me."

"Aw, don't cry. It's going to work out great. Now dry your tears and tell me what we're doing for dinner."

"We still have some meatloaf and potatoes left."

"Meatloaf again?" At this, we both burst out laughing, remembering a scene from *The Rocky Horror Picture Show*. By the time we stopped laughing, we were home.

After dinner, we were too tired to do anything. Abbey had hung up and put away all her new clothes, and we settled down to watch TV. Abbey dozed off.

As I sat there, my mind once again drifted back to Ches and all the time we'd spent together. Details that I had blocked out over these months came floating back. God, I missed her. My heart gave a jolt just thinking about her. *Forget her, Eddie. You have a new life now.*

Among the happy moments I recalled was how Ches used to do a kind of striptease for me after she'd bought something new and wanted to model it for me. I'd lie on the bed and watch as she stripped. She'd be sassy and sexy as hell. She used to tell me that an important part of sex was the tease. Getting the appetite worked up. Prolonging the moment. The anticipation. Yes, I must teach that to Abbey. Tomorrow.

I turned off the TV and fell asleep dreaming about Ches all night long, wishing she was next to me instead of Abbey.

‗‗

AS WE ATE BREAKFAST THE next morning, I outlined my plan for Abbey. "Today you'll spend the day learning how to do the striptease in all your new clothes."

Abbey stared at me. "What?"

"Learning how to do a striptease. See, here's the thing. The john is paying you to do your job. Now he wants to get his money's worth. This whole thing is about sex, right? So watching a woman pull a dress over her head isn't very sexy. But watching a woman undress in a provocative manner is. This is different than what you've been doing."

"O . . . kay, go on."

"You're going up to a hotel room. You didn't just pick him up off the street. When he lets you into the room, you're fully dressed. You don't know each other. It could be a little awkward. This is a way of easing the awkwardness and making it fun."

"I see. So what do you want me to do?"

"First, put on your evening makeup and fix your hair. Then put on one of the new black bras and panties. And the black stockings, the ones with the lace tops that have the elastic in them. We'll practice some moves with those on and then we'll work on the dresses."

Abbey shrugged. "You're the boss." She finished eating her egg and toast and drank the last drop of coffee. Then she got up from the table, curtsied, shook her butt suggestively, and sashayed to the bathroom.

"Funny, Abbey." While she was getting ready, I cleaned up the breakfast dishes and made the bed so we would have room to practice.

I pulled out one of the kitchen chairs and set it up as a viewing stand. The other chair I set out as a prop for Abbey to use while stripping.

When she came out, I said, "Okay, you sit on the chair and I'll show you what I think you should do with the bra."

Now while I'm six feet tall and have a very athletic build that some women would find sexy, I don't have that natural, easy movement that sexy guys have. I'm often quite clumsy. Plus, since I've been taking judo class, my movements tend to be precise, strong, and chop-chop. Apparently, I wasn't coming off very well because Abbey was rolling on the floor belly-laughing so hard that tears were rolling down her face.

"Okay, I get it. I'm never going to make it stripping. Stop laughing, and I'll just walk you through it."

"Sorry, but you really were just too funny."

"Yeah, yeah. Look. You've got mascara running down your face now. Go fix it and then we'll start over. And put on that first black dress we bought."

When Abbey came out in the first black dress, I told her to turn around a couple of times so I could check everything out. She did look great.

"Okay. Now all the dresses I picked out for you have one thing in common. They're all easy to take off. This one has that long zipper in the back. So just reach back and pull it down in one easy movement."

Abbey did that.

"Now, look at your right shoulder, let the dress slip off a little, then look at me."

I watched her as she made that move. I shook my head. "Not quite right, too jerky. Make it a little sassy. Try again."

After she did it for the fifth time, she finally had the movement right. "Okay, now hold it there and do the left one, same thing."

Perfect the first time. "Okay, now let the dress drop. Bend your knees, pick it up, lean back, and let it hang over the chair."

"Too stiff. Try it again." Again, after a few times, she finally managed to do it in one fluid movement. "Now, sit down on the chair. Think about how the ladies take off their stockings in the movies. That's what I want you to do."

I didn't want to try and demonstrate again and set Abbey off into another bout of hilarity, so I did my best to give specific verbal cues.

"Get your leg higher," I instructed. "Roll the stocking down your leg. That's it. Now the other leg." Her movement was a little jerky and the angle not quite right, so we tried again.

"This time, turn your body just a little and try to make your movement a little smoother."

"That was much better, but let's go through it a couple more times."

After she made adjustments according to my instructions, Abbey stuck her tongue out at me. "I hope you're having fun."

"I am. Now let's move onto the bra. Same thing as with the dress. Look at your right shoulder. Let the strap fall. Look at me. Reach back and undo the bra. Don't let it fall off. Now do the left shoulder while you're still holding it up. Now let it fall off, lean back, and put it on the chair. Great, you did it just great."

She winked at me. "Okay, what about the panties?"

"Leave the panties on. Let the john take care of those."

"Okay boss. What's next?"

"Get the next black dress and put it on."

This dress was a wraparound, so we had to do it a little differently. First one side, expose, close. Then the other side, expose, close. Then open both sides and let it fall off. By now Abbey had gotten the whole concept and seemed to be really enjoying herself.

"Okay, get the next dress." Now it was easy. It only took Abbey a few minutes to figure out the most provocative way to slip out of each dress. We finished, and I told Abbey it was time to relax.

Abbey hung up all her clothes and put on her jeans and a T-shirt. "I'm really not hungry for lunch. So why don't we go for a walk up to the Dairy Queen and get an ice cream."

"Sure. An ice cream sounds good."

We walked without talking for several minutes. Then Abbey said, "I actually had fun doing that strip. Do you think it will really work . . . and how did you ever get that idea?"

I sure as hell didn't want to reveal anything about Ches and me, so I answered in a vague way. "Oh, I just listen and observe what goes on around the hotel. And, yes, I think it will work."

We left the conversation at that. The rest of the day we spent relaxing and watching TV.

= =

MONDAY MORNING AT BREAKFAST, I told Abbey that I wanted her to get a manicure and pedicure. I had noticed while she was practicing the strip that both were scruffy looking.

"Wow, I've never had a real . . . I mean a professional . . . manicure and pedicure. I wouldn't even know where to go."

"First to the yellow pages. I'm sure there's a place near here that must do both."

"Of course, how stupid of me."

I ignored that comment and went to get the telephone book. It didn't take me long to find a place on Colorado Boulevard, not far from the apartment. I wrote down the number.

"Call and make an appointment," I told her. "While you're doing that, I'll get the washing done."

She made an appointment for ten o'clock. "I'd better hurry, it's already nine-fifteen."

"If you have some stuff you want washed, get it out now and I'll do both."

Abbey scurried to get her dirty clothes and get dressed. She was ready to leave within thirty-five minutes.

"Get a pink color, not red," I shouted as she ran out the door.

Abbey came home just before lunch. She couldn't wait to show off her nails and toes; she was so excited at having her first professional manicure and pedicure.

I admired both. "Now you're complete, from your head to your toes."

She grinned and gave me a hug. "I only hope it won't take me the rest of my life to pay you back for everything."

"Don't worry. We're going to be a great success."

After lunch, I sat Abbey down and said, "I want to continue the conversation we were having yesterday."

She made herself comfortable on the sofa. "Shoot," she said.

"Remember how I talked about how this was all about sex yesterday and how you wanted to give the john his money's worth?"

"Yeah, I remember."

"Well, there is a little more to it than that. Even though it is about sex and not making love, there is another part of it that you should think about."

I wasn't exactly sure how to put it, so I just sort of rambled. "Every guy wants to believe he's sexy. Every guy wants to believe that he's a good lover. Every guy worries about the size of his dick. So it's part of your job to make the guy believe that he is sexy and a good lover and that his dick is just great. You need to be a good actress and get into the part. You want to put your brand on the john so that when he comes back, it's only you he wants. That's where the money is to be made."

Abbey gave me a solemn look. "Wow, I never thought about it like that."

"I know you can do it."

It was time for me to take a little nap before dinner, since I was working the early night shift. "Wake me up at four so I can get ready and have a little dinner before I go to work."

"Sure thing."

I reminded Abbey before I left that my shift ended at two so I would be home around two-thirty.

"Please try to be quiet in the morning. I really need the sleep."

She gave me a kiss on the cheek and said, "I'll remember."

SIXTEEN

I WAS IN THAT HAZY stage somewhere between still being asleep and trying to wake up. The house was still, so Abbey must have gone out to do the grocery shopping so she wouldn't wake me. It surprised me that I had only known Abbey for just a few days because it seemed as if we had known each other for a long time. And the transformation we had accomplished in such a short time really amazed me.

It occurred to me that I'd been so busy trying to remake Abbey, I'd never given any thought to how little I really knew about her and her life before we met. I realized it was because, ever since I met her, it had been all about me. I was so needy when Abbey came along that all I could think about was what I needed and wanted. And then Ches intruded on my thoughts, as she had done so much in these past few days. I was reminded of all the things she had taught me about women and their desires and needs.

Then it dawned on me: With Abbey's past being what it was, she probably never had any man treat her with love or respect. Her dad had been abusive, and since coming to Denver and immediately becoming a prostitute, she'd had no chance of discovering her own needs.

Based on Abbey's responses, I ventured a guess that she'd probably never experienced an orgasm or even knew what it was. Well shit, that was going to change.

Because I had exchanged schedules with Art so he could take care of family business during the day, I would be working the graveyard shift for the next couple of nights. That would leave me free in the early evening. I decided that the following night would be Abbey's graduation present. A night planned just for her.

Since it wasn't yet time to get up, I drifted back to sleep. I don't know how long I slept, but the rustling of grocery bags and cupboards being opened and shut woke me up.

"Did I wake you? I'm sorry, I was trying so hard to be quiet."

"No problem, time to get up anyway." I yawned, stretched, and got out of bed. As I showered, I reviewed my plans for the next day. Then I tried to decide whether to reveal at least part of my plan to Abbey before I left for work, or to wait. I decided to wait until the following morning.

"So what plans do you have for me today?" Abbey asked.

"Nothing much. I thought we could have some discussion about different scenarios you might experience and how to handle them."

"What's there to discuss? I get undressed, we have sex, I leave. End of scenario."

"Abbey, Abbey. Some guys are a little awkward and shy. You need to learn to make them comfortable and get the ball rolling, so to speak."

"I don't know why I just can't do what I do."

"Here's the thing. I'm trying to be a businessman, not some . . . some pimp who just throws girls out on the street. Because now you're not going to be a streetwalker. You're going to be a high-class call girl."

"Yeah, high-class call girl." She snorted and made a face.

What? She's smart-assing me? This has to stop right now. She needs to know that I'm the boss and we do it my way. I stared at her but didn't speak. After a few minutes of silence, she paled and fidgeted with her T-shirt.

"Hey, nobody's making you do this. There's the door. Feel free to leave."

She trembled, looked down, and stuttered, "I'm sor . . . sorry."

"Okay then."

Chastened, she added, "Whenever you're ready, Eddie."

I left it at that, got dressed, and had some breakfast. While I read the paper and ate, Abbey busied herself putting away the groceries. Then she tidied up the apartment. It was enjoyable having someone take care of me. I felt a little like royalty.

Then Abbey curled up in the lounge chair and prepared for our discussion. It was obvious she had just about reached her limit with all this additional preparation, so I did my best to keep it low-key and easy. I really did like Abbey and I wanted her to feel comfortable.

I tried to show her how to have a casual and comfortable conversation to make a john feel at ease. After a short time, I told Abbey that I wanted to go to the library and get some new books. Her face brightened. "I'd like to get something to read. It gets a little boring around here when you're gone."

I was happy to hear that she enjoyed reading too—something we could share that reminded me of my mother. We spent a couple of hours browsing at the library. Abbey picked out a few romance novels and a mystery. I picked up a copy of the Kama Sutra, thinking I might get some ideas to pass on to Abbey. I also checked out a couple of mysteries. They were good to read on the graveyard shift, which was generally fairly quiet. Occasionally there might be a late night drunk who needed assistance getting to his room, or a complaint about noise from other guests. Other than that, there was usually plenty of time to read.

When we got home, I took a quick nap, had some dinner, and left for work. Once again, I reminded Abbey to try and be quiet in the morning and not wake me.

═ ═

I WOKE UP ABOUT TEN-THIRTY. Abbey was curled up in the lounge chair, engrossed in her book.

"Good morning."

Startled, she jumped up. "Wow, you just about scared me to death. I didn't expect you to be up so early. Can I get you some breakfast?"

"I'm going to shower first. Have you had breakfast yet?"

"No, I was waiting for you."

"Good, then we'll have breakfast together."

While I showered and got dressed, Abbey fried up some bacon and eggs. The smell made me realize I was ravenous. Conversation could wait.

When my hunger was satisfied, I said to Abbey, "Do you know what today is?"

She frowned. "Did I forget something? Is today something special?"

"It is. Today is graduation day. A couple of more points I want to go over with you, and then I proclaim you ready."

She grinned. "Really? You think I'm ready?"

"I know you are. And, because this is your day, I'm going to take you out to dinner."

Abbey leaped up and came over and gave me a hug and a kiss on the cheek. "You are the best, Eddie. Thank you."

"Let's get things cleaned up and then we'll go over some final points."

After we finished, we settled in our usual places.

"Shoot," she said. "I'm ready."

"There are three final rules that must never be broken," I said. "First, always get your money up front."

"I already know that one."

"Second, never give the john your telephone number or address. And, third, never give the john your real name. We should decide what name you want to use with guests and that will be your business name."

"You do know that I know all that. I'm not totally stupid. And the name I use is Vicky."

"Sorry, I didn't mean to imply that you're stupid. Just being sure, Vicky. Now I'm going to go to the gym for my judo lesson, and then I'll work out for a bit. Then my plan is to take a little nap before we go to dinner. Remember I'm working the grave-yard shift tonight. We'll have an early dinner, so I can catch a nap before I go to work."

I debated whether to tell her about my plans for her after dinner. It might make her a little apprehensive, so I decided to wait until we were ready to leave the restaurant.

"Do you have any plans?"

"I think I'll just hang out here and read my book."

"Okay. I'll see you later then."

═ ═

"WEAR THE NEW BLOUSE AND skirt we bought," I told Abbey. "I made a reservation at Roberto's at five-thirty."

I figured an early dinner would give us plenty of time to have dinner, sex, and a nap for me before I had to go to work. I had already shaved and showered at the gym so all I had to do was get dressed. While I waited, I watched TV. When she came out, I gave a low whistle.

"What a lucky guy I am to have such a beautiful girl with me tonight." I knew that she felt insecure. Couldn't hurt to build up her ego a bit.

Abbey blushed. "Thank you."

Roberto's was one of the restaurants on my list of recom-mended places that I gave to guests who asked me. The owner recognized me when we arrived.

"Eddie, my friend, it's a pleasure to see you." He ushered us to a table.

Abbey's skirt swished as she walked, and she looked quite sexy. She received several appreciative glances as we walked to our table. However, she seemed to be oblivious to it all. I realized then how young and naïve she still was. Just a kid.

I had determined that I would encourage Abbey to talk about her life during dinner. After we ordered, I started asking questions.

"You know, Abbey, I really don't know anything about your life. Tell me about where you lived and about your family."

"There's not much to tell. We were what you call trailer trash. My dad never seemed to be able to earn much money. He was a mean man. I guess his dad was mean too and beat his wife and kids all the time. So my dad did the same. He beat my mom and me constantly."

"And your mom, what about her?"

"My mom was a fairly good woman. I don't know how she ever decided to marry my dad. After I was born, she couldn't have any more kids, so that's why I was an only child."

Our soup arrived and we ate silently for a few minutes. While we waited for our main course, Abbey told me how they did a little backyard farming and how her dad worked at the local hardware and feed store. He repaired farm machinery in the winter. She described how the kids teased and bullied her at school because she was always bruised and her clothes were ragged.

A sad story, much like mine in some ways. It's no wonder she ran away and took to the streets.

"That's pretty much it, Eddie. I don't really want to talk about it anymore. I'd rather just enjoy this wonderful dinner."

"Sorry, you're right." We had ordered chicken marsala, and it was delicious. "I hope you have room for dessert because they have the best cheesecake."

"I'm already stuffed. But I guess I could have a bite."

While we waited for our check, I decided it was time to tell Abbey what else I had in mind.

"So Abbey, since this is your special day, tonight before I go to work, the focus will be on you and your pleasure. I plan to do things to you that will make you feel good." I winked at her.

She gave me a strange look and let out a strangled, "Oh . . ."

I couldn't tell if that was a question or a statement or what. I wished I could see what she was thinking. Obviously it wasn't what she was expecting.

"Just leave everything to me." I picked up the check and helped Abbey from her chair. Suddenly it felt a bit awkward because she was so quiet.

After we were in the car, she turned to me. "Thanks for a truly wonderful dinner," she said, and I noticed a tear in her eye.

She was quiet during the rest of the drive. When we got home, as she started undressing, I said to her, "Most every guy in the restaurant was jealous of me tonight and wished he were in my place."

She turned a bright pink. "What?"

"You heard me. You looked beautiful and sexy and the guys all noticed."

"You sure know how to soften up a girl." She paused for a moment. "What did you mean in the restaurant?"

"Exactly what I said. Tonight is your night. You don't have to do anything to please me. I intend to please you."

Once again she blushed but didn't say anything.

Even though we'd had sex many times, Abbey and I had never kissed, so I decided to start by kissing her. As I pressed my lips to hers, I could feel her stiffen and resist, but I kept softly kissing her and gently stroking her neck and back.

Soon I felt her relax and kiss me back. I kissed her eyes, her nose, and her neck. I found that place on the back of her neck where Ches used to love to be kissed. I felt the hair and goosebumps on the back of her neck rise as she gave a little shiver. I continued touching and kissing every part of her body. From the sighs and moans she made, I knew that she had surrendered herself to me. As I brought her to a climax, she shuddered. "Omigod, omigod."

A feeling of power swept through me. I felt like Svengali. She was mine. Afterward, as she lay basking in the afterglow, she whispered, "I didn't know, Eddie, I had no idea."

I smiled in the dark and said, "I know. Now I need to get a little sleep before I have to get up and go to work."

When I came home after work the following morning, I couldn't help but notice a change in Abbey. If I had to guess, I would say that the previous night was the culmination of the week's preparations. Her transformation was complete. She was no longer a child; she was now a woman.

I am her Svengali. She is bound to me now. She will never abandon me. Never.

SEVENTEEN

AT ABOUT EIGHT-THIRTY ON FRIDAY night as I was opening the door for some departing guests, I spotted one of our frequent guests coming up the walk.

"Tom Martin, what are you doing here on a Friday night?"

"Long story, Eddie. I have an uncle and aunt here in town. My uncle is giving my aunt a surprise fiftieth birthday party to-morrow night and my mom insisted that I be here. So, I decided it would be easier to drive in today after I finished my business. Then I can actually have a nice weekend relaxing and be ready early Monday morning for work."

"Sounds good to me." I grabbed his suitcases as we walked over for him to check in. "So where is this party going to be?"

"Some club downtown."

As we walked toward the elevator, I asked, "Would you like a snack? I think I can still get something from the kitchen."

"Nah, I had some dinner on the road. I just want to get some sleep. Long week."

"Sure," I answered as I opened the door to his room. "Anything else I can get you?"

"As a matter of fact, yes. The party starts at five-thirty tomorrow. I'm sure it'll be over by ten. How about getting me a girl for oh, say, ten-thirty?"

Elated, I said, "I can do that. I'll take care of it, Tom."

"Thanks, Eddie. See you later."

Tom always had us get him a girl whenever he stayed over. What a stroke of luck. He was the perfect guy for Abbey as her first customer. Young, nice looking, and a nice guy to boot. I could hardly wait to tell her.

I woke up early the next day. Abbey wasn't around. *Damn, she must be washing clothes.* I showered, shaved, and started breakfast. Abbey came in with a basket of clothes just as I finished my coffee.

I jumped up, grabbed the basket from her, and gave her a hug. "You'll never guess what happened."

"Okay, I'll never guess. What happened?"

I sang, "You have a job tonight."

"Really? Tell me about it."

So I told her about Tom, and she seemed totally excited. We decided that I would take her to the hotel, and while she was doing her job, I'd go over to the coffee shop on Colfax and then come back and pick her up. I hadn't told any of the other guys about her yet. I told her to go straight to the elevator, just like she was a guest. "Just smile at the bellman and say hello, but keep on walking."

IT WAS BOTH EXCITEMENT AND trepidation that I experienced when I left Abbey off at the hotel. "Don't forget. Just do everything you learned and you'll be fine."

She blew me a kiss and waved. To say that I was a nervous wreck would be putting it mildly. I had spent a lot of time and money on Abbey getting her ready, and now my future was in her hands. I drove over to the coffee shop and choked down a cup of coffee and a doughnut. *Great, that took a whole twenty minutes!*

I drove back to the hotel, found a parking space, and paced up and down the block, checking my watch every five minutes. Finally I saw her coming out of the hotel. I waved her down and jumped into the car. As I watched her approach, I knew that it had gone well. Her face was one big smile and her walk was jaunty.

"So how did it go?" I asked her.

"Oh, Eddie, it went just great. Tom loved the strip. He said he hadn't had so much fun in a long time. I did all the things you told me and I just had so much fun. And look, he gave me a twenty-dollar tip. Can you believe it?" She took a deep breath. "And, he wants me again tomorrow. And he wants to take me out to dinner first cause he said he hates to eat alone."

What was that? Did I just feel a pang of jealousy? Why? I don't love Abbey. Is it because now I have created and started something I can't change? Stop it, don't be stupid, Eddie. This is business. This is money, and money is what you want. Remember Stout Street. You never want to go back there again. Never.

"Fantastic, Abbey. I knew you'd be fantastic. I told you we'd be a great team. Did you tell him you'd go tomorrow night?"

"Of course, I did." She handed me the money as well as her tip.

"The tip is yours to keep, Abbey. You earned it," I said as I tried to hand the money back to her.

"Consider it my first payment toward the money I owe you."

"This is only the beginning. Only the beginning."

OVER THE COURSE OF THE next couple of weeks, Abbey had four jobs. We were still flying under the radar. I hadn't told anyone about Abbey, but now I felt confident that it was time to tell the other bellmen about her so we could get more jobs. The ski and holiday seasons, as well as several conventions, were coming up, and we were sure to have a busy season.

I told Mike, the bell captain, that I wanted to talk to all the guys. "Sure. Something up I should know about?"

"Yep, something you should all know about."

"Um, nothing serious, I hope."

"Nope, nothing serious." I tried to give him what I thought was a mysterious smile.

"Okay, you got it. I'll pass the word around. We'll all meet before the night shift starts. What do you want to do about the guys working graveyard this week?"

"I'll figure out a way to catch them."

Before the next shift started, everyone gathered in the employee locker room. Mike said, "Eddie has something he wants to tell all of us."

I cleared my throat. "So do you guys recall seeing a cute gal with brown hair coming into the hotel during the last couple of weeks?"

Art scratched his beard. "Yeah, I do remember her. I was on the night shift one of those weeks."

Then Hank shut his eyes and said, "I think I remember her. I guessed she was one of TT's gals."

"Well, actually she's my gal. I'm her . . . um . . . pimp. Her name is Abbey."

They all looked at me like I was some kind of lunatic. Then Hank started snorting and laughing.

"What's so funny?" I asked.

"Our Eddie is a pimp. No shit." Then Hank snorted again. "I don't believe it."

"Okay, enough. I am her pimp. And I wanted you guys to know. Hopefully you'll start to use her first before calling TT. Same deal as with him, I'll give you guys a finder's fee, which you can split."

"Sure thing, Eddie." Everyone but Art nodded. "We'd be happy to do that."

"Art?"

"I don't know, Eddie. TT gets wind of this, it could get pretty ugly. He's one mean S.O.B."

"Hey, you guys do what you think you have to do, but I'd appreciate it if you didn't mention it to TT. I doubt he'll even notice since it's just one girl. Now that you know, I'll bring her in and introduce her. You'll like her. She's a great gal."

They all agreed, and the meeting broke up so the night shift guys could get to work. The day guys hung around to ask me more questions, like how I met her, and how we got started. After I answered their questions, I made a hasty exit, eager to tell Abbey that the guys knew now and we should start seeing more business.

EIGHTEEN

BUSINESS REALLY STARTED TO PICK up. I knew that it was just a matter of time before someone would want Abbey for an all-nighter. It was important that she make it a memorable occasion, so I racked my brain on how Abbey could make it special. This was where the real money was, so I wanted Abbey to cultivate this kind of business.

I remembered how Ches taught me about food being sensual and how it really stimulated me. It seemed a good place to start. I talked to the chef and had him make up some little treats that had different textures and tastes. I took them home and tried them out on Abbey. She liked the idea, and we worked on our presentation until we felt like we had it perfected.

I found that the mall had a lingerie store that sold provocative underwear. I bought some sexy panties without a crotch. That should make the striptease more interesting.

We worked out a scenario. First the appetizer. Abbey would use the taste treats to start the evening, followed by a quickie. Just enough to satisfy. This would be followed by a nice dinner where Abbey would make sure that the john ate enough to be mellow. Then back to the bedroom where he could enjoy dessert for as long as he desired, starting with the striptease.

Just after Thanksgiving, the opportunity came. One of our older guests who had been widowed and who had enjoyed Abbey on a prior occasion wanted to spend the night with her. I could hardly wait until the next day to find out how it worked out. As soon as Abbey walked in the door, I jumped up and ran to greet her.

"So did everything work out as we expected?"

"Better than. He's such a sweet guy. He didn't even want sex this morning. He did order us a nice breakfast, though, and he promised that he'd ask for me again. Not to mention that he gave me a fifty-dollar tip!"

"Wow!" I yelled. "We're on our way, baby."

THE HOLIDAY SEASON WAS BETTER than I'd ever dreamed. If Tomcat noticed a drop in his business, I hadn't heard about it. Since I didn't want any trouble, I was grateful for that. Abbey worked every day except Christmas. New Year's Eve she got to go to an upscale party and got paid double as well.

We experienced a slight lull after the holiday season was over. Abbey still had plenty of jobs, but the pace had slowed. By Valentine's Day, she had paid back everything she owed. As

I counted my money, I was amazed at how much money we'd made in such a short period of time.

== ==

AFTER MULLING IT OVER FOR a few days, I concluded that it was time to get a new car. The Chevy, grand old lady that she was, was getting old and in need of repairs. Plus I wanted a car that was cool.

Mike's brother Walt had a new and used car lot in Greeley. Mike arranged for us to meet with his brother to see about getting a car. On a day off in early March, Abbey and I drove up to Greeley to meet him. As we drove, Abbey asked, "Do you have any idea what kind of car you want?"

"Not totally. I've kinda had some thoughts about getting a Mustang."

"Um. Yeah, I think the convertible is a great-looking car."

We followed Mike's directions and soon found the dealership. Walt looked a lot like Mike: same eyes, same chin, and same hair. Walt was a lot bigger, though, and had that slick salesman quality. My mom used to say, "The kind that could sell you ice in the winter."

Walt greeted us and invited us into his office. "So, Eddie, what did you have in mind?"

"Well, Abbey and I have talked about a Ford Mustang convertible."

"I have four on the lot right now. We'll take a look. Plus, I want to look at your car."

We strolled over to the Chevy. I had parked it in the visitor's lot.

"Wow, a 1956 Chevy. Everything still original?"

"Yes."

"It's in great shape. You've taken good care of it."

"I have. But it needs some repair work."

"No surprise."

"How much trade-in do you think you could give me?"

Walt scratched his head and walked around the car, checking it out. He got inside and started the engine. He checked the back seat and the trunk.

"Nothing," he said.

"Nothing?" I said, shocked. "Not even say . . . fifty dollars?"

"Now don't get excited. The reason I said nothing is because this car could be worth a lot of money."

"You're kidding."

"No. There are several collectors out there who would be extremely interested in this car in the shape that it's in. Let's go into the office."

While we waited, Walt went to get a collector's magazine. He handed me a copy. "Look this over. I think you can probably put an ad in for next month and sell the car for a substantial sum of money."

Shocked, I said, "I had no idea."

"I realize that. And since you work with my brother, I couldn't possibly take advantage of you. He'd kill me. Hang onto that, and we'll go check out the cars I have on the lot."

We viewed the four Mustangs as well as a couple of other cars. Abbey and I immediately fell in love with a red 1973 Mustang convertible.

"It's this one, Walt. No question."

"Good choice, Eddie. I can make you a good deal on it too. The sticker price is $2,500. I can let you have it for $2,000. I would suggest that you put new tires on it, though."

"If you think so, I'm good with that."

"While I fill out the paperwork, look over the magazine, and we'll talk more about it when I come back."

Abbey and I leafed through the magazine. I had no idea there were so many different kinds of collectors out there. There were Cadillac, Chevy, Packard, and Lincoln car clubs. The magazine was full of ads for original parts, restoration mechanics, and cars for sale.

Walt came back with the paperwork. "How do you want to pay for the car?"

I looked over the papers. "By check," I said as I signed where indicated. I wrote a check and handed it to him.

"Did you look over the magazine?"

"I did. Would you mind helping me with an ad?"

"Be happy to. I'd also be happy to keep the car here until you have a buyer."

"That's great. Thanks."

Walt checked his watch. "Why don't you go have lunch while I get the tires changed and do a final check. There's a nice restaurant about two blocks down the street."

We followed his directions and our noses and found Sadie's Chicken Restaurant. Man, I'd never seen so many different chicken dishes. I ordered fried chicken, and Abbey had a chicken salad. After we finished, we went back to the dealership. There was my new car parked right in front. I was so excited I could hardly wait to get in and drive it back to Denver. Now here was a car a guy could be proud to drive.

It was time to say goodbye to the Chevy. My heart thumped, and a knot formed in my throat. We'd been through a lot together. The old girl had saved my life many times. She'd supported my mom and me in our moves. And she was also my last connection to my dad. I gulped. Time to let the past go. Don't need that shit anymore. I patted the trunk as I went to the office.

We found Walt, and he had an ad ready to send to *Car Collector Magazine*. The address of the magazine was clipped to the top. He handed the car keys to me and said, "Any problems, let me know. And, let me know about the Chevy."

We shook hands before Abbey and I climbed into the car. It was too cold to put the top down, but it didn't matter. It was still a rush driving the car home.

Abbey gushed. "How much more perfect can things get?"

NINETEEN

A COUPLE OF WEEKS LATER, as I was lounging around watching TV, the phone rang.

"Eddie, this is Hank. You need to come down to the hotel right away. The john that Abbey was with beat her up pretty good. You might need to take her to the hospital."

"What? The john did what? Beat her up? Oh my God!" I could feel my heart thumping. What kind of a son-of-a-bitch would do that to Abbey? Everyone *loved* Abbey.

Rushing out to the car, I sped to the hotel. I parked in front and ran into the lobby. Hank was waiting for me.

"She's down in the employee locker room."

I ran down the stairs and burst into the locker room. Art was with her, holding some ice bags on her face.

"Oh my god."

Abbey opened her eyes. I took her hand.

"It's okay, Eddie. I'll be okay."

I checked her over. Her face and arms were bruised, but it didn't look like anything was broken. "Where else are you hurt, Abbey?"

She clutched her rib cage. "It hurts pretty bad."

I picked her up. "I'm going to take her to the hospital to have her ribs checked. Help me get her to the car."

Art took the ice bags and blanket he had covered her with and opened the door. I carried her as gently as I could, but she still moaned with pain. Carefully, I put her in the car.

"I'm going to take her to the emergency room at University Hospital."

"Call us as soon as you can," Art said as he waved us off.

"Will do." I turned to Abbey. "When we get to the hospital, let me do the talking. What can you tell me now before we get there?"

"Well, we were finished, and I got up to get dressed, ready to leave 'cause the time was up." Taking some breaths, she winced before continuing, "Then Ralph started screaming that he wasn't done yet, and I still owed him. He yelled that I'd wasted so much time doing the strip." She paused again and moaned.

"Hang on, we're almost there."

"Shit, it hurts so bad." She closed her eyes and took another long breath. "Then he grabbed me and started hitting me and I started screaming. I guess the people next door called the bell-man and Hank came up. He burst into the room with a passkey and fought Ralph off me. Then Art helped me downstairs to the locker room." She leaned her head back, trying to catch her breath again.

"That son-of-a-bitch. I'll kill him. Hold on, Abbey, we're almost there."

I carried Abbey into the emergency room and told the receptionist that she'd been mugged and maybe she had some broken ribs. We were shown into a room, and soon the ER doc came in and asked what happened as he examined her. I told him she had been beaten up. He ordered some X-rays to determine if there was anything broken or any internal injuries that needed attention.

It didn't take long for the doctor to come back with the X-rays. "I don't see anything broken or any other problems. Mainly she's been badly bruised. It will take several days for her to heal, but she'll be okay. I'm going to give her a shot that will put her out for several hours. I'll give you a prescription for some painkillers. Have her take it easy until some of these bruises begin to heal."

"Thanks, doc. Can you have someone help me get her to the car?"

"Sure thing. While you wait you can pay the bill. They'll have it ready for you at the front desk in a few minutes."

As I waited for the bill, my rage grew. I wanted to get back to the hotel and punch out the fucker that did this to Abbey. I paid the bill, and by the time I got back to the room, Abbey was out cold. An orderly came in with a wheelchair and we got Abbey in it and wheeled her out to the car. When we got home, I left Abbey in the car while I got the bed ready, and then I carried her in. She stirred a little as we entered the apartment. As I lay her on the bed, I assured her she was safe.

I sat with Abbey until I was sure she was out. Then I quietly slipped out of the apartment and headed down to the hotel. I wanted to take care of the bastard who did this to Abbey.

Hank was in the lobby when I drove up. He rushed out to the car. "How's Abbey?"

"Badly bruised, but she'll be okay." I got out of the car. "Now tell me what happened and where the bastard is so I can do to him what he did to Abbey."

"Calm down, Eddie. Let me tell you what's going on. Art and I were here in the lobby when the couple next door called to say that someone in the next room was screaming for help, and it sounded like there was a big fight going on. Art and I rushed up and went in and found Abbey. Art got her out of there while I confronted the john." Hank paused to open the door for a couple of guests.

After they were out of earshot, he continued, "I told him he could stay the night, but he was no longer welcome as a guest ever at The Montgomery. I told him that if he made any trouble, we'd press charges for assault and battery. I made him give me all the cash he had on him to pay for Abbey's care. Then I roughed him up just a little bit. Enough for him to know I meant business. So, just leave it be. Don't get into trouble." He reached into his pocket and pulled out the money he had gotten from the john and handed it to me.

I'd cooled down by then and realized Hank was right. "Thank you. You're right." I knew I should get back home and take care of Abbey. "You're a good buddy. I need to get back to Abbey. Thank Art for me. See ya."

⌐ ⌐

ABBEY WAS STILL ASLEEP WHEN I got up the next morning. Fortunately, I had the day off and wouldn't start on graveyard for another night, so I had plenty of time to take care of her. Looking at her face, she was one big purple mass of bruises. Her left eye was swollen and purple. She also had a small cut under her eye where the bastard had punched her. Her lips were swollen and she had a cut in her lip as well. It made me sick.

By the time I finished making breakfast, Abbey woke up groaning. "Shit, I feel like I've been hit by a ton of bricks."

"You look like you've been hit by a ton of bricks too," I teased. I walked over to the bed and sat down. "Do you think you can get up?"

"I think so." She tried pushing herself up. She moaned. I put my hand under her back and lifted her up. She sat there a moment and then said, "Wow, I feel woozy. What did that doc give me?"

"Some pretty strong painkiller. How's the pain right now?"

"Help me up. I need to go to the bathroom."

I helped her into the bathroom where she promptly threw up. "Oh, this is awful."

I helped her wash up and then led her to the kitchen table. "Sit down and have something to eat. I think that will make you feel better."

After she managed to down some tea and toast, she did feel better. "Do you think you want to take a painkiller now?"

"No. Just help me over to the lounge chair. I think I'd like to sit up for a while." I turned on the TV as she settled into the chair. Then I prepared a couple of ice bags for her to put on her face to help with the swelling. After I finished eating breakfast and tidying up, Abbey was ready to lie back down.

"I want you to take another painkiller now and get some more sleep. It'll help you heal faster."

As I watched her sleep, I asked myself why the hell I was in this business anyway. It's a dirty, ugly business. *Hey, asshole, you know why. It's the money. Remember, no going back to Stout Street. And Abbey is doing this of her own free will. I didn't force her to do this.*

I spent the rest of the day feeding Abbey and helping her up and down. My nerves were shot by the end of the day. I hoped tomorrow would be better.

═ ═

A HOTEL IS A TWENTY-FOUR seven business. We always had maids, maintenance men, bellmen, and desk clerks on duty. It surprised me to find out how many of these employees knew and liked Abbey.

When I returned to work, the maintenance men had bought a vase full of flowers for Abbey. The maids had purchased a pair of fluffy slippers for her, and the bellmen had pitched in to get her a nice robe.

Apparently Abbey hung out with the different employees in between jobs or when she had free time. It seemed that she knew the names of their spouses, children, boyfriends, and girlfriends. She often brought small treats for them, like Annie's special cinnamon rolls and other baked goods, including cookies.

Most employees accepted the fact that being a prostitute was her business, and that she was just a working girl doing her job just as they were doing theirs. Of course, there were those few others who thought she was evil, godless, and nothing but trash.

I thanked everyone profusely and told them I knew Abbey would be thrilled by their gifts and good wishes. When I

presented the gifts and good wishes to Abbey, she was overwhelmed by their kindness and burst into tears.

"I don't get it. Why are you crying?" I wanted to understand.
"I thought you'd be happy that everyone thought about you."

"I am happy, you stupid idiot. That's why I'm crying."

Would I ever really understand women?

===

BY THE END OF THE week, Abbey's bruises had turned from
bright purple to a greenish color. Some had even faded to a pale
yellow. Her ribs still hurt pretty badly, but that would take time.
Overall, she was feeling much better.

"As soon as you're better, I'm signing you up for a judo class.
This isn't going to happen again. Ever. You're going to learn to
defend yourself."

"I think that's a great idea. Too bad we didn't think of
it sooner."

===

THE TIME HAD COME FOR Abbey to get back to work. "I think
you're healed enough to work again. How about I tell the guys
you're ready to start tomorrow?"

"I don't know. I'm scared, and I'm not sure I want to do this
anymore."

"Really? Life is full of risks, Abbey. It's just like falling off a
bike. You need to get back on and ride. And what would you do
instead? I thought we had a good thing going here."

"Don't be mad at me. I just don't know right now."

I got up and left the apartment. I needed to be alone to cool off and think this over.

＝ ＝

WHEN I CAME BACK, IT was obvious that Abbey had been crying. I ignored her and went into the kitchen. I took some ham and condiments out and made myself a sandwich. Still feeling a little agitated, I sat at the table, read the paper, and ate my sandwich.

Abbey sat down. "I'm sorry. I understand what you're saying, but I can't help being afraid. Just tell me what you want me to do."

I put the paper down. "We'll sign you up for a self-defense class today. You'll go back to work tomorrow. You'll go to your class every day and learn to defend yourself. It's a tough world, Abbey. Deal with it." I tried to sound convincing. Deep inside, I hoped I was right.

"I'll do it."

＝ ＝

THANKFULLY, THINGS RESUMED THEIR NORMAL pace. Abbey started a judo class. We had fun practicing in the gym when I had time off. Surprisingly, she turned out to be tough and did quite well. I felt confident that she'd be able to take care of herself in the future.

TWENTY

THE AD FOR THE CHEVY appeared in the February issue of *Car Collector Magazine*. By the end of the week, I received a call from a Robert Miller in Goodland, Kansas. I answered all his questions, and he decided he would travel to Greeley to see the car.

"So how much do you think you want for the car if I'm interested?" he asked me.

Walt had said he thought I could get between $2,000 and $2,500, so I decided to go big. "I'm thinking in the neighborhood of $2,500," I said. "But I'd consider less."

"Um, well, let me look at the car first and then I'll think about it. I can plan to be there on Saturday."

I promised I'd call Walt to make sure he would be available. I took Robert's telephone number in case there was a problem. Then I thanked him for his call, hung up, and called Walt.

"I told him $2,500 for the car, but that I might consider less. I'll leave it to you to negotiate the best price."

"I'll do my best. I'll give you a call when I have something to report."

Since Abbey wasn't home, I decided not to tell her anything until something happened. At work on Saturday, we were so busy that I had almost forgotten about the car until Abbey called.

"Hey. Everything okay?"

"Fine. Walt called. He wants you to call him."

"Thanks. I'll call him right away."

I took my break and went to the employee locker room to call Walt.

"Good news, I hope," I said to Walt.

"Yep. Sold the car to Mr. Miller for $2,300."

"Whoa, Walt that's fantastic."

"I'll send you a check first thing Monday morning."

"I appreciate it, Walt. Take $250 for yourself." It was the least I could do.

"Thanks, Eddie. It's nice of you to do that."

"Hell, you deserve it. I'll let Hank know what a great salesman you are."

Walt guffawed. "I think he already knows that but rub it in anyway. Bye now."

I called Abbey next. "What time is your first job tonight?"

"Not until nine. Why?"

"Well then get dressed and be ready when I come home. I'm taking you out to dinner tonight. Walt sold the Chevy for $2,300."

"That's great news, Eddie. I was wondering if that was the reason for his call. I'll be ready. It'll be nice to celebrate."

IT WAS TIME TO OPEN a savings account. With the cash from the sale of the Chevy and the money that I had accumulated from my various enterprises, I had way too much money stashed at home, even with the various cash deposits I had made to my checking account over the last few months.

I found a savings and loan bank on Colorado Boulevard not far from home. After I had made my deposit, the new accounts person told me that I was entitled to a free gift.

Huh, how about that? Deposit money and get a gift. I like it. She handed me a small box that said: 1 Revere Bowl. I thanked her, took my gift, and left.

When I got home, Abbey was getting dressed for work. "Hey, Abbey, come look at what I got."

"In a minute."

I opened the box and found a silver bowl. I had a vague recollection of reading about Revere bowls in a novel, and I remembered that Revere was a silversmith and had designed some kind of Liberty Bowl, but this was the first time I'd ever seen one.

Abbey came out of the bathroom fresh from her shower. "Yeah, what did you get?"

I showed her the bowl. "What is it?" she asked.

"It's called a Revere bowl. I got it as a gift for opening a savings account."

"Very nice. What are we supposed to put in it?"

"I have no clue. What do you think?"

"How about we put it on the coffee table and put nuts in it?" she suggested.

"Okay, nuts it is."

After I thought about it for a while, I realized that it was more than just a silver bowl I got as a free gift. It was a symbol of what money can buy. Things that I'd only read about but had never seen, experienced, felt, or touched before. It's one thing to read a glorious description of a purple sunset in a novel, but if you've never seen or experienced a purple sunset, you only have a shallow understanding of the experience and the deep feelings that such a sunset can provoke.

This was a step to a richer life. I was at a point where I could choose to follow the same kind of life as Tomcat or L.T. A life of drugs, alcohol, gambling, and sex. Or I could choose a life more like I had experienced with Ches. A life of good food, good friends, rich experiences, and greater knowledge and understanding of the world. A chance to be a better man. *I choose the latter.*

TWENTY-ONE

"GOD DAMN IT, ABBEY, WHEN are you going to pick up all this mess in here? Surprise, I live here too. I'm sick of trying to find my own stuff."

She rolled her eyes at me and gave me that look. Then she sighed. "I'll try to get around to it soon."

"Soon? How about now?"

"I'm busy right now. I said I'd get around to it and I will."

"See that you do." Frustrated, I picked up my stuff and left, slamming the door as loudly as possible.

AS I SAT AT A table in my favorite coffee shop on East Colfax on a cold, dreary day in March, I finally came to a decision about something I'd been thinking about for several days. It was time to move.

I could no longer live with Abbey in our buffet apartment. As much as I loved her as my best friend, and as much as I appreciated the fact that she was my ticket out of the Stout Streets in my life, she was driving me crazy. The hanging space in the closet was jammed with all her clothes. The floor was covered with her shoes. The dresser drawers were stuffed with her things. The top of the dresser was covered with her cosmetics and jewelry. The bathroom rod always had her bras, panties, hose, and garter belts hanging over it.

I needed my own room. I needed my own space. I had lived so much of my life in cramped quarters, that all this closeness was too much. I needed someplace where I could be alone with myself. I decided I'd talk to Abbey about it when I got home from work that night.

== ==

I WAS IN BED WATCHING TV when she came home. "So how was your evening, Abbey?"

She yawned. "Good. I'm beat though. I had two very, uh, enthusiastic customers tonight." She yawned again as she began to undress.

"I have something I want to discuss with you if it's okay."

"Jeez, can it wait till morning?"

"Sure, I guess so." I sighed.

"Okay, I know you. You need to tell me now. Spit it out."

"We have to move."

Alarmed, she jumped up and said, "Did I do something wrong? What's happened?"

Dumb ass . . . that came out well. "No, you didn't do anything wrong. Sorry, that just came out wrong. What I meant was that we've outgrown this place. You need your own room and closet, and I need my own room and closet. We have plenty of money now to do it. So, I want you to start looking tomorrow. I want to be out of here by the end of the month."

"For Chrissake, you scared the hell out of me. Fine. You're right. We do need more room. Let's talk about it more tomorrow. Right now I need to get some sleep."

Satisfied that Abbey would take care of things, I rolled over and fell asleep.

In the morning, we discussed what kind of place she should look for. I began, "I'd like to stay in this neighborhood. It's close to the bus so I can still take the bus to work most of the time. And it's nice and convenient to everything we need. Two bedrooms, of course. Not too big of a building. Anything else?"

"How about covered parking of some kind?"

"Absolutely. I do want covered parking for the Mustang. Good thinking. Anyway, pick out three or four that we can look at together on Thursday."

"Thursday? Wow, you don't give a girl much time. I'll get started on it right away."

"Thanks, I know you'll find the perfect place for us."

I went to take my shower and get ready for work. When I was ready to leave, Abbey was already writing down addresses of available apartments.

"By the way, don't forget we're still brother and sister sharing an apartment."

She smiled. "Right. I remember."

I waved goodbye and said "good hunting" as I left.

When I came home from work, Abbey was waiting for me with a list of what she'd found.

"Wow, I had a wonderful time today. So far I've found two great places for us to look at. The only problem is that all the two-bedroom apartments are unfurnished. And we don't have any furniture."

"Not to worry. It's time we bought furniture anyway. We have the money. I figure we'll each pay for our own bedroom furniture and then share the cost of whatever else we buy. If you don't have enough, I'll loan it to you, and you can pay me back."

She hesitated. "You know I don't know anything about furniture. I don't mean to be stupid, but we never really had much of anything when I was growing up."

"I know. Me neither. But we'll figure it out."

She seemed to relax. Then she told me about the apartments she'd looked at so far.

"I have four more to look at tomorrow. I'm certain that by Thursday I will have four lined up for me to show you."

"Good girl. Let's watch TV now and then get some sleep."

══ ══

WE GOT UP EARLY ON Thursday to begin our day of apartment hunting. The first apartment was on Colorado Boulevard.

"Nice apartment, but it faces west. We'll fry from the afternoon sun in the summer. Plus it faces Colorado. When we open the windows, we'll hear all that noise from the street."

"I guess you're right." She looked wistfully at the apartment as she checked it off her list.

The next apartment was okay, but they wanted twenty dollars extra for covered parking, and that wasn't even a garage. It was just some poles with a cover over the top. Didn't seem like it was worth twenty bucks to me.

I really liked the next apartment. It was spacious and very nice. The building was bigger than I wanted, but I figured I could live with that. Then we found out that there were no garages available, but we could get on the waiting list. I told the agent we'd think about it.

The fourth apartment was off 8th Avenue. It seemed to have around twelve units, give or take. Just the right size, in my opinion. The owner was an older, short, rotund, balding man with glasses. He wore suspenders that he kept snapping. His name was Irving. I liked him immediately.

"I have two apartments available," Irving informed us. "One on the first floor in back and one on the second floor in front."

"We'll look at both," I told him.

It was an older building but seemed to be in pretty good shape. Both apartments were large and appeared to be the same size and floor plan. I liked the one on the second floor because I could look out and see the mountains from the living room. It also had a real honest-to-goodness garage. It would be the first real garage I'd ever had, so that sealed the deal for me. I did notice a couple of things that could be done in the apartment to make it nicer, so I decided to mention them to Irving.

"Irving, I noticed that the faucets in both the kitchen and bathroom could stand to be replaced. They're looking a little old. The kitchen and bathroom floors are also starting to look a little worn. And the kitchen countertops and the hardware on the kitchen cabinets are looking a little rundown too. So, here's what I propose." Irving was fidgeting a bit, but I went on.

"I'm good at fixing that kind of stuff. If you'll pay for the materials, I'll do the repair and installation."

Irving scratched his head, adjusted his glasses, and snapped his suspenders. Finally, he said, "That sounds good, Eddie, but I want to see what you pick out first and approve it before I let you do it."

"That's only fair. I know you're worried about the cost, but I'll keep it reasonable. Speaking of reasonable, I won't charge for my labor if you'll take five dollars off the monthly rent for one year." I eyed Irving to see if I could tell how that went over.

Once again, Irving adjusted his glasses and snapped his suspenders. Then he said, "Let's see how much everything costs first. If it's reasonable, then I will take five dollars off each month. Do we have a deal?"

"We have a deal." We shook hands. "We'll want to move in by the first."

Irving whipped out a contract and quickly filled in the details. I looked at Abbey for her okay, and she nodded yes. I signed the contract and gave Irving a check for the deposit and the first month's rent.

As we walked to the car, Abbey gave me a hug and said, "Wow, I'm excited. It's a great apartment."

"Yes, I can hardly wait to get to the hardware and tile store to start picking out stuff. We have a lot to do this next couple of weeks, so we need to spend our free time getting everything ready. Let's go to the tile store on Colorado first and see what we can find."

"Sure."

The apartment was painted a pale gray with gray carpeting. The kitchen cabinets were painted off-white with a gray cast, and the countertop was also off-white. The tile in the bathroom was gray, trimmed in white. To stick with the current color scheme, for the kitchen and bathroom floors, I picked out gray-colored tile with white streaking and silver sparkles running through it. For the countertop, I picked off-white laminate Formica with silver sparkles in it. I took samples of each as well as a price list.

At the hardware store, I found cool brushed silver faucets and hardware for the kitchen cabinets. I purchased a sample of the hardware and took the brochures and price lists for the faucets. I could hardly wait to get home and call Irving.

Irving was surprised that I had already picked out everything we needed. We arranged to meet the following day so he could check out the samples and prices before he decided.

═ ═

IRVING WAS WAITING FOR ME in the apartment. "So, Eddie, you're mister hurry-up-and-get-it-done."

"Yes sir," I said as I unpacked the samples I'd bought and laid them out for him to inspect.

He checked everything and went over the price lists. "Nice job, Eddie, I think we can do this. The prices are reasonable, so I will take five dollars off the rent for a year, providing the job is well done."

Enthusiastically, I pumped his hand. "Thanks, I promise you'll be pleased, Irving."

With Irving's okay, I headed back to the tile and hardware stores to purchase the materials and supplies I would need. I also rented the equipment necessary to get the job done. I was excited to get started.

Working with my hands, measuring, and figuring out just how things should go together pleased me, and I enjoyed every part of the renovation process. Installing the cabinet hardware and new faucets went quickly. The floors and countertop were a little trickier, but I got the job done and was pleased and satisfied with the result. I looked forward to showing Irving what I had done.

Once again, we met in the apartment. Irving had a smile from ear to ear as he appraised my work.

"Well done. It looks better than I had imagined. You've got your five dollars off. And I hope that maybe you'll do some more work for me."

"I'll consider it, Irving. Let's plan to talk about it later."

TWENTY-TWO

IT WAS TIME FOR THE next task before we could settle into our new apartment: buy furniture. I went to the library and loaded up on books about furniture, including books that depicted furnishings of different periods and different styles. Abbey and I poured through the photos.

"I definitely don't like period furniture, or ornate furniture with little flowers and other fussy stuff. I like simple lines and bright colors," I told Abbey.

"That suits me," Abbey replied. "Simple and bright is good. So I guess that means we're ready to go shopping."

At the first two furniture stores, we wandered about without finding anything we liked or anyone to help us. Discouraged, we drove to the next store on our list, Modern Décor.

As soon as we walked in, I knew we would find what I wanted-ed. A salesman immediately approached us. "Good morning," he said. "Can I help you?"

I explained to him what we were looking for.

"Yes," he said. "I believe what you need to do is talk to our interior designer, Marianne. I'll get her."

While we waited, we wandered around and saw several pieces of furniture we liked. After a few minutes, the salesman came back with Marianne and introduced her.

"Hi, I'm Eddie and this is Abbey. We just rented a new apartment and need to furnish the whole place."

She nodded. "Let's sit down and you can tell me about your place."

"Here's the floor plan, along with the measurements of each room." I spread it out in front of us.

Marianne listened to our ideas and studied the plan. "I have some ideas for you. First, I want you to tell me what colors you like and what kind of furniture you like."

I told Marianne that we'd already spotted some pieces we liked, so she asked us to show her. Afterward, she suggested, "Now that I have a better idea of your preferences, why don't you two go have some lunch, and I'll have sketches and other pieces of furniture ready for you to look at when you come back?"

We agreed and left. As we sat eating our sandwiches, I said to Abbey, "I think we've hit the jackpot. I feel certain we'll find what we want today."

"I think so too."

We finished our lunch and walked back to the store. Marianne was waiting for us with a few sketches for where we might place our furniture, some fabric samples, as well as items of furniture she had picked out that she thought we might like even more than what we'd first seen. She was right—she'd picked the perfect pieces. "I really like this off-white rattan bedroom set," Abbey said.

"And this black set will work really well for me."

Together we decided on a sofa and two chairs, along with the fabrics they'd be upholstered in, plus a couple of tables and lamps for the living room. Last, we chose a kitchen set.

When Marianne quoted the price to us, I looked at Abbey, whose face was white. I wondered if I was as white as she looked. To us it was a staggering sum. Almost $3,000. Marianne explained that we could pay it off in three payments. My blood pressure went down slightly.

"I'll leave you two alone to discuss it," she said.

"We can do this," I whispered to Abbey. "We'll just have to work hard. I already have almost all of it in my savings. How much do you have?"

Abbey gulped. "About a thousand dollars. I'm scared to spend all of my money, though."

"This is a new plateau for us. Our start on a new life. Something better than what either of us has ever had. I think it's time to do it. And we can make payments, as Marianne suggested, rather than spend everything we've saved," I urged.

Abbey sighed. "If you say so. I guess I'm alright with doing this."

I called Marianne back and told her we were ready to make our purchases.

"While you were talking, I checked our stock and the materials we picked out. We have most of the bedroom pieces. The upholstered pieces will have to be ordered. I do have the tables, the lamps, and the kitchen set. So, I'll need a deposit and then we'll bill you for the things we deliver. We won't bill you for the other pieces until they arrive. That way, you don't have to pay for everything all at once."

I realized that with this pay-as-you-go arrangement, we should have the money to cover the entire cost by the time all the furniture arrived.

"Okay. How much of a deposit do I need to make?"

"We require a twenty percent deposit."

I wrote a check. "Done," I said.

We then discussed delivery dates before Abbey and I thanked Marianne for her help and left the store. As we walked to the car, I wasn't sure who was shaking more-Abbey or me. "That was some day we just had," I commented.

"I'm scared out of my britches. I just hope we're doing the right thing."

"I know we are. You'll see. It'll all work out."

TWENTY-THREE

IRVING HAD GIVEN US THE keys to the apartment after I finished the remodeling, so Abbey and I moved whatever we could toward the end of the month. When moving day arrived, we were able to load what few things were left into the car with no problem.

Abbey cleaned our old apartment. We turned in the keys and were on our way. Our excitement was high as we drove to our new home and, hopefully, a better life.

The furniture delivery van arrived promptly at nine-thirty. With Marianne's plan in hand, we were able to direct them where to put each piece.

When they finished, we surveyed the results. "The living room looks a little weird with just lamps and tables, doesn't it?" I said to Abbey.

"Everything looks strange to me," she said. "You know I've never had my own bedroom set. All I ever had was a rollaway with a mattress. It just feels so . . . so funny."

"I know. For me too."

After we finished putting the rest of our things away, Abbey went to the store, as we had no food left in the house when we moved.

Making dinner proved to be an adventure. We still were not used to where we had put everything.

After dinner we made a nice soft bed on the floor so we could watch TV. When it came time to go to bed to our separate rooms, we weren't sure what to do. This would be the first time Abbey and I hadn't slept together since I first picked her up by the bus stop. It just didn't feel right somehow.

I didn't know about Abbey, but I tossed and turned all night. When I woke up in the morning, I had misgivings about our move. The whole thing just didn't feel right.

"How did you sleep last night?" Abbey asked as she yawned.

"Not very well. And you?"

"Me either. That bed just seemed so big."

"It's not home yet, is it?"

"No. But we'll get used to it."

In a few weeks, the rest of our furniture arrived. As we surveyed the apartment, we found that we still had mixed feelings.

"Looks like it came right out of a magazine," Abbey said.

"Uh, yeah. It does, doesn't it? Kind of uncomfortable, huh?" I sighed. "I'm sure once we get used to it, we'll like it."

Abbey looked doubtful. "Sure, I guess so."

Over the course of the next few weeks, Abbey started adding little things here and there. Knickknacks, she called them. She also bought curtains for the kitchen window that made it look cheerier.

"I'm getting used to it," I told her.

Abbey smiled back at me.

There we were. The pimp and the prostitute. All cozy in a nice two-bedroom apartment. *This has got to be the strangest arrangement ever.*

TWENTY-FOUR

SO FAR, WE'D BEEN OPERATING under the radar. Tomcat didn't seem to notice that he had a little less action from our hotel. Obviously, with just Abbey, we weren't digging into his business that much.

I'd begun thinking about how to expand our little business, and I'd been mulling over my thoughts for several days. I decided it was time to discuss it with her.

When I came home for dinner, I was surprised to find another girl there.

"Eddie, this is my friend, Colleen. I ran into her today after I left the hotel. Seems Tomcat threw her out too." She paused to look at me. Then she took a breath and went on. "Anyway I brought her home and told her about you and me and about how you taught me stuff and how we're doing, and I thought maybe you'd do the same for her." Out of breath, Abbey looked at me intently.

Is this coincidence or what? I checked Colleen over. It was obvious that Abbey had her take a shower before I arrived. She had a clean face and her curly red hair was still damp. I could see that she had a sprinkling of freckles on her face, which had that transparent porcelain look to it. She wasn't especially pretty, but her eyes were a sparkly green with flecks of gold in them, giving her face a memorable quality.

I let my eyes run down her body. Nothing special until I came to her legs. She had legs up the ying-yang. *Yeah, I could enjoy getting between those.*

Finally I spoke. "So Colleen, do you think you'd like to work for me?"

With downcast eyes, she mumbled, "Yes."

Since I had been thinking about this for the last several days, I'd already formalized a plan for how I would get a girl ready for business. I outlined my plan to Colleen. "Do you think you can do this?"

She looked up at me. "Yes, I think so."

"Good. Abbey, tomorrow first thing, you'll take her to the clinic and make sure everything is okay. If it's a go, then you'll do the beauty thing. Hair, nails, and makeup. Will that work with your schedule tomorrow?"

"No problem, Eddie."

"Okay. Next thing. Colleen, do you have any money and a place to stay?"

Again the downcast eyes. "No to both."

"It's okay," Abbey said. "She can share my room with me until she gets going."

"Are you sure?"

"Sure, Eddie."

I looked at Colleen and said, "You understand that the money I put out for you has to be paid back? Also, we share expenses for the apartment. But, unlike with Tomcat, you will get a fair share of the money that you earn."

"I understand. And, I'm grateful for the chance. Thank you both. I had no idea what I was going to do when Tomcat kicked me out."

Abbey had a job that evening, so that left me alone with Colleen. "So, Colleen, tell me about yourself."

She shrugged. "What do you want to know?"

"Like, where are you from? How did you get here? How did you hook up with Tomcat?"

She sighed. "Well, I'm from Goodland, Kansas. My dad got hurt in an accident about four years ago and hasn't been able to work."

"Sorry to hear that."

"Yeah, well that left me looking after him and my brothers while my mom worked. Anyway he's gotten pretty mean and I finally couldn't take it anymore so I ran away." She sniffled and a few tears fell. I found a tissue and handed it to her.

"So how did you get here?"

"I hitched a ride with a trucker and he dropped me off here in Denver. I ran out of money real fast and then Tomcat found me on the street and took me in."

Same old story. Dad probably abused her too. I wasn't sure what to say in response, and I didn't want to press too hard, so I decided it was time to change the subject. "Okay, we'll talk more later. Let's watch some TV."

After watching TV for a while, I told her I was going to bed. She said goodnight and headed for Abbey's room.

＝ ＝

BEFORE I LEFT FOR WORK in the morning, I gave Abbey a few thoughts about how I wanted Colleen's hair and makeup. Then I headed out to work.

The girls were waiting for me at the door when I came home. Abbey had done a great job with Colleen. Her hair was dyed a darker red with blonde highlights. It was still long but fell in soft waves just below her shoulders. Yes, quite sexy looking. Her makeup made the most of her green eyes and porcelain-white skin.

"Colleen, you look fantastic!" I enthused. "Good job, Abbey."

The girls giggled, thrilled that I was pleased. "What's next, boss?" Abbey asked.

"I don't have a day off until Thursday, so tomorrow I want you to sign Colleen up for judo class and then I want you to work with her on the strip. We'll shop for clothes on Thursday."

Since Abbey was busy each night, I worked with Colleen in the evenings. She was thrilled with the new clothes and anxious to please. Unlike Abbey, Colleen was so quiet I could see why Tomcat threw her out. Obviously, she couldn't have been very successful at soliciting.

After a couple of nights, I invited Colleen to go to bed with me. She was much like Abbey the first time. Young, inexperienced, and not particularly good. Definitely not up to the standard I had set in my mind for a call girl. Once again, I became the teacher.

Ches had taught me that every person is different and that one should strive to find what it is that's special about each one. Every woman has her own distinct perfume, and the feel of each body is just a little different. As I lay with Colleen, I asked myself: What do I feel and smell about Colleen? What makes her different? What makes her special?

Colleen seemed like a wounded bird, so I spoke and instructed in a soft, quiet voice that seemed to calm her down. She responded and even improvised some on what I told her. I was pleased. It seemed she would be a good asset. I would just need to spend more time with her to discover her special talents.

Afterward, I asked her if she wanted to stay with me or go to Abbey's room.

"If you don't mind, I think I'd rather go to Abbey's room."

"No problem. See you in the morning."

The next time I worked with her, I asked, "What did you always want to be when you grew up?" I hoped to get her to open up a little.

She didn't even have to think about it. "A swimmer. When I was little, I saw a movie about this lady who swam the English Channel. It was wonderful. I decided I wanted to do that. So I learned to swim and practiced all the time. Then my dad had the accident and that was the end of that. I had to take care of the family. No time to swim." She sighed.

"Yeah, I know all about that."

I asked her a few more questions, and I realized that she was a good listener and responded intelligently. Afterward, I worked on developing a script for her that would help her during those first few awkward moments with a new client.

The next morning, I gave her the script. I told her to study it and then we'd practice. "Does this really work?" she asked.

"There's a huge difference between what you did for Tomcat and what you're going to do now. You've been invited by a gentleman to please him. You aren't hustling on the street. You will be in a nice room in a nice hotel wearing pretty clothes and looking beautiful. So, yes. It does work, I promise."

"Okay. I'll do my best."

Finally, after three weeks, I felt that Colleen was ready. It was time for her to get actual experience to gain the confidence and additional skills she needed. I planned her special evening for Friday night, since I was working day shift and would then have the following two days off.

Abbey had an all-night gig, so it would work out great. I wanted Colleen to have the full benefit of her special night. I had told Abbey not to tell Colleen too much about the evening.

Colleen dressed up in her favorite new dress. I was proud to be taking her out in public; she looked so beautiful. We had a delicious dinner and a nice slow drive home. Once we were in the apartment, I put on soft music and put my arm around her.

"This evening belongs to you, Colleen. You don't have to do anything to please me. Tonight is for your pleasure alone."

I felt her shudder. Just as Abbey had been nervous, so was Colleen. She obviously did not know quite what to expect. I kissed and touched every part of her. I hadn't done anything like this in a long time, and I was enjoying myself.

Is that Colleen? I suddenly thought to myself. The sound she had begun to make sounded somewhere between a hum and a purr. *Yes, she's getting into it.* I could feel her body asking for more. I became more insistent with my kisses, teasing her in every way I knew. Soon, she was panting and her body arched to meet mine and I knew it was time.

Once again, I felt that overwhelming sense of power as I brought Colleen to a climax and bonded her to me. Afterward, she smiled. Her eyes heavy, she whispered thank you and promptly fell asleep.

She will never abandon me either. She is mine forever.

TWENTY-FIVE

I INTRODUCED COLLEEN TO THE gang at the hotel. She got some jobs immediately.

The feedback from johns was that she was sensuous as hell and the sex so smoldering it left a guy melted to his core and wanting more. That certainly surprised me. I hadn't felt that at all, but I was pleased that she had turned out to be such an asset. I considered that perhaps I needed to have sex with her again real soon, although there hadn't been time for that. We were busy and the money was pouring in. I felt strong and powerful.

It wasn't long before another of Tomcat's girls asked to join us. I was in the middle of updating one of Irving's apartments that had been recently vacated, so once Kim joined us, I instructed Colleen and Kim to rent it.

Now that I had three girls, I needed to consider where I was going with this business. When I first started, I hadn't thought beyond Abbey. Did I want to keep expanding? Was this a business that I wanted to stay in? I wasn't entirely sure. Even though I'd been lucky, I knew it could be an ugly business. On the other hand, I was making really good money and I knew Abbey, Colleen, and Kim were happy. With those thoughts, the decision was made. I would stay the course.

To make sure that everything continued to go well, however, it was time to develop a set of rules to keep discipline and order. I suspected that soon I would have more girls employed, and I wanted to make sure they would always be top-notch. I wanted them to always look and behave like ladies. Ches had taught me that it was important to know the rules of the social set you wanted to belong to. Once I had settled on what those rules needed to be, I called a meeting of the three girls.

"Ladies, since there are now three of you in my employ, I called this meeting today to review the rules you must follow. These are non-negotiable, and I want to make sure they are adhered to at all times. First, when you are out in public, you will always look and act like ladies. Second, you will always be discreet. Third, you will make sure to stay out of trouble. You must never be recognizable to law enforcement. Fourth, you will always treat your customers well. I don't want any trouble with johns. If any of these rules are broken more than once, you can expect to lose your job immediately." I was dead serious. The girls knew it and didn't challenge me.

= =

AS I HAD PREDICTED, TWO more girls defected from Tomcat. A few days after they arrived, Mike, the bell captain, approached me. "I heard that Tomcat is furious and plans to come over to the hotel and take you down."

I wasn't too worried. I'd continued to take martial arts classes at the Y, and I was certain that I could take Tomcat easily. Rumor had it that he'd been enjoying the good life too much. Too many late nights of drinking, doing drugs, and having sex with anyone and everyone had left him in bad shape.

Two days later, Mike called me over as I was returning to the lobby. "Word has it that Tomcat is on his way. What are you going to do?"

"I'll handle it. Don't worry."

"Whatever you do, keep it away from the hotel."

I gave him an okay and went out the front door. Hank was on duty in front of the hotel, and said, "Hey, man, what's up?"

"Word is Tomcat is on his way over to take me down."

"Shit. He's one mean son-of-a-bitch. What's your plan?"

"As long as he doesn't have a gun, I think I can take him. So, I'll steer him away from the front of the hotel. Get Fred out here to cover and you come with me. Make sure he doesn't shoot me or something. I don't want you to be involved. Just be a witness."

"Sure, Eddie."

At that moment, I saw Tomcat's canary yellow caddie drive up and park on the street. Tomcat got out of the back, and his two goons got out of the front.

"Quick, Hank, go get Fred and Mike. Tomcat has his goons with him."

Hank ran into the lobby. At this point, I felt apprehensive. I'd only planned to have to deal with Tomcat. Thankfully, the hotel was quiet. Mike, Hank, and Fred all came rushing out the front door.

"What do you want us to do?"

"Mike, you stay here and cover the hotel. Hank, Fred, you come with me. We'll meet them near the sidewalk." We quickly made our way down the driveway and met at the bottom.

I faced Tomcat. He sneered at me. "So you're the little fucking bastard that's been stealing my girls."

"No, Tomcat. I haven't been stealing your girls. You threw them out, I took them in. You gotta problem with that, too bad."

"Listen, you little fucker, nobody takes anything from Tomcat," he said, slurring his words.

I figured he was either half drunk or doped up. I desperately wanted to solve this without a fight and hoped he wasn't too far gone. "Listen, guy. There's plenty of business out there for both of us. I'm not trying to do you any harm. Girl comes to me, wants to work for me. Fine. I'm not going out and soliciting your girls."

"You're nothing but a son-of-a-bitch and I'm going to teach you a lesson," he replied as he pulled out a knife.

I reacted quickly and kicked the knife out of his hand, but not before he nicked my arm. Shit, that stung! Then I grabbed his arm and twisted it at the same time that he managed to get in a punch to my gut. That really made me mad. I kicked him in the balls. Writhing in agony, he fell to the ground. His guys came toward me, but Hank and Fred blocked the way, hands balled and ready to fight.

"This is between me and Tomcat," I said. "Stay the fuck out of it."

The boys started to make a move, but Fred and Hank didn't budge. With their fists at the ready, they stared down the goons, who finally backed off. I put my foot on Tomcat's chest the same way I'd seen Jeff do to L.T.

"Now you listen to me, Tomcat. I'm gonna let you go. You leave me alone and I'll leave you alone. As I said, there's plenty of business for both of us. We start a war, we'll have the police all over us and our girls. That's not what we want, so just cool it."

Tomcat got up slowly. "You just don't get it, you little shit. You take a girl, you gotta pay for her. It's $500 a girl."

Fuck, now I get it. I didn't know that. It's about money and saving face too, I guess. I stared at Tomcat and said, "Have one of your boys at the hotel tomorrow. The money will be waiting."

He gestured to his boys, got in the car, and they drove off.

The three of us just stood there shaking. Then we started laughing. "Damn, Eddie, you were fucking great," Hank said.

"I hope this is the end of it, and we don't have any more trouble. I don't want the hotel to have a problem."

We hurried back to the front door where Mike was anxiously waiting to find out what happened.

Fred roared, "Mike you should have seen Eddie. He laid Tomcat flat out. Whoa, I never saw anything like it. He was fast as a bolt of lightning."

Mike mopped his forehead. "I was plenty worried. Thank God, you're okay. Now, let's get back to work."

WITH FIVE GIRLS, I NEEDED to generate more business. I had Art take photos of the girls and made an album with the photos.

Then I went to several of the nearby hotels and schmoozed the bellmen, like I was a real press agent, and left my business card with my name and phone number.

Before I'd even finished training the two new girls, phone calls from other hotels started coming in. "Shit, we're going to be a huge organization in no time," I told Abbey.

"Wow, I had no idea when we started that it was going to get so crazy. Did you?"

"I didn't have a clue. Now we just need to keep it tight so everything doesn't fall apart. I'm depending on you to help keep the girls straight."

Abbey gave me her most solemn look. "You know, Eddie, there isn't anything I wouldn't do for you."

I hugged her. "I knew I could count on you." Abbey had turned out to be my best friend, a good organizer, and a trusted advisor. If she had been given the chance, she could have been a top executive in a large corporation.

In the meantime, another couple of apartments became vacant and I began remodeling them. Irving really liked what I'd done to the other apartments and had asked me to transform them all as each place became available. This was the work I most enjoyed doing. I assured Irving that Abbey had friends who would rent the vacant apartments as soon as I finished.

"Eddie, you've been a godsend. Now I have a proposition for you. Before you say anything, I want you to think it over." He adjusted his glasses, snapped his suspenders, and waited.

"Sure, Irving, I'll listen."

"I'm thinking that I'm ready to retire and move to Florida. So I'm thinking, what am I going to do with this building? So I'm thinking, why not sell it to Eddie? He already lives there and has remodeled most of it. I'd make him a good deal and I'd still have some income in Florida and he'd have a nice investment." He peered at me anxiously.

This was something that had never crossed my mind. But the prospect excited me. Why not own the building? I already had all my girls here. And, as the rest of the apartments vacated, I'd probably be able to fill them with more girls. *Owning my own piece of real estate. Would that be coming up in the world? Damn right. But how did Irving know I had any money?*

"Well, Irving, I'd never thought about it, but the idea intrigues me. Put a proposal together and let's discuss it."

Irving slapped me on the back. "I'll call you as soon as I get something together."

While I waited for Irving to call me back, I counted all my various stashes of money. I figured I could put together about $10,000, give or take, as a down payment to Irving. I thought that would be enough to make the deal work.

Two days later, Irving called. "Eddie, I've worked out a deal. When would be a good time to get together?"

"I'm working day shift this week, so any evening would be fine."

"How about tomorrow evening?"

"Fine. What time?"

"How about seven in your apartment?"

I checked everybody's schedule for the following night. The two new girls would be home, but I could make sure they stayed in their apartment.

"Sounds good, I'll see you then."

I could hear Irving snap his suspenders as he said okay and hung up.

＝＝

NERVOUS, I PACED AROUND THE apartment. Could I really do this? Was it a good idea? After all, what do I know about real estate? Nothing. But it sure seemed like a good idea. I thought about calling Mr. G to talk it over with him; he'd know what I should do.

Yeah, sure. I haven't talked to him in months. That's right, Eddie, only call when you need help. Shit, why haven't I kept in touch? You know why, because you don't want him to know what you do. I guess I'll just have to take my chances. I know I need help.

The doorbell rang and interrupted my thoughts. "Irving, hi, come in."

He walked in waving a sheaf of papers. "So, Eddie, I think I've worked out a deal that will work for both of us."

We sat down at the dining room table and Irving straightened the stack of papers. He picked up the first page and handed it to me.

"I propose a price of $75,000 for the building at seven and a half percent interest for twenty years." He pointed at each of the figures as he spoke. "And this is the monthly payment if you put down $5,000." He pointed at another figure. "And this is the payment if you put down $10,000. Either one will give you enough to cover the maintenance if ten of the twelve apartments are rented. That will give you some leeway in case of major problems."

I gulped. That number sounded like a fortune to me. I couldn't even visualize that number, it sounded so large. "And what are the rest of these papers?" I asked.

"Legal stuff, which I don't totally understand, but my lawyer says they're necessary to make a proper contract. Now this means that I'm going to carry the loan." He handed me another paper. "You won't have to borrow money from the bank if you have the down payment. I want to have the income, not the whole amount at one time."

He continued going through the papers, but by now my mind was reeling. I definitely needed some help.

"Irving, I need to have some time to study all this and get some advice."

"No problem. Take all the time you need. If you have any questions, give me a call."

"Thanks. I'll do that."

As I escorted him to the door, he said, "It's a good deal, Eddie. You'll never be sorry if you do this. Real estate is good."

I mumbled something and shut the door. Feeling sick to my stomach, I drank a glass of water and tried to calm down. As I sat looking over the papers, it came to me that I could talk to Jeff about the deal. After all, he had bought the motel, so he had some idea about how all this worked. Plus I'd kept in touch with him, sort of, over the past year. *Yes, I'll call him and stop by the motel tomorrow. Eventually, I need to get back in touch with Mr. G too . . . once I'm the owner and manager of an apartment building.*

TWENTY-SIX

THE NEXT DAY, I CALLED Jeff and made arrangements to see him after work. I could barely concentrate on my job, eagerly waiting for the day to end.

After I parked, I took the papers out of my trunk and hurried into the office where Jeff was waiting.

"Long time, no see." He came around the counter and we shook hands. "So what's up? You sounded pretty urgent over the phone."

We sat down in the lobby. I handed the papers to Jeff and told him about Irving and the deal he was offering me.

"I don't know anything about contracts and real estate stuff. I'm hoping that you can help me. I don't know if this is a good deal or not."

He took the stack and said, "I'm no lawyer, but I'll do my best to look it over and give you an opinion. My first question is: Does Irving know you're not twenty-one yet? I don't think it's legal if you're not."

"Shit, I never even thought about that. I've been on my own for over a year now, and I figure since I'm on my own that I'm an adult."

"And you are, but not in the eyes of the law."

"But since Irving is carrying the loan, wouldn't that make a difference?"

"If he's willing to take the risk. Now grab a cup while I look this over."

It had never occurred to me that not being twenty-one would have any effect on my life and the decisions I made. I hoped Irving would not consider my age to be a deal-breaker. Just thinking about the deal had my adrenaline going nonstop, and I'd already started to consider business plans based on the possibility that I could have my own place to house my girls.

Jeff finished perusing the documents. "It looks to me like Irving is offering you a very good deal. Certainly it's a fair interest rate, considering current rates. I think he's made the payments low enough that even if you run into problems with rentals or repairs, you'll still be able to make those payments. However, I strongly advise that you have a lawyer check everything over. I've got a guy that I've worked with for years. Here's his information, if you decide to go ahead with this." Jeff handed me a piece of paper with a name and number written on it.

"Thanks a lot, Jeff. I appreciate your help and I will contact your lawyer, but first, I'm going to give Irving a call."

I couldn't wait to get home to call Irving and settle this matter.

"Hello Irving. This is Eddie."

"Yeah, Eddie, have you come to a decision already?"

"Not yet. I want to have the papers looked over by an attorney, but before I do, there is something I need to tell you first."

I heard Irving pause. "Yes, what is it?"

"Did you know that I'm not twenty-one yet?"

I heard a sharp intake of breath. I could visualize him adjusting his glasses and snapping his suspenders before he answered.

"No, I had no idea. I just assumed you were. You seem so grown up to me."

"I've definitely been on my own for a while now. So . . . would you be willing to take a chance on me knowing all that?"

Silence. Then, he continued, "I appreciate your honesty, Eddie, but I have to think it over. I'll give you a call tomorrow. Okay?"

Now I was the one to take a breath. "Let me just say that I won't let you down. This opportunity means everything to me and, if we do go through with what you've offered, I give you my solemn oath that I will pay you back."

"Thanks for that, Eddie. Let me sleep on it and give you a call tomorrow."

⸝═ ═⸝

I WAS SO NERVOUS THAT it was time to have some mind-blowing sex to take my mind off the deal. I considered that it would be a good time to see if what they said about Colleen is true.

I went over to her apartment and knocked on the door.

"Yes, who is it?"

"It's me, Eddie."

Surprised, Colleen opened the door. "Hey, Eddie, c'mon in. What's up?"

"I thought if you don't have too many jobs tonight you'd spend the night with me."

She arched her eyebrows and gave me a questioning look. "Really?"

"Really. You know we haven't had sex since you, ah, graduated. I've heard a lot of good things about you."

She grinned. "Thank you. It's because of you, you know. Your graduation present did it. I learned a lot. Now I work to get as good as I give." She stared at me.

I felt my face grow hot. *Fuck, I hope she didn't notice.* "What time do you think you'll be finished?"

"I should be through by midnight, if that's okay with you."

"I'll plan to see you then. I'll leave the door open. Just come in."

I figured I'd catch a few z's before she came home, since I had to get up and go to work in the morning. Unfortunately, it had been more than a few days since I'd had sex—between the remodeling, work, and the business with Irving—so I was pretty horny. Instead of sleeping, I fantasized about Colleen. I could hardly wait until she got home.

I heard the door creak and then I saw her creep into my room. She whispered, "Are you awake?"

"Awake and waiting," I said.

She slipped off her clothes and climbed in beside me. We began caressing as soon as she settled in. I couldn't believe what she was doing to me. She would bring me to the brink and then stop. "Not yet, baby," she whispered hotly into my ear.

Holy shit, soon we were doing things I'd never done before, and she was doing things nobody had ever done to me. The girl was insatiable. By the time we finished, I was totally spent. My last thought before I passed out was that I needed to raise her rates. She was totally worth it.

⸺ ⸺

THE NEXT MORNING, I AWOKE thoroughly rested and clear-headed. *Man, I needed that.* Colleen was gone. I had no idea when she'd left. *When I see her, I must remember to tell her I'm raising her rates.*

Later, Irving called me at work and said that if it worked for me, he was willing to take a chance.

"I have good feelings about you, Eddie. I know you're trust-worthy, twenty-one or not."

"Thanks. I'll have a lawyer look over the contract and get back to you as soon as I can."

"I'll wait to hear from you."

⸺ ⸺

I FOUND BRIAN BARNES'S OFFICE with no problem. It was just a few blocks from the Monty. Since it was after five, there was no receptionist at the desk. I found a bell and pushed it.

A tall, red-haired man with glasses came out into the office. "I'm Brian," he said, as he extended his hand.

I took his hand and said, "I'm Eddie Anderson. Thanks for taking the time to see me."

We went into his office, and he sat down at his desk. "So, Eddie, what is it you want me to look over?"

Handing the contract to him, I explained about the apartment building and Irving and what he had offered. "I know zip about contracts, so Jeff told me I'd better have a lawyer look it over to make sure it was okay. He said you've helped him through the years, so here I am."

While I talked, Brian leafed through the documents and jotted down a few notes. I watched, fascinated as he ran his fingers through the pages, stopping his fingers at certain places for several seconds and then moving on.

After what seemed like forever, but was actually only about twenty minutes, Brian looked up and said, "This is pretty much what we call a boilerplate contract. The thing that I want to make sure you understand is that if you miss any payments, Irving has the right to take back the property. You could lose all the money that you're putting into this apartment if something goes wrong."

I let this sink in. "Irving is taking a chance on me because I'm not twenty-one yet, so I think I'm willing to take a chance that he'll be fair with me if I run into any problems. I don't think I'll have any issues keeping the apartments rented, though, and Irving told me that he is keeping the payments low so that if anything goes wrong, like the furnace going out, I should have enough to cover those kinds of extras."

"All fine and good, but how do you know you'll be able to keep the apartments rented?"

How do I answer that question? Of course I know they'll be rented. My girls will rent them. "Well, the location is good. It's close to the hospitals, and there are always lots of hospital personnel looking for apartments close by."

"Good point. It sounds to me like you have your bases covered. I've circled a couple of places and changed the wording a bit. If that will fly with Irving's lawyer, then I think you have a deal. Good luck to you."

Handing the papers back to me, he got up and shook my hand. "Anything else I can help you with, just let me know."

"Thanks. How much do I owe you?"

"Nothing, it was no big deal. I'm always happy to do a favor for Jeff."

"That's really nice of you. I won't forget."

"No problem," he said as he ushered me out the door.

I walked back to my car feeling happy. I did a little dance before getting in. *This is going to happen. My own apartment building. Eddie Anderson is going places.*

TWENTY-SEVEN

SHORTLY AFTER IRVING AND I concluded our deal, I had a chance to find out about another pimp, Jazz Man. He had the territory east of Colorado Boulevard. Plenty of business there. Tons of motels. Lots of military guys and hospital personnel from Fitzsimons Hospital.

One of his girls heard about me and came to see me. Her name was Samantha, and she was one statuesque beauty, with dark brown hair, big dark brown eyes, and lots of curves. She looked to be about five feet ten inches—one big girl.

"So tell me, Sam, why do you want to come to work for me?"

She ran her fingers through her hair. "That neighborhood is way too rough. I never know if I'm gonna get home all right or end up stabbed or shot. There are too many hoods in the area, and it seems to be getting worse. I'm honestly scared to work there anymore."

"Um. So tell me about Jazz Man. I know nothing about him. Will he come after you?"

"Nah, I don't think so. He has plenty of girls, and he's become pretty mellow since he got off the drugs. He plays a hot sax, and since he got clean, he's gotten sidetracked with his music, doing pickup with some of the groups around town, but he still keeps the business going cause the money's good. I honestly think he'd rather be in the music biz, so one less girl won't bother him."

"Okay, well I hope you're right. To get started, I'm going to turn you over to Abbey. She'll tell you the rules and get you ready. Have you heard anything about me?"

"Are you kidding? All us girls know about you, Eddie. Everybody wants to work for you, but mostly they're just too scared to leave their pimps. And they're scared they can't meet your requirements. Then what would they do? Their pimp is a sure thing. Besides, what you hear and what you get can be two different things."

I had to laugh at that. Smart girl. "Well, you'll let me know what you think when, and if, you get through with Abbey." I stared at her.

She took a deep breath and answered, "I'm ready, take me to Abbey."

With Sam, the building would now have at least two people in each apartment. I also had two tenants leftover from Irving. Once their leases expired, I wasn't going to renew them. I needed the two apartments in order to expand my business.

I called Abbey, who was over at Kim's apartment, and told her to come and get Sam. Abbey did everything with the new girls except the sex part. I still checked their performance to make sure they were up to my professional standards. At the same time, I had begun looking for that special girl, the one who would replace the hole left by Ches. I still thought about Ches, not as much as I had in the past, but I couldn't seem to let her memory go. I wondered: *Will I ever find that special someone?* I doubted it . . . especially not amongst the "street girls turned call girls."

After Sam, I got a couple more girls from Jazz Man. I'd learned my lesson and made sure he got paid for each girl who joined us. I took it out of their pay until the debt was paid off.

Then a girl from Goldilocks approached me. Goldilocks controlled all of West Colfax. Rumor had it that he got his moniker because he had blonde hair, which was dyed, and wore it down to his shoulders. People also said he was powerfully built, worked out incessantly, and thought he was Adonis.

When I asked a couple of girls about him, they told me they'd heard that he abused his girls. He beat them often and sexually abused them too. They feared for their lives, so it surprised me that one of his girls got up the nerve to come and see me.

Her name was Cassandra, and it was hard for me to tell much about her looks. When she took off her sunglasses, she had a huge shiner on her right eye. She also had other small bruises on her face, but they were nothing compared to the bruises on her arms and legs.

She could barely speak, her voice just a whisper. My heart went out to her; she seemed so pathetic. I sat quietly and waited for her to tell me her story.

It seemed she had become ill for a day, an unforgivable offense in Goldilocks's mind. Cassandra ended up in the hospital for several days with broken ribs, a concussion, and several deep cuts, along with the bruises. When she was ready to be released, she sneaked out of the hospital before Goldilocks came to get her. That's when she showed up on my doorstep.

I pondered what to do. I didn't want any trouble with Goldilocks, but I couldn't let her go back to him.

"Cassandra, I can see that you're still in pretty bad shape. You can stay here and recover for the next few days. When you're feeling better, we can talk again. I don't want either of us to make any decisions until then."

She burst into tears. "Thank you so much. I just can't go back to him. He'll kill me, I know."

"You do know that he'll probably come after you. From what I've heard, he's mean and won't give up anything easily that he thinks belongs to him. What do you plan to do about that?"

Her face changed and a defiant look replaced the tears. "I swear on my life that if he comes after me, I'll go to the police. I'll tell them everything I know about his operation."

"I understand. Right now you need to recover." I went to find Abbey. I instructed her to put Cassandra in with Kim and told her to take care of Cassandra and help her recover. I also asked Abbey to find out anything else she could. I wasn't looking for any trouble.

==

CASSANDRA'S RECOVERY WAS RAPID THANKS to the extra care the girls gave her. While she recuperated, there hadn't been any signs of trouble from Goldilocks, or any rumors about Cassandra. I told her that if she wanted to work for me, it was okay.

"Thanks, Eddie, I appreciate the chance."

The girls all seemed happy too. Once she was herself, Cassie (the name we had all begun to call her) had a mischievous and sparkling personality and kept the girls upbeat with her pranks and stories. The girls had bonded and become like one big family. I kinda felt a little left out.

＝＝

I NOW HAD SO MANY girls that I needed to make several changes. To begin with, I needed an office with a real receptionist. Having an answering service was no longer viable—because of our expansion, there was too much risk that something might go wrong.

When the first floor front apartment became vacant, I immediately went to work remodeling it so that the front could become a small reception area, and the rest of the living room could be used as an office.

I asked Abbey if she would run the office full-time. Since she still had calls from her special clients, we decided that one of the other girls could manage the phone whenever Abbey needed to be out. I also wanted the living room area to serve as a place where prospects could come in to look through our albums and pick the girl of their choice.

Since I wanted to provide services to local clients in addition to the hotel trade, I needed a place for those encounters. I remodeled the bedroom so that it looked real high-class, with fancy moulding, chandeliers, and fancy wallpaper. Abbey and I then added an ornate king-size headboard, a plush mattress, fine linens, a luxurious velvet bedspread, and plenty of pillows to complete the look. We also purchased a sofa and coffee table and installed a mini-bar that we kept well stocked.

I also redid the bathroom with lots of mirrors, lights, and gold fittings, and an oversize bathtub with jet sprays and a separate shower with surrounding spray heads.

The bathroom turned out to be a nightmare to remodel. Not being able to do the job myself, I had to hire a specialty remodeling firm. It cost an arm and a leg, but the finished product was worth it. The bedroom and bath were decadent to the nth degree. A place worthy to bring high-paying johns.

To emphasize our upscale services, I had fancy cards printed, which read:

E. A. Anderson Escort Services
Escorts for any occasion
Telephone: 343-7968

I had to laugh. Like everyone didn't know what escort services meant. But that seemed to keep the vice squad out of our hair, so who was I to question it.

We also started having weekly meetings to discuss any problems the girls had with any of the johns during the week. We compiled a list of johns who could no longer receive our services. We also discussed how we could improve our services, especially now that we were soliciting local clientele.

Cassie suggested that we offer massage. It seemed that the all-night guys enjoyed a relaxing massage as part of their bennies. All the girls agreed, so I called a local massage school and set up a four-week series of classes for the girls.

Massage school turned out to be a lot of fun for the girls, as well as a good way to learn about the anatomy of the body, something they made good use of. I also added an extra charge for a massage.

The amount of money rolling in was unbelievable. I was able to make double payments to Irving so the debt would be paid off in half the time, maybe even sooner. With the prospect of paying Irving off early, I began to contemplate the purchase of another apartment building. When opportunity knocked, I hoped I'd be able to answer the door.

TWENTY-EIGHT

MY TWENTIETH BIRTHDAY WAS QUICKLY approaching. *Has it only been two years since I started this business? It seems like years ago.* How different this year would be. I wouldn't be spending my birthday alone and horny.

I couldn't remember looking forward to a birthday since I was five years old. I planned that for my twentieth, I would take all my girls out to dinner. I told Abbey to have them all hold the date. No early jobs that night. It would be our night to celebrate.

Abbey came back a couple of days later with a downcast face. "Gee, I'm so sorry, Eddie, but almost all the girls have jobs that night. So maybe we could do it the next week. Most of the girls are free a couple of nights then."

"You're kidding me, right? They're all busy already?"

"Not kidding. You know how popular we are."

Disappointed, I said, "Well, shit, let me see what I can figure out."

"Sorry, Eddie, I truly am. But I'm free on your birthday. Let's you and I go out and have a great dinner."

I kissed Abbey on the cheek. "Thanks, I can always count on you. Sounds nice."

"Good, I'll make the arrangements. It'll be my surprise."

DETERMINED TO MAKE THE BEST of my birthday, I took the day off. The girls floated in and out of my apartment during the morning, delivering birthday cards and greetings and apologies for being busy that night. I tried my best to feel grateful for their thoughtfulness.

By the afternoon, though, when things had quieted down, I began to feel somewhat depressed. With all the good things that had happened during the past year, I had been looking forward to a big party. I tried to console myself by remembering that Abbey and I would still be going out together for dinner.

Abbey blew in a couple of hours later. "I have reservations at Tiffany at six, so put on your best suit and tie and we'll have a super time. I promise."

"Thanks, I'll be ready," I told her, trying to sound enthusiastic. I knew she was trying her best to make me happy.

As I dressed for dinner, I reviewed the past two years. So many things had happened, both good and bad. Meeting Abbey had been the beginning of the good things. *It's fitting that we should celebrate together.*

As I waited in the living room, Abbey came out, and I let out a loud whistle. She looked positively stunning. A far cry from the girl I picked up off the street. She wore a short deep-red cocktail dress with feathers on the sleeves and the original pearl necklace and earrings I'd bought for her. Her hair was swept back in a French twist and showed off her face. The red of her lipstick matched her dress.

"You look sensational, Abbey. Are you ready?"

She smiled, kissed me on the cheek, took my arm, and we headed out the door. When we arrived at Tiffany, I couldn't help but notice that every male we passed was appreciative, and I felt truly lucky that I was her escort.

We followed the host through the dining room to what seemed to be a second dining area. It turned out to be a private room. When the host opened the door, all my girls were there throwing confetti and shouting "Happy Birthday, Eddie!" Balloons floated from the ceiling, and each table had a flower centerpiece and candles.

Overwhelmed, I didn't know what to say. I'd never had a surprise party, or any party, and I was touched. When I finally found my voice, I said, "I don't know how to thank you, so I'll just say thank you for this fantastic evening."

As I surveyed the group, I couldn't help but feel satisfied. I had done this. They were all mine. Bound to me. They would never leave me.

The girls all clapped and chattered away. We sat down as the waiters brought the first course. I turned to Abbey. "You had me fooled, Abbey, completely fooled." I gave her a hug and a light kiss. I didn't want to spoil her makeup.

As we ate our dessert, Abbey stood up and called the group to attention. "On this special occasion, does anyone have anything they want to say to Eddie?"

One by one, each of the girls stood up and thanked me for taking them in when they had reached bottom. After the last girl spoke, Abbey once again stood up.

"Now I'd like to present you with this birthday present from all of us."

She handed me a small box. When I opened it, I found the most beautiful gold watch I'd ever seen. It must have cost the girls a fortune! Speechless, I could only blow kisses to each of them as tears of happiness welled up in my eyes.

By nine, the party broke up. Most of the girls had jobs and needed to get going. Only Abbey and I were left, and we sat and drank another cup of coffee.

"Thanks again. I just don't know what to say. Nobody has ever done anything this nice for me before."

"No, thank you. I don't know what would have happened to me if you hadn't talked to me and taken me home that day. I know each of us feels the same way about you, Eddie. You've changed all of our lives."

After we got home, we watched TV for a while. Then Abbey crawled in bed with me and I had my last birthday present of the day. Since it was my day, Abbey went all out to please me. I was indeed one lucky man.

TWENTY-NINE

WE WERE JUST ABOUT FINISHED with our regular weekly meeting. Ready to conclude our meeting, I asked, "Anyone have anything else they want to talk about?"

Kim cleared her throat. "I have something to say."

"Go ahead."

"Well, we girls have been talking and we've all had some johns who want us to do things that we don't usually do. And . . . well, we feel uncomfortable. We talked it over, and we think we should get someone who does that kind of thing, you know, S&M."

Kim's words surprised me. This was the first time any of the girls had said anything. I needed to think about it. First I had a question.

"Do they generally let you know up front what they want, or do they ask for it once you're engaged?"

"Usually up front." Kim checked with the girls and they were all nodding their heads yes.

"Okay. I'll need to think this over. Do any of you know any girls who do this? You know I can't exactly advertise for this in the newspaper."

The girls all giggled. Then it got out of hand with obscene gestures and jokes. Finally, everyone was gasping for air, and I called for order.

"I'll nose around and see what I can find out. Check with your friends and the johns who are looking for a dominatrix, and see if they know someone. I'm sure once we let it be known that we're in the market for someone practiced, she will show up."

We put the word out about what we were looking for. Nothing. I began to wonder if we would ever find someone. Patience, I told myself. Sooner or later, someone will show up.

<hr>

IT WAS MY DAY OFF and I had decided to sleep in. I got up at about ten and found Abbey waiting for me in the kitchen.

"I think we've found our girl. One of the johns told Cassie about her. Cassie got her name and called her. She said she'd be willing to talk to you." Excited, Abbey waited for my answer.

"Good morning to you, too, Abbey. Coffee first." She poured a cup for me. "Thanks, of course I'll talk to her. So, what's the deal? Do I need to call her to set up a meet or what?"

"She said she could come this afternoon if that's okay with you."

"Fine." I checked the time. I had a couple of things to do. "Let's say one in the office."

"Okay, I'll have Cassie call and set it up." She hurried out of the apartment.

This should be interesting. How do you interview a person like this? And does she do the regular stuff or does she just specialize? Shit, this is giving me a headache. I need to think about this some more.

I tried to relax. *Let it hang, Eddie. Maybe the best thing to do is just play it by ear. Meet the girl. See what happens.*

I went to the gym and did my workout and felt better. Afterward, I ran a couple of errands and then returned to the office to work on payroll. I was just finishing when the doorbell rang. "Come in," I yelled.

The first thing that came to my mind when I gazed at the woman in front of me was "Teutonic." Something from my history class, I guess. She was the weirdest looking female I'd ever seen. Severe looking, you could say. Her hair was coal black, straight, and didn't quite reach her shoulders. She wore straight bangs that stopped just above her eyebrows. Her face was square and her eyes were odd-looking, kind of slanted and black as her hair. She had dark black eyebrows and wore black eye makeup. Her lipstick was a deep blood red, almost black. As I looked at her, I thought of Halloween—she was kind of ghoulish-looking.

She had the build of a wrestler and wore a black silk shirt, black leather pants, and a black leather jacket. The cuffs were bordered by small silver spikes that glittered. *Shit,* I thought, *is that a tattoo I see peeking out of her bra?* She seemed like someone who would fit right in with the biker crowd—like someone who could take care of herself and then some. She carried a large black bag. Her bag of goodies, I assumed.

"Hello, I'm Eddie," I said by way of introduction.

"Sydney," she answered. "Sydney Marsden."

"Please sit down." I indicated the chair in front of my desk.

She sat down and stared at me with those black eyes. I noticed her belt buckle. It was a big silver disk with some fancy scrollwork around it. Her initials, "SM," were engraved on the disk. I almost laughed out loud. What kind of joke is that? I wondered if that was her real name or if she was using it because of the initials.

I looked her straight in the eye. "So, Sydney, tell me something about yourself."

"Nothing to tell. I understand that you're looking for someone to satisfy some of your clients' special desires. That's what I do." She held up her bag.

"And how long have you been into the S&M scene?" I asked.

"Long enough to be an expert."

Holy shit. This one doesn't mince words, does she? "Who have you been working for?"

She got a strange look in her eyes. I wish I knew what that meant. She didn't speak for a few seconds.

"I've been working up in the North Denver area."

Oh fuck. I had a bad feeling about this. North Denver was off limits to every pimp. Nobody ever even talked about it. All the north side, up to God knows where, was run by the local mafia head, Tony Morelli, and his three brothers. They ran gambling, prostitution, drugs—and whatever else there is that's illegal. No questions, shoot first, or end up in the bottom of the lake. I didn't want to tangle with them.

"You work for Tony Morelli?"

I saw a funny look come into her eyes. "Worked, past tense."

Um. What does that mean? "Tell me what that means."

"It means that son-of-a-bitch cheated me and I won't work for him anymore."

"And that's okay with him?"

"I didn't ask." She sat and waited for me to respond.

Okay, now what? I tried to clear my brain. "So do you, how do I put this, do plain sex or do you just specialize?"

She smirked. "Only specialize. I keep ninety percent of the money I make. I give you a ten percent finder fee."

Who the hell does she think she is? The rage rose in my throat. I stood up, glared at her, and said, "That's not the way I work." I moved to see her out.

She didn't get up. "Hold on, you don't have to pitch a shit fit. Give me your deal."

That's more like it. "Normally I take seventy-five percent, but since you perform a special service, I'd be willing to do seventy."

"How about forty percent for me?"

"No," I said firmly. "Final offer." I again stood up.

She remained seated. "Deal. Sometimes I need a place other than a hotel room. Do you have such a place?"

I grinned. "Just step right this way, Sydney." I led her to the room I had recently finished.

Her eyes lit up as we walked into the room. She stood for a minute and took in the total view and then moved around the room, touching each piece of furniture, feeling the textures of everything. I led her into the bathroom.

"Wow, this is fantastic. Perfect. I'm gonna love working here. Would you like to see some of my toys?" she asked with a smirk.

I could feel the heat climb through my body, but I tried to remain cool. I shrugged my shoulders. "Sure."

She retrieved her bag from the office. When she came back into the bedroom, she started laying things out. A leather whip, a braided whip, and what looked like a suede flogger. Then there was an assortment of cuffs and silk scarves. A couple of vibrators.

"Okay, you can put it away. I see that you're well equipped."

She smirked again and put her toys away, and we went back into the office. "So Sydney, I'd be willing to give you work on a trial basis. If my clients are happy, then we'll talk about a permanent arrangement. Right now, I'll need a way to get in touch with you."

She reached into her pocket and pulled out a card and scribbled a couple of numbers on it. "The first number is my answering service. They can usually get in touch with me right away. The other two numbers are places where I often hang out if the service isn't quite sure where I'm at. I guarantee your clients will be satisfied. I'll wait to hear from you."

I showed her to the door and went back to my desk. The alarm bells were still ringing in my head. *I'm not sure this is going to turn out to be one of my best decisions.*

That evening, I let all my girls know about Sydney and told them we were now open for kinky sex business.

THIRTY

WITH MY HANDS BEHIND MY back, handcuffed to a chair, and with Tony Morelli pointing a gun at my head, I tried to make sense of what was happening. *This has got to be the worst day of my life,* I thought to myself, realizing what an understatement that was. I was facing the wrath of a mobster. *Why the fuck didn't I listen to my gut and not hire that bitch Sydney?*

Scrambling to mentally sort out the last few hours . . . or maybe even days . . . I tried to piece together what was happening. I thought back to the events of the previous week. Things might have worked out just fine with Sydney if she hadn't almost killed one of my clients. Too bad I didn't look her over when we met. I might have seen the needle tracks on her arms. From what the girls told me after the incident, she was totally whacked out and got so caught up in what she was doing, she damn near beat the john to death.

Sydney called me in the middle of the night, screaming hysterically that I had to help her get out of town. She'd run away and was hiding out in a cabin just outside of Evergreen. What I really wanted to do at the time was kill her, but I took the telephone number and address and told her I'd get back to her.

Naturally, the story hit all the papers the following day, giving details about the incident and Sydney. I'm not sure how Morelli made the connection to me or tracked me down . . . or how I ended up tied up with him pointing a gun at me. The last thing I remembered was waiting for Abbey who had gone into Walgreens to pick up a prescription for Colleen.

I've got to get my head together, I thought, *see if I can talk to this maniac and get him to stop pointing that fucking gun at me.*

I stared up at him and said in the calmest voice I could muster, "So, Mr. Morelli, why am I here and why are you pointing that gun at me?"

"You fucking well know why you're here. Nobody takes anything from Tony Morelli. You thought you could get away with stealing my bitch, Sydney, well you're wrong, you SOB."

I glared at him. "I didn't steal your fucking bitch. She told me she didn't work for you anymore. And if I had known she was a fucking druggie, I sure as hell would have kicked her ass right out my door. Your fucking bitch damn near killed one of my clients. If I could get my hands on her right now, I'd fucking put a bullet in her head."

For some reason, this struck Morelli as funny, and he laughed a big belly laugh. "So you want to kill my bitch, and I want to kill you. Great, we'll have one big party and I'll kill both of you, you son-of-a-bitch."

Oh, shit. I'm a dead man. I gotta figure out a way to stall. "Well, then, you're gonna have to wait until you find her. Hell, before you kill me, it's only fair you let me kill her."

Morelli appeared to think this over. He holstered the gun. "Maybe you're right. I'd enjoy seeing you kill her, and I'd like to be a part of that. I'll torture her first, then you can finish her off, and then I'll kill you. Yeah, I'd like that. Two birds with one stone." He kicked me and left me sitting there.

After he was gone, I tried to figure out where I was. I listened to see if I could hear any voices or street noise. I could hear muffled voices nearby. There were no windows, so I couldn't hear any outside sounds, and I couldn't tell if it was night or day. I didn't know how long I'd been there. I did know that I had to pee.

"Hey, someone, I gotta pee!" I shouted as loud as I could.

No answer. I banged my chair on the floor and screamed again. "Ya hear me, I gotta pee!"

The door opened and one of Morelli's goons came in and smacked me. "Shut up. Here's a bottle. Pee in that." He undid the cuffs so I could manage.

Not what I'd wanted, though. I'd hoped to get out of this room so I could get an idea of where I was. I peed in the bottle. "Thanks," I muttered.

After he left, I tried again to get my wits together. What kind of deal could I offer Morelli so he wouldn't kill me? I had the feeling that what he really wanted was Sydney. At that point, the only thing I could do was wait.

I guess I dozed off because I woke up when I heard someone shouting at me. I opened my eyes and Morelli was sitting on a chair facing me. His two goons were guarding the door, Goon Number One who had helped me relieve myself, and a second guy.

"I've been thinking it over. I want Sydney. I'm guessing you know where she is. You tell me where she is, and I'll think about how you can pay me back for stealing her."

I glared at him. "Yeah, I know where she is. I also know if I tell you, you'll kill me. I don't give a fuck about Sydney. You let me go, you can have the bitch."

Morelli punched me in the gut. "Don't try to make any deals with me, punk. I make the deals. If I want to kill you, I'll kill you."

"Look, Mr. Morelli, I'm not trying to steal any part of your business. I'm happy minding my own business. There's room for all of us. You have your territory. I have mine. It's not smart to start an all-out war or get the police involved. You let me go, I'll get Sydney for you. If I'd known better, I would have never gotten involved with that bitch. I don't want any part of her. Think about it. All you want is Sydney. You don't really want to bother with me."

"Don't tell me what I want." He slugged me again, got up, and left.

My insides felt like a truck had just run over me. *Probably have a busted rib. It hurts like hell. Am I ever going to get out of here?* I sure as hell hoped so.

I must have passed out after that because I was startled when someone started shaking my shoulders. I hadn't heard anyone come in.

"Here, kid, here's something to eat." Goon Number Two released the cuffs.

The food smelled surprisingly good. Rubbing my wrists, I realized I was starving. I looked at the plate piled with spaghetti and meatballs. *Of course! What else would it be?* I devoured the food and then asked to pee again before Goon Number Two put the cuffs back on.

A while later, Morelli came in and stood over me. "Okay, punk, here's the deal. My guys will go with you and you'll get Sydney. Once they have her, they'll let you go."

"How do I know they'll let me go?"

"Because you have my word, you little shit. Morelli doesn't go back on his word."

I knew in that instant that he wasn't going to kill me. He didn't care about killing me. This whole thing was about Sydney. He needed Sydney. She was his dom. Yep, he had to get Sydney back. I prayed that I could deliver. If only I could talk to Abbey and make sure Sydney was still in hiding.

"Can I make a phone call to one of my girls to make sure Sydney is still there?"

"Oh sure, so then your girl can call the police. Do you think I'm crazy? You just better hope Sydney is still wherever the hell she's hiding."

"I'm ready. Let's do it." *Well, here goes nothing.*

"Not yet. We'll let you know when."

"Well, can I at least go to the bathroom?"

"Yeah." He motioned to Goon Number One, who came over, untied me, and removed the cuffs. Then he led me to the door. Goon Number Two opened the door and led me up some stairs to a hallway. Down the hallway was the bathroom. I spotted a window at the end of the hall and could see that it was dark out. *That's why Morelli isn't ready for me to go yet. He probably wants to go real early in the morning when everything will be quiet.*

Afterward, I was led back to the room, tied up, handcuffed, and left alone. *I need a plan*, I thought. *I'm not out of danger yet. If I can't get Sydney, Morelli will kill me for sure. Shit, I wish I knew if Sydney is still at the cabin.*

I fell asleep after that. I don't know how long I slept, but I was rudely awakened when someone threw water in my face. "Wake up. It's almost time to go." Goon Number One untied me and removed the cuffs. Number Two Goon handed me a cup of coffee and a piece of toast.

"Eat, we're ready to go."

Starved, I grabbed the toast and wolfed it down with gulps of coffee in between. "I gotta pee before we leave."

"Yeah, in the bottle. And then put on this shirt," he said as he handed me a clean shirt.

Guess they didn't want me to look like a bum. I sighed and peed in the bottle. As we walked out of the room, I rubbed my wrists. They were stiff and sore from being in handcuffs for so long. I could barely stumble as I tried to walk, my legs and ankles stiff from sitting in a chair for so many hours. The parts of my body where Morelli had repeatedly punched me in the gut hurt badly. *At least it doesn't feel like anything's broken.*

Once we were nearing the turnoff, I told them the address of the cabin, trying to figure out how I was going to approach Sydney so she would come out. When I spotted a gas station just off the turnoff road, I felt relieved to know that if they left me at the cabin, I could probably get myself back to the gas station.

"Park where she can't see the car and wait there. I'll go in and check things out."

"No way," said Goon Number One, who'd been driving. "The boss said we should stick to you like glue."

"Think about it. If I don't turn Sydney over to you, Morelli will kill me. Do I strike you as some kind of fool? Would I risk that over a bitch like Sydney? Not likely. She sees the three of us, she'll run. Be cool, guys. I want to get this over with."

They looked at each other. Goon Number One shrugged, then Goon Number Two said, "Okay, but you'd better play it straight or you're a dead man."

I nodded, got out of the car, and limped to the front door of the cabin. I could feel the perspiration from my armpits dripping down the sides of my body. Sydney opened the door and pulled me in. I stared at her for a moment—without makeup and obviously going through withdrawal, she looked old.

"Thank god you're here, Eddie," she seemed panicked. "I prayed that you'd come to get me."

I felt the rage building up in me. As much as I wanted to hurt her, I knew I had to keep my cool. "Sure, Sydney. C'mon, let's get out of here."

I took her by the arm and led her out the front door. I couldn't believe how easy it was. When we got to the car and she saw the two goons inside, she tried to bolt, but the two of them jumped out and grabbed her.

"Fuck you, Eddie, you bastard."

"No, fuck you, Sydney. You almost got me killed. I never want to see you again."

The two guys forced Sydney into the car, and I took off toward the gas station. Now that it was over, I felt my body falling apart. I hoped I could get to a phone and call Abbey before I collapsed.

The gas station attendant pointed me to the phone. I dialed and waited for Abbey to answer. "Abbey, this is Eddie. You need to come and get me."

"Eddie," she shrieked. "Are you okay? We've been trying to find you for two days."

"I'm okay, Abbey, just come get me. I'm at Phil's Gas Station just outside of Evergreen. Please hurry."

"I'll be right there, Eddie."

I hung up and my knees started to shake. I steadied myself against the wall until I felt strong enough to move. Then, I headed for the front door to wait for Abbey. *Hurry, Abbey, hurry.*

When she drove up, she flew out of the car and ran over to me. "My god, Eddie. What happened to you?"

I stumbled into the car and pretty much passed out. The next thing I knew, Abbey and a couple of the other girls were helping me out of the car and into the apartment.

"I need something to drink right away. I'm really thirsty. I could use some food too." I winced as the girls helped me into our apartment.

As they helped me into my bedroom, Abbey turned to me. "Are you hurt bad, Eddie? Should we take you to the emergency room first?"

"I think I just have some bruised ribs. I'll be okay. I just need to get my strength back."

"Okay, Eddie, I'll get some food going. Colleen and Kim, could you help Eddie get undressed and showered while I make some breakfast?"

"Sure, Abbey. Eddie, we'll be careful, I promise," Colleen said. Then she and Kim pulled off my clothes slowly. They led me to the shower and both got in with me to help me wash and make sure I was okay. *Hey, this is kind of cool. Two girls and me in a small hot shower. Gotta try this when I'm well.* Even in extreme pain, I couldn't help but appreciate the experience.

The hot water felt wonderful and revived me. We all got out and the girls dried me off and helped me into a robe. They then led me to the table where Abbey had breakfast ready. As I scarfed down the food, I told the girls about Morelli kidnapping me and wanting me to get Sydney back to him.

Abbey gave me a gentle hug. "Wow, you're just damn lucky. Thank god. I hope we never see her again. I'm going to get you some painkillers now and let Colleen and Kim help you into bed so you can rest."

I winced as the two of them helped me hobble to my bed. Abbey came in with some pills and water that I swallowed and then I lay down. "Thank you for your help. And please let everyone know that we'll have a meeting first thing tomorrow morning. Now I need to rest."

"Of course, Eddie," they said in chorus and left.

Abbey lay down beside me, and I immediately fell asleep. When I woke up, it was still light out. Abbey was still beside me.

"You okay?" she asked.

"Sure, help me up." I felt a little better.

"Hungry?"

"Starved."

"Good, I'll get you some dinner."

I realized I had to pee. "Can you help me out of bed so I can use the bathroom?"

Very gently, she helped me ease out of bed and led me to the bathroom. When I finished, I hobbled into the kitchen. "Meatloaf, my favorite."

After dinner, I was half in and half out watching some kind of crime show on TV. Then I went to bed. My last thoughts were, *What now?*

THIRTY-ONE

THE GIRLS WERE ALL GATHERED in the living room chattering away when I came in. No doubt gossiping about what had happened.

"Good morning, everyone."

After murmuring things like "Glad you're okay" and other sentiments, they quieted down.

"The first thing I need to know is if any of you have anyone, anyone at all, father, brother, boyfriend, john, pimp, whatever, after you for some reason? I need to know now 'cause I sure as hell don't want a repeat of the last two days."

One of the newer girls, Tracy, raised her hand.

"Tracy, let's hear it."

"Goldilocks might be after me," she said softly, looking down as she spoke.

"Goldilocks? You didn't tell me you worked for Goldilocks."

"Well, it's a long story," Tracy answered.

"I have all day." The girls were now all waiting expectantly to hear Tracy's story.

"I wanted to get away from Goldilocks so I told him my mother was ill and dying up in Wyoming. I asked him if he would loan me the money for a bus ticket so I could go up and see her before she died. He was pissed, but I cried so hard he finally agreed to let me go." She paused and took a deep breath and continued.

"Anyway he came with me to the bus station and bought me a round-trip ticket. He only let me take a bag with a few things. He told me he expected me back no later than a week or he'd come up and get me. I took the bus as far as Cheyenne and then came back here. I wandered around for a few weeks, sleeping in shelters and stuff. Finally, I remembered hearing that Cassie worked for you. I asked around until I found her and you know the story from there. If he ever found out that I'm here and working for you, he'd probably come after both of us."

Shit. Goldilocks. Of all the pimps, he is probably the most vicious. "Thanks for letting me know, Tracy. I'll have to think it over and come up with a plan."

I took a few minutes to get my cool back, and then I said to the girls, "We're now out of the kinky business. I don't want any more of that shit. You girls are free to do whatever you want in that direction, but no more 'specialists.'"

Colleen raised her hand. "Yes, Colleen."

"Uh, I became kind of friendly with Sydney and she taught me a few things, so I'd be willing to take care of those johns who are into that."

Of course, Colleen, who else? No big surprise really. If she wants to do that, who am I to say anything? "Okay, Colleen. We'll adjust your price accordingly. Talk it over with the girls and decide how you all want to handle it and let me know. I still have final okay."

There were no further topics to discuss at the moment, so I declared the meeting over. After everyone left, I called Mike.

"Mike, this is Eddie."

"Eddie, how ya doing, buddy. Pretty scary thing happened. Are you okay?"

"Much better. I plan to come to work tomorrow if that's okay. I'd like to do the night shift since my ribs are still pretty bruised and I don't want to be doing any heavy lifting."

"I'm sure Art or Hank will change with you. I'll call you and let you know."

"Thanks, Mike. Appreciate it."

I went to my desk to try and come up with a plan to avert a showdown with Goldilocks. I didn't think paying him for Tracy would work. From what I'd heard, he'd rather have her so he could beat her up good as an example for the rest of his girls. I wouldn't be surprised if he beat her to death. Who would care? Another whore dead. Big deal. *God, some days I really hate this business. Is it worth it?* After much thought, a plan that might work occurred to me. I called Tracy.

"Tracy, can you come down to the office?"

"Sure thing, I'll be right down."

When she walked in, she apologized again. "I'm so sorry. I didn't mean to cause any trouble."

"I know that, but it doesn't solve the problem. Here's what I want you to do." I put a sheet of paper and pen in front of her. "Now write what I dictate."

She picked up the pen and waited.

Boss,

> *After my mother died and I finished settling her business, I decided to go to North Dakota where I have some cousins. I like it here and I have decided to stay. I'm sending you the money back you loaned me for my bus ticket.*
>
> *Thank you for letting me be with my mother.*
>
> > *Sincerely,*
> >
> > *Tracy*

"You think he'll buy this?" she asked.

"I think so, especially if the postmark is from North Dakota. I want you to take a bus to Minot and mail the letter from there and then come back. Now put the letter in an envelope and address it, but don't include a return address."

She sighed. "I hope this will be the end of it. I really thought it was going to be okay."

"This is on your dime, by the way. Your problem, you pay for it."

"Sure thing, Eddie, I didn't expect you to pay."

"Good, now get to it and let's get this over with." I sincerely hoped this would work. In the future, I planned to be more careful to check out the stories of any new girls.

THIRTY-TWO

I STOOD LOOKING OUT OF the window of my new apartment. It was hard to believe that five years had passed since I first became a pimp. The business had become so successful that I quit my job as a bellman almost two years earlier.

My new apartment was located in the building I'd recently purchased. Since I was close to paying off Irving, I decided it was time to take the plunge and buy a second building when it came up for sale. Now that Abbey was basically running the business, I could get more involved in doing what I liked best: remodeling.

I'd spent a great deal of time renovating my apartment, and once it was finished, I couldn't help but give myself a pat on the back. This was a home to be proud of. I'd made a large combined living-dining area that included a real dining room set. I'd also created a large kitchen with ample eating space. My bedroom was spacious with its own bathroom. I still had the same black bedroom set and Mom's angel figurine still held a place of honor on the nightstand. I'd made the second bedroom into an office-TV room with the second bathroom next to it.

As each apartment became vacant, I planned to do renovations to update and modernize them. I also planned that any new girls I hired would live in the new building, since my first building was at capacity already. I liked to keep everyone together as much as possible so that I could keep close tabs on them. Abbey still lived in our old apartment and kept an eye on the girls in that building.

Although Abbey ran the day-to-day business, I continued to oversee operations and the money. Some days I felt bad that I had dragged Abbey back into being a prostitute, but that was water under the bridge. She had turned into quite the businesswoman.

As I worked on the renovations for the latest vacant apartment, Abbey came to me one day with a new idea. We'd been receiving calls from businesswomen who wanted male escorts for various functions they had to attend. Additionally, they wanted the services of the escorts afterward. We'd also received a few calls from women who just wanted a guy to have sex with.

Abbey thought it was time to bring on a man, but what kind of guy should we hire? And how would we find him? An ad in the paper or word of mouth? I considered how we did things. Up to this point, we had our program to teach the girls how to please a guy. So what kind of program would I have for a guy, and who would oversee it? I certainly wanted any male escorts I hired to live up to the same standards I had set for the girls.

As I sorted through the questions this new venture brought up, I realized that I'd probably have to hire two guys. One would have to be forty to fifty years old for the older, established businesswoman. Then, I would need a younger guy for the rest of the ladies. They would have to have day jobs, since this seemed unlikely to turn into full-time work. So far, we'd only received a handful of calls.

I decided I needed to talk this over with Abbey before I made any final decisions, so I called her and asked her to come for lunch.

"Sure thing. I'll be there around twelve-thirty, if that's okay."

"Perfect. See you then." I checked the fridge to see what I could make us for lunch. Since I'd been living alone for the last couple of years, I'd become quite the cook. I found some good leftovers. As I assembled a couple gourmet sandwiches and a special side salad, I continued to puzzle over how to make this work. Some of what we did to prepare the girls should work the same with the guys, like how to make conversation and make them feel special. I could at least go over with them some of the things Ches taught me.

A knock on the door interrupted my thoughts, announcing that Abbey had arrived. "Come on in," I yelled. "Door's open."

Abbey breezed into the kitchen and gave me a kiss on the cheek. "How's my favorite brother?" She grinned.

"Some brother," I said. "Good. I've been thinking about your idea and decided we should discuss how we might do it."

She sat down and checked out lunch. "Um, looks good." She took a bite out of her sandwich. "Tastes good too. So, what are your thoughts?"

"Well first, I want to hear your ideas about how you think we could find a couple guys to bring in."

"Actually, I think we already have one possibility." She paused as she took another bite out of her sandwich. After she finished chewing, she said, "His name is Scott Thomas. He's a widower, in his forties, good-looking, smart, and sexy. Long story short, he's one of our clients. That's how he met Kim, Sam, and Cassie. Anyway, he's interested."

"Using a client. Hmm . . . interesting."

"When Kim mentioned to him that we are thinking of expanding the business, he thought it might be something he'd actually enjoy doing. It would give him a chance to meet women who aren't interested in getting married, women who want to have sex with no strings attached."

"He sounds promising, and obviously some of the girls like him, so let's set up a meeting. My only reservation is whether or not he knows how to please a woman. These women will be paying us to have their desires met. We can't have a slam, bam, thank you ma'am."

"That's for sure. Well, I'll get him over here in the next couple of days so we can find out more about him."

"Good. See you tonight?" In the last year, I'd basically only been having sex with Abbey. For a change, I sometimes had sex with Colleen, but that was it. As the business grew, it became too complicated to try and have sex with all the other girls. Abbey and Colleen both knew what I liked, so it was simple. And I'd pretty much given up hope of ever finding that special thing I'd had with Ches.

"Yes, I'll be here," she answered as she left.

= =

SCOTT AND I MET THE following week. We liked each other immediately and quickly came to an agreement. Talking man to man, it was clear he knew what to provide to make a woman feel special. I had a good feeling about this new direction and having him join us.

"Thank you, Eddie. I look forward to our arrangement," Scott said, as we walked toward the door.

"I do too, Scott. Go ahead and talk to Abbey and she'll take care of getting things going." We shook hands and he left. Now we just needed to find that second man.

A few days later, I was in the office doing paperwork and answering the phone because our receptionist was out sick. I fielded and scheduled the usual requests, and enjoyed having the chance to catch up with a couple of the johns from my hotel days.

Later in the afternoon, I got a phone call from a woman. She was looking for an escort for the final evening of dinner and dancing at a convention she was attending. She also wanted to hire him for the night.

"I need someone under thirty, decent looking, and not stupid," she said. "Do you have a gentleman who fits that description?"

Shit, we aren't quite operational and I don't have that younger second man yet. I wasn't sure what to do. The only thing I knew for certain was that I didn't want to lose this opportunity.

"Yes, I have your man," I said with as much confidence as I could muster. "Give me the details and I'll make sure he understands exactly what you want."

"Cocktails are at six at the Brown Palace. He can pick me up in my room then. It's business formal, so he needs to wear a dark suit with a white shirt and a tie. Make sure his shoes are polished, too, and his nails are clean . . . and that he's showered and shaved as well."

Damn, what kind of operation does she think I run? "We run a high-class operation," I said in my most insulted tone of voice. "Our escorts are all gentlemen of the highest quality."

"Sorry, I didn't mean to offend you. What is his name, please?"

I needed to come up with a name quick for what I had in mind. Looking at the bills on my desk, I honed in on Ron's Lock & Key and Connor Plumbing. "Ron," I responded. "Ron Connor. He'll be there promptly at six."

"Thank you. My name is Carla Warren, and I'm in room 650. I look forward to a special evening, if you get my meaning."

"It will be," I promised and hung up.

When Abbey came into the office, I told her what I had done.

"What," she roared, "the boss is doing tricks. Let me know how that works out." She giggled and left.

———

SUDDENLY NERVOUS, I WONDERED WHAT the hell I'd been thinking. It was one thing to run an escort service, but to become the escort? *I should have just told her we were in the process of setting up our services. I could have invited her to use us next time she's in town by offering her a discount. No, I didn't want to miss the chance to start getting our name out there. It's done, so just go with it.*

There was no going back—it was time to execute my plan. I dressed in my best black suit, fancy white shirt, and black-and-gray striped tie. I put on the special gold cufflinks Abbey had given me for my birthday. I checked myself one last time in the mirror and decided that I looked quite presentable. I had maintained myself by working out regularly and continuing my martial arts training.

I arrived at the hotel a few minutes early, so I went into the men's room and checked myself out again. *What the hell, you know how to please a woman,* I coached myself as I stared at my reflection in the mirror. With that, I took a deep breath and headed toward the elevators.

When I reached room 650, I hesitated for another moment and then knocked. Carla answered the door promptly. She gave me an appraising look and said, "You'll do. Come in."

I'll do? I checked her out. Tall, blonde, blue-eyed, nice looks, good figure. But those blue eyes were hard and her mouth had a pinched look to it. *A tough cookie.* "Thanks," I answered as I entered the room.

"Drink?" she said.

"No thanks. Business first. I always get paid up front."

"Certainly." She got her purse and handed me five one hundred-dollar bills. I put them in my wallet.

Then I said, "I'd like to know a little bit about the function we're attending and what you expect of me."

"Of course. Sit down." She motioned to a chair.

"This is a communications convention. All the media people are here, TV and radio people. Also journalists from magazines, papers, that kind of stuff. The people involved in script writing, directing, and production are also here. So it's a huge crowd."

"Interesting."

"Okay, it's show time, Ron. Do your best not to act stupid."

Back to tough cookie Carla. I stood up, opened the door, and ushered her out. We maintained silence as we rode down the elevator. When we got to the ballroom, Carla put her arm through mine, plastered a smile on her face, and took a deep breath. Several people recognized her as we entered and came over to say hello. They waited for her to introduce me.

"This is my escort for the evening," she said, "Ron Connor. And a pretty penny he cost me!"

Shit, how humiliating is that! Apparently, everyone knew that Carla hired escorts. So I smiled and said, "Yes, and worth every one of those pennies."

"Well said," one of the girls giggled as a few applauded. I bowed.

Carla put her arm through mine and led me away. During drinks, she chatted with a few other people before we sat down to dinner. Right after our salads were served, Carla took off to make the rounds of the tables. She obviously knew how to work a room.

I found out from the girl sitting next to me that Carla had come up from the bottom. As a female in a man's world, she endured all kinds of harassment. *No wonder she's so hard.*

During dessert, we all suffered through the usual boring speeches and kudos to the various people in the biz. Afterward, when the band started to play, I invited Carla to dance.

"You dance too?" she asked.

"I do and I'd very much like to dance with you."

She gave me a strange look but got up and followed me to the dance floor. I remembered what Ches had taught me: that dancing helps us get the feel of each other's bodies and being close helps to fuel the senses.

After a couple of dances, I felt her begin to relax and enjoy herself. I kept her close and didn't talk. I just let her feel the beating of my heart.

When the band took a break, she said, "I'm ready to say my goodbyes."

We made the rounds and she said goodbye to several people. Once again, we rode the elevator up in silence. When we reached her room, she handed me the key and we went in.

"I'll be happy to get out of these clothes," she said as she kicked off her shoes and quickly began to undress.

I took off my jacket. "No," she said. "I expect you to do a strip for me."

What? She wants me to do a strip tease. Why am I so surprised? I suddenly remembered the time when I tried to show Abbey how to strip and she rolled over on the floor howling with laughter. *God, I hope I don't embarrass myself with Carla by looking stupid.*

In the meantime, Carla had stripped down to her bra and panties and was lying on the bed waiting for me. I kicked off my shoes and then I turned my back to her, looked over my shoulder, and took off my jacket. Then I turned around, took off my tie, and threw it to her. She smirked and draped it around her neck. Slowly, I unbuttoned my shirt and discarded it. Once again, I turned around, unzipped my pants, and slowly let them slide down. Then I showed one cheek and then the other. Then I let my boxers fall to the floor, revealing the *pièce de résistance*.

"Not bad. Now turn off the light and get in bed." I did.

"Now take off my bra and panties." I did.

She continued to give me directions. *What the fuck? Does she think this is a show and she's the director? I don't like this.* I stopped and put my finger on her lips.

"Did you pay me to give you pleasure tonight?"

She stared at me. "Yes."

"Then let me do it my way. I promise you I won't hurt you and that you'll like it."

She sighed and whispered, "Okay."

"Now close your eyes." *Time to play some of the games that Colleen and I play.* I found the sash Carla had worn and wrapped it around her eyes.

"Hey, why are you blindfolding me?"

"Because I want you to feel every sensation." Once again, I put my finger over her lips to silence her. Then I got up and I went to the closet and took out a hanger. I hung it over the headboard and then I took her hands and, using my tie that was still on the bed, I tied her hands over the hanger.

"I'm not sure I like this. I don't want to be tied up."

"Shhh, it'll be okay." I did everything that Ches had taught me that women liked, as well as a few tricks that Colleen had taught me.

Soon, she started panting. I picked up the pace. It didn't take long before she began to convulse and moan.

"Oh, Oh, OH. MY. GOD."

A couple more thrusts and I let go. Afterward, we lay there for a few minutes. Then I untied her hands and massaged her arms and wrists. Then I took off the blindfold. Her eyes were closed. I whispered into her ear. "Worth every pretty penny?"

She smiled.

I got up and went to the bathroom. When I came back, she was passed out. I crawled in beside her and did the same.

⇒⇒

I WOKE UP TO THE feeling that someone was attacking me. Carla had turned and her arm and knee had hit me in the back. I looked at the clock and saw that it was seven. I got up, called room service, and ordered breakfast. Then I showered, shaved, and dressed. When I came out, Carla was still asleep.

"Carla, wake up. It's seven-thirty and I'm ready to leave."

Her eyes stayed closed, but she mumbled something. I shook her and said in a soft-spoken voice, "Carla, wake up."

Her eyes opened. "What time did you say it is?"

"Seven-thirty. I've ordered breakfast. Should be here any minute."

She got out of bed and headed into the bathroom. By the time she came out, breakfast was delivered. I'd already downed two cups of coffee.

"Unless you need something else, I'm ready to leave."

"Fine. You can tell your boss you were satisfactory." She got her purse and handed me a $100 bill. "Tell him I'll call next time I'm in town."

Damn, she couldn't even give me the satisfaction of telling me I was great. I guess I'm just another piece of meat. "Thanks," I said and left.

━ ━

CARLA TURNED OUT TO BE a wake-up call for me. It made me wonder how my girls felt. Did they sometimes feel less than human afterward? I'd always viewed prostitution as recreational sex, even though it was paid sex. Like a movie or concert or any other entertainment you pay for. This was the first time I'd felt . . . I'm not sure what the right word is . . . ugly, bad, dirty, used

. . . after having sex. Did my girls ever regret being in this business? Did it make them hate me? Hell, did I still want to be in the business after this experience? Something to think about.

They say different strokes for different folks. This wasn't my stroke. It wasn't my thing. I didn't like it and never would. It was time to hire another guy fast. I needed to tell Abbey to get on it.

WHERE ABBEY FOUND TONY I have no idea, but he certainly fit the description I was looking for. Reasonably tall, five feet eleven inches, dark, good-looking, and he had a rock hard body. At twenty-two, Tony was not looking for a wife. He wanted to drink, smoke, and have sex. He wasn't interested in doing the dating scene: first date, second date, third date, and maybe a little petting, but usually no sex. What more perfect job for a young man like this. *If his mother knew what he planned to do, though, I'm sure she'd want to kill him.*

Tony's dad was a snack food vendor, and Tony had been learning the business from the bottom up. He was working in the warehouse, receiving and filling orders. It was hard work, which accounted for his hard body.

He itched to get into the sales and management area, but his dad wanted him to cool his heels and learn the basics. Tony's plan was that while he learned the basics of his dad's business, he would also learn the ins and outs of this business.

Tony turned out to be a good acquisition and helped add more money to the pot.

THIRTY-THREE

ANOTHER APARTMENT BECAME VACANT. I had pretty much gutted it and was trying to decide why what I had planned didn't seem quite right. I pored over the sketches in front of me, picked them up, and began to walk around. As I continued to look at the plans and the room, I finally got a couple of ideas. I rushed back to my card table so I could get my thoughts down before they slipped my mind.

Suddenly, I heard footsteps in the hall, followed by a knock on the door. *Who could that be?* "Door's open. Come in." Wanting to finish getting my thoughts down, I didn't look up. "Be with you in a minute."

When I finished, I raised my head and found myself looking into the eyes of the most drop-dead gorgeous woman I'd ever seen. My blood raced, my heart pounded, the hair stood up on the back of my neck, and my mouth went dry.

Under the longest eyelashes I'd ever seen were big black eyes. Her jet-black hair cascaded down to her shoulders in soft waves. When she brushed a loose strand away from her face, I saw her shining pink lips. All I could think was how much I wanted to take her in my arms and kiss those gorgeous lips. *What the hell is going on here?* I tried to calm myself. Finally I cleared my throat and said, "Yes?"

"I'm Alexandra Turner. My friend Kim spoke to you about me, and she said you'd be able to talk with me today, that you'd be expecting me."

Oh yes. I remember now. Something about her freelancing and looking for some extra business. I stood up and looked for a place for her to sit down. There was a table and lone chair behind some boxes of tile.

"Why don't you grab the chair and I'll get the table and we'll move over to the corner there?"

I moved the table in front of the boxes and said, "Please sit down." I sat down on the boxes.

My brain felt scrambled. I wasn't sure where to begin. "So why don't you tell me what it is you're looking for?"

She looked at me with those big black eyes and I felt myself melt. *She can have whatever she wants.*

"I work for an interior design showroom part-time and go to school nights. I . . . uh . . . freelance to earn extra money so I can go to school, since I don't make much at my job. I don't have many customers and I need to earn a little extra money, so I was hoping I could kinda do some . . . part-time work for you?"

She seemed a little apprehensive, so I decided to probe a little more. "And what did Kim tell you about my business?"

"Well, first she told me it's high class. I wouldn't have to worry about the kind of guys I'd meet. She also told me about your, uh, program. How you expect the girls to act and dress. She also told me about your performance standards."

"I see." I couldn't believe the desire I was experiencing to make love to this girl right then and there. I had never felt like this before. There was something different about her and I wanted to know more. "I'm free this evening," I blurted out. "Why don't you come over for dinner and we'll discuss it?"

Surprised, she said, "Come over for dinner?"

"Yes, I get tired of going out, so I cook. You can tell me exactly what it is you think I can help you with."

She blushed. "Okay. Kim said you want to see a girl's wardrobe. Do you want me to bring my clothes?"

By the way she dressed, I knew I didn't need to see her clothes. She wore a black-and-tan striped summer dress that fitted her slim figure perfectly. She'd accessorized with a jet-black bead necklace with matching earrings and black patent pumps. She looked as though she belonged in one of those society page pictures of women who attend those fancy charity luncheons. I couldn't put my finger on it, but I didn't think she was meant for what she was proposing—to come work for me as a call girl.

"No, I can see that I won't need to see your clothes. Tonight, why don't you just wear what you'd wear on a classy date?"

"Fine. What time and where do you live?"

"I live here. The apartment on the top floor. Say six." I was having difficulty forming complete sentences.

She had been glancing around the apartment as we talked. "Can I ask you a question?"

"Sure."

"What exactly are you planning to do here? I'm not being nosy, I'm just interested."

I took the sketches, spread them out, and pointed out to her basically what I had in mind. "I've been sitting here trying to decide what changes to make. Somehow these plans just don't seem right."

She picked them up and walked around the space. "Look here," she said. "If you move this wall over here, then I think you'll find that the space works the way you want."

Surprised, I checked out her idea. "You're right. So simple. Right in front of my nose."

"Sometimes you're just too close to see what's obvious. Also, I think if you change this part right here and make it a hallway, your space will work better."

Amazed at how quickly she had seen what needed to be done, I said, "I can't thank you enough. I can hardly wait to make these changes."

"You're welcome." She checked her watch. "I have to leave now. I'll see you at six."

"I'm looking forward to it." I walked her to the door and watched her until she got on the elevator. I immediately worked on my menu for dinner. I had totally lost interest in my plans for the moment. I was too excited to see her again to think about something as mundane as floor plans. All I could think about was making a good impression.

AFTER I DECIDED WHAT I would make for dinner, I took my list and headed out to the grocery store, flower shop, and bakery to purchase what I needed.

I spent the rest of the afternoon cooking, arranging the table, and deciding what I would wear. *My god, you'd think I was taking my girlfriend to the prom the way I am acting.* I had no idea why this female made me so crazy. I only knew that all my senses said yes from the moment I first laid eyes on her.

By five, I was ready. The anticipation of seeing her again kept my heart racing, and I kept looking out the window so I could see her when she arrived.

I was doing my last-minute check when the doorbell rang. *Shit, I missed seeing her arrive.* I took a deep breath and answered the door.

The sight of her left me breathless. She wore an ice blue halter dress that showed off her tanned arms and cleavage beautifully. She wore a chunky kind of white necklace and earrings to match. Her beautifully manicured toes peeked out of her high-heeled white sandals. Shivers ran up my back.

"Alexandra, good evening."

"Good evening. My friends call me Alix. You don't need to call me Alexandra."

"Alix it is then. I like that. Have a seat. Can I get you a drink?"

"Sure, whatever you're having would be fine." She glanced around the living room. "This is a really nice apartment. Did someone help you decorate it?"

"Thanks, mostly it's stuff from my last place, but yes, I did have some help from the decorator at the store."

"Well, I really like what you did."

I went to the kitchen and poured each of us a glass of wine. As we sat and sipped, I felt my nervousness ease. For some reason, I felt immediately connected to her. When we finished our drinks, I invited her to the dining room table and went to the kitchen to get our first course.

"I'm awed, Eddie, the table looks beautiful." As I set down the shrimp, her eyes grew big. "How scrumptious this looks."

I had put cocktail sauce in the bottom of two martini glasses and arranged five shrimp on the lip around each one. Her comments pleased me and made me feel warm. After the shrimp, I served my special spinach salad and then lamb chops and mashed potatoes. As we ate, I asked her about herself and listened intently as she told me her story.

"My dad was an office equipment and supply salesman. We were never rich, but we were always comfortable. I was an only child, and my parents made sure I had every advantage they could afford.

"We lived in Littleton, and life was always pleasant. The summer I graduated high school, my parents were killed in an auto accident. My father had a decent life insurance policy, so I was able to pay off the house and have enough money left to live on and start college. It didn't take me long to realize that the money wouldn't take me all the way through school, so I started working a couple of part-time jobs."

"When was that?" I asked, realizing we had both suffered losses in our lives and tried to find ways to go on.

"A little over a year ago." She took a sip of wine. "I'm studying to be an interior designer, and I was lucky to find my current job as a gofer for this firm. I usually only work three days a week, which doesn't bring me enough money to take more than one course at a time."

"So, I don't understand. How did you get into this business?" I was reluctant to say "prostituting."

"By chance, actually. The showroom serves the Rocky Mountain Region, so we get clients from Nebraska, Wyoming, Kansas, New Mexico, and Idaho. The boss usually takes these clients out to dinner. One night, he asked me if I wanted to earn a little extra money. I said, 'Sure, what do you want me to do?' He explained what he wanted. I was shocked, but desperate. He promised me that these were nice guys and they'd treat me okay." She looked down.

"What happened after that?" I asked, hoping to make her feel comfortable.

"So I went. It was okay. And it served a purpose. So whenever clients come into town, I'm one of the girls. Unfortunately, out-of-town clients usually only come in once every couple of months, so I only have maybe three or four jobs a month. With tuition going up and maintenance problems in the house, I need to make more money." She gazed at me hopefully. "So, I thought this might work." I could tell her heart wasn't in it completely.

"I'm sure we can work something out." I cleared the table and served dessert. Vanilla ice cream with peaches poached in a sugar-and-cinnamon mixture. The smell was intoxicating.

"Umm, this is *so* good, Eddie, this is the best dinner I've ever had. I'm in complete awe of you."

I felt happy all over and gave her a huge grin as I cleared the table.

"You cooked, I'll do the dishes," she offered.

"No, I'll do the dishes tomorrow. Why don't we sit down and get to know each other better."

She blushed. "Of course."

Damn, I hope I didn't just offend her. Sometimes I have a stupid mouth. "I didn't mean . . ." I stammered. "Okay, tell you what, we'll do the dishes together. I'll wash, you dry."

She brightened, obviously relieved. "Done."

As we did the dishes, we talked about various topics. I even told her about my dad having left when I was little and my mom's death. It all felt so easy and comfortable. But, being so close to her and smelling her wonderful fragrance, the urge to make love to her came to the forefront. Something held me back, though.

When we were finished cleaning up, she turned to me. I could tell she wondered what was supposed to happen next. Not having entertained any potential new girl over dinner before, I found myself at a bit of a loss too.

"Do you want me to leave now?"

With her question, I realized I didn't want to have sex with Alix. I wanted to make love to her. To kiss her, to caress her, to hold her, to please her. I knew that I couldn't do that now. We'd just met. And I didn't know how she felt about me. What if I scared her or made her angry? It just didn't feel right. Not having experienced this before, I wasn't sure what I should do next. The only thing I knew for certain was that I didn't want her to leave.

"Could you stay for a little while longer? I'm not tired, and we can just talk if it's okay with you." I was beginning to feel that I didn't want her to ever leave, but something told me to go slow.

We sat back down on the couch and talked for another two hours. Finally she said, "I really have to leave. I've got to get up early for work tomorrow."

"Gosh, I'm sorry. I didn't mean to keep you."

"It's okay. I've really enjoyed spending time with you, Eddie."

She got up to leave. As I walked her to the door, she turned to me. "Thanks for an incredibly special evening. One of the best evenings I've ever had. I enjoyed every minute. Will you call me and let me know what you decide about me working for you?"

I escorted her to the door. "I'll call you tomorrow." I wanted desperately to kiss her and to make her stay. Instead, I opened the door and waved as she walked to the elevator.

THIRTY-FOUR

I COULDN'T SLEEP. THERE'S NO way I can let her sleep with an-other man. I must figure out a way to keep her for myself. Fi-nally, I thought of a solution. Exhausted, I fell asleep.

When I woke up in the morning, I could hardly wait for the time to pass so I could call Alix and present my idea to her. In the meantime, I prayed she would accept.

After tinkering around and doing busywork for a couple of hours, I decided it was time to call.

"Inspired Ideas, how may I help you?"

It was Alix. "Alix, this is Eddie. I know you're busy so I won't keep you. I'd like to have lunch with you today. Can you make it?"

"Lunch? Uh . . . sure . . . okay. My lunch hour is at elev-en-thirty."

"Great, I'll be out in front at eleven-thirty."

"I'll be there."

Now all I had to do was practice what I was going to say and make sure she took me up on my offer. I took a deep breath and repeated my pitch out loud.

I arrived about fifteen minutes early, so I had plenty of time to sweat while I waited for her. As soon as she came out, I confirmed what I'd already suspected. I was crazy, madly head over heels in love with this woman and ready to marry her. All I had to do was convince her.

I jumped out of the car, greeted her, and opened the door for her. "Hi, Alix, glad you could make lunch. Is there a place nearby where we can eat?"

"Just down the block there's a burger joint. Is that okay?"

"Sure."

Once we were seated and the waitress had taken our order, I began my proposal. "I was so amazed yesterday at how much you helped me with my plans that I decided what I really want is for you to work with me on my remodel. I'll pay you what you would make in my other business. It would really make me happy if you said yes."

"Really? You really want me to work with you on the apartment? Gosh, that would be super. I can't think of anything I'd rather do. It fits in perfectly with my career plans."

"I take it that means yes."

"Absolutely, yes." She colored as she said, "Actually, I'd much rather be doing that than . . . you know."

"I understand." I was giddy with anticipation of the next few weeks. "If it's okay, you can work for me Tuesday, Thursday, and Saturday. Does that work?"

"Yes. That works out great, because my class is also on the same days I work for Inspired Ideas."

"Then I'll see you tomorrow. Is eight-thirty too early? If it is, you can come at nine."

"Eight-thirty is great. I'm excited about doing this, Eddie."

"Me too." We finished our lunch and I took her back to work. I spent the rest of the day imagining what the next three or four weeks would be like.

As it turned out, it was both heaven and hell. We had a great time working together. Alix was a big help, and we had a lot of fun both during and after work. We had lunch together each day, sometimes heading over to the nearby park for a picnic. At night, we ate dinner together, and on a few of the nights, we went to the movies and attended a comedy revue. I didn't remember ever enjoying summer so much.

The hell part was that I didn't dare touch her. I was too freaking scared. I didn't try to kiss her or attempt to have sex with her. It was total hell. And now, the apartment was almost finished. Desperate, I needed to figure out a way to let her know my feelings. I hoped it wouldn't scare her off. Most of all, I hoped that she shared some of the same feelings.

On the third Saturday we'd been working together, we knocked off early. Alix invited me to dinner at her place. This had to be the night. I had to tell her how crazy I was about her. Like some stupid schoolgirl, I stood in front of my closet and tried to figure out what to wear. Wanting to look my best, I changed my mind three times. I couldn't believe how one little female could fuck with one's mind.

‗‗ ‗

I RANG THE DOORBELL, AND when she opened the door, her face broke out into a big smile as she took the bouquet of flowers that I presented to her. She smelled the flowers and said, "They're gorgeous, Eddie. Thank you. Come in."

She led me into a small homey living room. Even though everything looked neat and clean, I could see that the furniture had become somewhat shabby. For sure she had been living frugally. No surprise that she had resorted to having sex for money.

"Can I get you a drink?" she asked.

"Whatever you're having is fine." This sounded just like the first time she came to my place.

Evidently she thought so too, because she remarked, "Haven't we had this conversation before?"

I laughed. "Yeah, I guess so." Then we both relaxed and started talking away, like we'd been doing the last few weeks.

I didn't even notice what she made for dinner. I was struggling with how to tell her how much I loved her. After dinner, she led me to the living room.

We sat down on the couch. She gazed into my eyes. "Eddie, is there something wrong?"

"Wrong? No, why would you think anything's wrong?"

"Well," she took a deep breath, "we've been together for the last few weeks, working and playing together. I thought you really liked me, but during this whole time, you've never tried to kiss me or . . . anything. I just wondered if it's just me or what?"

Oh. My. God. I couldn't let the words come out of my mouth fast enough. "Not only is anything *not wrong*, everything is *all right.* I love you so much Alix. I've been crazy in love with you since the day you walked into the apartment. I was just afraid that you didn't like me or . . ." At that point, I just shut my mouth and kissed her, and kissed her some more.

We finally stopped kissing long enough to make it to her bed. At last, I was able to make love to her as I had dreamed about for the last few weeks. Man, it was fireworks! What I'd had with Ches was one-dimensional compared to what I felt for Alix.

Afterward, I realized that all the money I'd earned and all the power I felt meant nothing compared to what I felt for this woman.

══

THE NEXT EVENING AFTER WE finished dinner, we sat down on the sofa and I put my arm around her.

"So Alix, when did you know that you loved me?" I ran my fingers through her hair and kissed her on the neck. She shivered.

"If you don't stop doing that, I won't be able to tell you."

"Okay, I'll behave."

"Do you remember the first day we met?"

How could I forget? "Yes."

"Well, you were sitting there concentrating on your plans. Then you looked up at me and I swear my heart just started to thump."

"Um, really."

"Yes, and then when you got up to set up a place to sit, I couldn't help but notice how sexy you looked in your T-shirt and jeans. And I thought, 'He sure doesn't look like a pimp.' Not that I'd ever met any. But, from what I'd read and seen in the movies, I couldn't help but think, 'What's wrong with this picture?' You weren't dressed like some peacock and you sure didn't look like someone who was mean and abusive. And when we were walking around with your plans, I just knew you were someone special."

I kissed her fingers. "Really? Go on."

"And then when we were having dinner, suddenly I thought, 'I'm going to marry this guy.' And then I thought, 'Why did I even think that?'"

I could feel my goofy grin start to spread across my face.

She stared at me. "What's so funny?"

"Just go on, I'll tell you later."

"Anyway, then when you asked me to stay for a while, I was never so happy. Now your turn."

"My story is pretty much the same as yours. When I looked up and saw you, my whole body went into a tailspin. I knew I had to see you again as soon as possible, which is why I invited you to dinner. I wanted so much to make love to you that first night, and I didn't want you to leave. It almost killed me to let you go."

Now Alix blushed and giggled. "And then what?"

"When you left, I knew that I couldn't let you have sex with any other man. I spent half the night trying to figure out how to keep you from being one of my girls. When I finally figured it out, I could hardly wait until morning to call you and ask you to work with me on the apartment."

"Yeah, I was thrilled when you called and really relieved when you asked me to work for you."

"I knew then that I had to figure out a way to get you to marry me. I hardly slept the whole time we were working together. Thank goodness you finally asked me about our relationship last night at dinner."

She put her arms around me and kissed me. I picked her up and carried her to bed. Total meltdown. Wow.

THIRTY-FIVE

ONE OF THE FIRST THINGS a pimp learns is discretion. Our back room continued to do a brisk business. Along with Colleen's special services, the girls had developed a couple of scenarios: a French maid evening that included a special meal, and a "Little Red Riding Hood meets the wolf" experience. Both got a lot of action. Because so many of our clients liked them, Sam, Cassie, and a couple of other girls wrote more scenarios, so it was a continuing story.

Our client list now included doctors, lawyers, judges, bankers, prominent businessmen, and for all I knew, maybe even a candlestick maker. If their names ever got out, the scandal would rock Denver and ruin not only them, but also me.

At our weekly meeting, I stressed once again to the girls the importance of secrecy. "Never, ever reveal the name of any of our clients to anyone."

Just then, Goldilocks burst into the front door. I stared at him and said, "What the hell do you think you're doing?"

"I'm here to get that little bitch Tracy back," he sneered.

I got up and stood between him and Tracy, who was cowering behind Kim. "Tracy doesn't work for you anymore, so get the fuck out of here."

"Listen, Mr. Easy Eddie, you can't just steal anyone else's girls. She's mine and I'm taking her back."

"You're not taking her anywhere. You get outta here right now or I'm going to call the police."

Goldilocks wound up, ready to throw a punch. I ducked, and his punch grazed my shoulder. Before he could even get his arm forward for a second punch, I kicked him in the balls and followed up with a kick to his knee, and he crashed to the floor.

I picked him up, drove my fist into his jaw, and dragged him to the door. "Don't you ever come here again, you bastard, or I'll kill you next time."

Tony and Scott had rushed over to help me. Between the three of us, we got Goldilocks outside and dumped him in front of his car. I thanked them for their help. When we got back into the office, the girls were sitting there, subdued.

"Okay, Tracy, how did Goldilocks find out you were here?"

"I'm so sorry, Eddie. I didn't mean for this to happen. I ran into Linda, one of Goldilocks's girls that I used to know. Well, we got to talking, and I let it slip that I was working for you." The tears ran down her face.

"You know you only get one mistake, Tracy. Screw up again and you're out. I can't have these kinds of threats. This is a dangerous business, and I need to protect all of us."

"I promise, Eddie, I'll never talk to anyone again."

"I hope for your sake it works. Now that Goldilocks knows you're here, he may come again. I can't protect you forever, nor do I plan to."

Everyone remained silent, waiting to see what I was going to say next. Cassie put her arm around Tracy.

"Let's get back to what we were talking about before. Now you can see the price of not keeping secrets. Let this be a lesson to all of you. I've noticed lately that some of you have been getting a little sloppy. So, next week Abbey will run some *required* meetings. I'm sorry to have to do this, but we can't have this kind of thing happen. It's too damn dangerous. So you can do this the easy way. Come to the meetings and get your heads on straight. If you choose to do it the hard way and not come, go find another job."

The girls sat there, shocked. No one said anything.

"Okay, that's all for today. I have other plans." I got up and left.

It shook me up more than I let on that Goldilocks had burst into my place of business. *Can't let that bastard ruin my day.* I needed a few minutes before I got on with my day's plan, which was to go down to Keystone Jewelers and buy Alix a ring. The owner of the jewelry store was a client of mine and promised me a good deal.

I looked forward to picking out a ring. I'd never bought any expensive jewelry, and I had to admit it scared the hell out of me. I planned to ask Alix to marry me the following Saturday night.

BY THE TIME I REACHED Keystone Jewelers, I had calmed down. Steve, the owner, greeted me with a friendly handshake. "I've picked out a few diamonds that I thought would work for you. It's easier than having you try to look at too many stones."

Grateful, I thanked him. "I really don't know anything about diamonds, so I'll rely on you to help me."

Steve patiently explained the basics of diamonds to me. He showed me several and explained details about each one. Surprisingly, I found it fascinating. I got down to two diamonds.

"Of the two, Eddie, I recommend the one carat round stone. It's a beautiful stone and one that most women favor. We can pick out a nice setting that will enhance the appearance even more." He gave me a questioning look.

"I agree." Then we looked at settings and I picked one out that had two small baguettes on each side of the main stone. "What do you think?" I asked.

"I think she'll be one happy woman. It's a good choice."

"Okay, now for the scary part. How much?"

"Four thousand dollars including the setting."

I gulped. I'd never spent that much money on one thing. But if it would make Alix happy, then it could be $10,000 and I wouldn't care. "I'm planning to propose Saturday night. Can you have it ready by then?"

"I'll take care of it personally. You can pick it up later this afternoon."

"Thanks, I'll be here."

Since I had a couple of hours to waste, I decided to go to The Montgomery and set things up for Saturday night. I schmoozed with the guys for a few minutes and then headed up to the restaurant. I went in the back and found Ray, the restaurant manager.

"Ray, I'm planning to bring my girl here on Saturday night. I'm going to propose to her, and here's what I want you to do."

I explained what I had planned. Ray clapped his hands. "I love it, Eddie. I'll make sure it's done just how you want it. By the way, your favorite band will be playing. If you'd like, I'll set it up for them to play your favorite song at the same time."

"That would be great." We shook hands and I left.

The ring should be ready by now, I thought. Luckily, I found a parking space right in front. I dashed in the front door, eager to see it. Steve was just coming out from the back room with the ring in his hand.

"Good timing, Eddie. I just finished." He laid it out on a velvet board.

I gasped when I saw it. It had to be the most gorgeous thing I'd ever seen. I hoped Alix would love it.

Steve smiled. "You like it?"

"It's perfect. I can't thank you enough." I took out my checkbook and wrote him a check. He put the ring in a box and tied it up with a silver bow.

"Good luck, Eddie."

＝＝

ABBEY AND I HAD PLANNED to meet for a drink and dinner later that evening. After picking up Alix's ring, I had just enough time to get there. We'd both been so busy these past few weeks, we hadn't had time to talk to each other. Since it was a school night for Alix, we'd decided it would be a good time to get together.

Abbey was already seated and waved me over. I must have had my goofy grin on my face because she took one look at me and said, "So, what's going on?"

"I just bought a ring for Alix." I pulled it out of my pocket, opened it, and showed it to Abbey.

"Wow, it's just gorgeous! I know she's going to love it. I'm so happy for you, Eddie." She hugged me and kissed me on the cheek.

After I put the ring away, I sat there with my goofy grin for another few minutes while Abbey talked about what was going on. Since we had begun doing business with the locals, we had found another revenue source. Once the businessmen got acquainted with our girls and found that they were not only pretty, but also socially acceptable in their manner and dress, they used us for conventions and meetings, either acting as hostesses or handing out goodie bags, brochures, and other materials. The money wasn't as good, but it provided us with less downtime for each girl, especially during the week when business was a little slow. It also gave us a whole new list of contacts.

By this time, I employed twenty girls and four guys. I had decided that was enough. It was getting too difficult to handle that many people and keep them in line.

"I'll tell you, Eddie, while you've been busy making goo-goo eyes at Alix, we've been doing a very brisk business."

"I know. I'm sorry I haven't been around much lately, but I just couldn't help myself. I had to make sure that I could get Alix to marry me."

"I know, I know. Although I don't think it took that much convincing. We could all see that she was just as crazy about you as you were about her."

"Yeah, I guess. I think it's probably time we had another meeting to discuss any problems we've been having."

"Definitely. When are you planning to propose? No point in trying to get anything done until that's over."

"Saturday night," I said. Then I told her my plan.

"Fantastic. I wish I could be the mouse under the table when it happens."

"I know. In a way, I wish you could be there too. You know how special you are to me. We've come a long way, Abbey, since I found you on that bench."

A tear trickled down Abbey's face. She took my hand and said, "You're very special to me too."

I coughed. "Okay, enough with this crap. Let's plan to have a meeting next Tuesday. Anything else going on I should know about?" Abbey blushed. *Aha, something else is going on.* "Out with it, girl."

"Well, Tony and I have been kinda seeing each other." She gazed into my eyes. "I really like him, but I'm not sure if he likes me or not. I know for sure he's not looking to settle down right now, so I'm just trying to play it cool."

"He's a nice guy. Just a little wild still. But he'll get over it. You're smart to play it cool. You want to make him think he has to catch you or you'll get away."

She sighed. "I suppose. I'm ready to order dinner now. How about you?"

We ordered, ate, and finished talking. I promised her that once Saturday was over, I'd get down to business again. In the meantime, I was anxious to get home, gaze at the ring, call Alix, and talk to her before she went to bed.

THIRTY-SIX

SATURDAY FINALLY ARRIVED. I HAD told Alix we were going to celebrate our second month anniversary by going to the top of The Montgomery. "And, by the way, my favorite local band, The Mellowtones, are playing. So we can dance too." I knew Alix loved to dance.

I put on my new beige suit with a lavender shirt and purple tie. Carefully, I put the ring in my inside pocket. Nervous, I checked myself in the mirror. Already the sweat had begun its trip down my armpits. *Calm down, Eddie. You know she's going to say yes. I think.*

When I arrived, I stood at her door a moment, once again trying to calm myself. When she opened the door, I felt my mouth go dry, she looked so beautiful. She wore a white lacy sundress with a lace jacket over it. At her waist was a hot pink ribbon sash. She wore a single strand of pearls and small pearl drop earrings.

When I was able to talk, I said, "You look exquisite, Alix. Like a beautiful white frosted cake."

She giggled. "White cake, hmm . . . good enough to eat?"

"Absolutely." *Damn, wipe off the goofy grin.* "We have a reservation at six-thirty. Ready?"

"Yes." She locked the door and took my arm, and as we walked to the car, I smelled her intoxicating perfume.

On the way to the restaurant, she did most of the talking. I was too nervous. I hoped she didn't notice.

Once we were seated, I excused myself. "I promised Ray I'd say hello when we got here so he could come out and meet you."

I found Ray, gave him the ring, and he assured me that he would take good care of it until it was delivered to Alix. "I'll be out in a few minutes to meet her," he told me before shooing me away.

Smiling, I rejoined Alix. Now that my plan had been put into action, I tried to relax. We ordered drinks and an appetizer and sat and enjoyed both while we waited for the band.

A short time later, Ray came out and I introduced him to Alix. Being the perfect host, he told her some funny stories about my missteps when I first started working as a bellman. We all had a good laugh and then he excused himself. "Time to get back to work. It was a pleasure meeting you, Alix."

"I enjoyed meeting you too, Ray."

The waiter came to take our order. I was beginning to have a good time. After he left, I invited Alix to dance. It felt so good holding her in my arms and dancing. Seeing our food arrive, we sat down to eat. The dinner was wonderful, but I was still a little too nervous to really enjoy it.

"This has been one delicious dinner. I don't think I could eat another morsel." Alix patted her stomach.

"Sorry, you must have dessert. Ray has prepared his special wine sundae for us." *Shit, she can't refuse dessert.*

"Okay, one bite. Can we get just one and share it?"

As we discussed our dessert, the waiter cleared the table. At that moment, Ray came out with the dessert. Just before he got to the table, he lit it and it was transformed into a gorgeous flaming sundae.

"Ooh, Ray, how beautiful."

Ray set the sundae in front of Alix. When she looked at it, her eyes grew wide and she gulped. "Oh, my, god, it's . . . it's a ring."

I jumped up and took the ring from its nest in the whipped cream, got down on my knee, and said, "Alexandra Turner, I love you more than anything. Will you marry me?"

"Yes," she squealed. "I love you too." We kissed and the band played "Celebration." Of course, everyone around us heard the proposal and clapped.

"I'm the happiest woman in the world tonight. Can we leave now, though? I want to be alone with you and share our happiness privately."

"Yes, me too." We found Ray and thanked him. He was all smiles.

"I was happy I could do this small thing for my friend," he said. "I wish you both all the happiness in the world."

When we got home, we celebrated in the way that made us most happy. It still surprised me that making love and just having sex were two very different things. I hadn't done much kissing since Ches, and I'd forgotten that kissing could be so intimate, sexy, and very, very hot.

～＝＝～

"WHEN DO YOU PLAN TO get married?" Abbey wanted to know.

"We thought we'd get married at the end of September."

"Any plans yet?"

"Yes and no. I think we'll rent one of the large rooms at The Montgomery. It won't be a huge wedding since neither Alix nor I have any family. I know Alix plans to call you to see if you'll help with the plans."

"I'd love to. It's going to be so much fun."

"I knew I could count on you."

"Of course, Eddie, anything for you."

"So, how are things progressing between you and Tony?"

Abbey frowned and sighed. "I wish I could answer that question. Sometimes, I think great. Other times, I don't know."

"Well, just keep playing it cool. I know he'll come around."

She gave me a hug. "I hope you're right. Now, I have things to do. See ya later."

THIRTY-SEVEN

ALIX AND I WERE SEATED at my kitchen table working on our wedding plans.

"Honey, there's a couple of people I'd like for you to meet."

"Sure, Eddie. Any special reason? Friends of yours?"

"Special, yes. The Greensteins. He gave me my first job. Remember I told you about them?"

"Of course, I remember. I also remember you told me how kind he and his wife were when your mom died."

"Yes. And I'm hoping that if you like Mr. G, you'd want him to give you away since your dad is dead and you don't have any other family."

"What a great idea. I've been wondering what to do about that."

"Good, then we'll drop by and see them later today, if that's okay with you."

"Let's do it then," she said. "By the way, I talked to Abbey yesterday and we're going to get together to look at table decorations and stuff. I think she's as excited as I am."

"I know she is. I really need to leave now, so I'll be back right after lunch and we'll go meet the Greensteins."

We both got up, and I put my arms around her and kissed her. I didn't want to leave, she tasted so good, but there were a few items that needed attention. I still had to mind the store. There was too much money involved. I couldn't let myself be totally distracted by my love.

When I got back to the apartment later that day, Alix had cleaned up and gotten dressed and was waiting for me. As we drove down to Stout Street, I told Alix more about the Greensteins. I had called before we left, so Mrs. Greenstein would also be there to meet Alix.

When we walked into the store, both Mr. and Mrs. G rushed over to greet us. I got a hug and Alix got the once-over.

"Eddie, how did you ever get so lucky to get such a beautiful girl?" Mr. Greenstein asked as he gave Alix a hug.

"And you, Alix, I want you to know Eddie's a good boy. He'll take good care of you, like he took good care of his mom."

Alix blushed as Mrs. G gave her a hug and echoed Mr. G's sentiments.

"So," Mrs. Greenstein said. "Tell us everything. How you met, when you plan to get married, you know, the whole story."

Since Mr. and Mrs. G had no idea how I earned my living these days, we told them the cleaned-up version of our meeting that we had practiced: how Alix and I met when I hired her as the interior decorator on a remodel I was doing. Alix concluded the story that was founded in the truth of our early relationship. Then she said to Mr. G, "And so since both my parents are dead, Eddie and I are hoping that you'd walk me down the aisle and give me away."

Mr. G was overwhelmed. He clamped his mouth down on his pipe. For a moment, he was speechless. A very unusual condition for him.

Finally he spoke, "My dear, nothing would give me greater pleasure. I'd be most honored to walk you down the aisle."

Alix had written down all the details and gave them to Mrs. G. "The invitations are in the mail today, so you should receive it in the next day or two. Thank you for doing this for me."

Then we all hugged and said our goodbyes, as we still had a lot of details to take care of.

＝＝

OUR WEDDING DAY FINALLY ARRIVED. The girls had spent the previous day decorating. I peeked into the room. From the chaos that had been going on, I wasn't sure what to expect. It had turned out great. A ribbon runner of hunter green ran down the center of each table. Fall colors of green, red, and yellow were in the centerpieces with candles set on each of the tables.

Around the room, the girls had arranged huge baskets of fall flowers. They'd also hung tiny twinkling lights around the stage where the band would be playing. I stepped into the room where the ceremony would be held. Down the aisle was a white runner. On the sides of the aisle were tall white baskets filled with flowers of yellow, white, and orange.

As I stood there, I felt a strange sense of peace come over me. I knew that finally I could forgive my dad for abandoning me, forgive the Johnstons for abandoning me by moving away, forgive Ches for abandoning me for another man, and forgive my mother for abandoning me by dying. My life had turned out just fine, and I was about to marry the most beautiful woman in the world.

It was time for me to get dressed. I went to the room I had rented for the men. Tony and Scott were already there preparing to get dressed.

"Where have you been?" Tony asked. "I was beginning to worry that you'd deserted the ship."

"Nope, just checking things out."

There was a knock on the door, and when I opened it, there stood the man who had loved me like a son. "Mr. G, I'm so happy you're here."

He took his pipe out of his mouth, put it in his pocket, and said, "From the grave, I'd be here, Eddie, you know that."

"I know, Mr. G. Where's Mrs. G?"

"She went down to the girls' room to say hello and see if there's anything she can do."

I excused myself so I could dress. Afterward, we all went downstairs to wait for the wedding party. Abbey came down and signaled that it was time for me to walk down the aisle. Then Jeff, my best man, and Molly, Alix's maid of honor, walked down the aisle, followed by Mike and Abbey and Hank and Colleen.

As the band played the wedding march, Mr. G escorted my bride down the aisle. I swear my heart stopped when I saw her, she was so beautiful. Mr. G gave her a hearty kiss and then she joined me.

Doug Parsons, the pastor from the Baptist church, officiated. As I repeated the words of our wedding vows, I looked lovingly into Alix's eyes so that she would know that I meant every word, that I would love and cherish her and take care of her the rest of my life. I placed my mom's wedding band on Alix's finger, and Alix placed the band she'd gotten for me on my finger as we repeated our vows. Looking at the band on her finger, I was grateful that I could give Alix something from my mom—I knew my mom was smiling down on us.

When the pastor announced that I could now kiss the bride, I literally swept her off her feet and gave her an enthusiastic kiss to the delight of everyone.

The rest of the evening went by in a blur. It was a small crowd of our closest friends, and we had a great time eating, drinking, and dancing. I did notice Tony following Abbey around, helping her with all of the special reception details. *He's hooked. Things are looking good.* I smiled and silently willed Abbey to keep up doing what she'd been doing.

＝＝

FOLLOWING OUR WEDDING, WE LEFT for our honeymoon in Cancun. The next ten days were a series of firsts for me. My first vacation, my first time on an airplane, my first time out of the country. Since that summer with Ches, I hadn't had any dates or done much besides work. At first, when Abbey and I started making money, I used to go out to dinner all the time, but after a while, I found it too lonesome to always eat by myself. That's when I started cooking at home. Occasionally, Abbey and I would go to the movies, but other than that, I did a lot of reading.

I didn't realize how much fun I'd been missing. And until our honeymoon, I didn't know that I could be a fun and social person. On our second day, we took a trip to some Mayan ruins—the name sounded like Chicken Itska. We met two other couples that we liked, and we quickly became a group.

We had a junior suite with a beautiful patio at the Fiesta Hotel. The six of us, Meg and Tim, Dotty and Jason, and Alix and I met in the late afternoon on our patio where we had drinks and appetizers and watched the sunset. Afterward, we went to dinner and then clubbing, where we drank, danced, and laughed until the wee hours of the morning.

During the day, we went to the beach, swam, and walked along the shore, enjoying the sand crunching beneath our toes. In the evening, we walked the streets and shopped. I loved shopping and buying things for Alix.

In years past, I had hoarded the money I made. I had made a vow that I would never be poor again and never have to go back to Stout Street or any other place like it. Being with Alix, I was happy to have so much money and be able to spend it on my beloved because it made me feel so damn happy.

"Honey, you don't have to keep buying stuff for me. I'll love you even if you never buy me anything."

"I know that, but please don't spoil my fun."

She shook her head, giggled, and gave me a kiss. "Okay, go ahead, spoil me. I love it." And so I did.

Sadly, our honeymoon came to an end. As we sat on the plane on the way home, I said to Alix, "I want you to promise me that we'll take a vacation every year. I had such a great time."

She snuggled into me. "You can count on me to keep that promise."

THIRTY-EIGHT

ALIX HAD QUIT HER JOB after we became engaged so she could go to school full-time. Our life was full and busy. The first thing we had to do when we came back was to decide what to do with Alix's house. We discussed various options. We could sell it, rent it, or live in it. We decided that we should sell it. It was too far away from the apartments where my girls were housed and where I did most of my business. I also still had a few apartments that needed remodeling in the second building.

Since the house was quite old, we knew we would have to do some cleanup, repairs, and remodeling before we put it on the market. We spent several weeks going through all the stuff in the house, separating what to give away, what to sell, and what Alix wanted to keep. Alix had a difficult time giving away things that were of no use anymore but held fond memories of her childhood. Finally, we had the house cleaned out and began the work to fix it up.

Alix had been poring over some of my plans. "Honey, I've been looking these over and I think what we need to do is tear out this wall in the kitchen so that we have a nice large kitchen with an eating space instead of a small kitchen, laundry room, and large dining room. The whole space will work much better."

I looked at her sketch. "Hmm . . . yes, I think you're right. We'll do it," I said and kissed her on the top of her head.

"Okay, I like everything else, so I think we're ready to begin."

It took us the better part of a month to finish. We had a lot of fun working together. When we finished, we did a walk-through. "I think we did a fantastic job. I'll bet we get top dollar for it," I said to her.

"I agree."

We found a realtor and put the house on the market. It sold within a week. We took the money and put it in the bank. "This is for a down payment on a home of our own someday," Alix declared.

"You want a house someday?" I'd always lived in apartments and didn't yet grasp the concept of a home of my own.

"Absolutely, there's nothing like your own home with your own yard."

"Whatever you say."

"That's what I say," she said and gave me a hug.

＝＝

I REALIZED THAT OUR FIRST anniversary would be coming up soon and I thought about what I'd like to buy Alix for a present. My first thought was jewelry, so once again, I went down to Keystone Jewelers to see Steve.

After looking at several pins, necklaces, earrings, and bracelets, I found a gold necklace with matching earrings that I liked.

"I'd like to sleep on it," I told Steve. "I just don't feel sure about it."

"Take all the time you'd like," Steve said. "I want you to be satisfied."

"Thanks, I'll be in touch."

As I drove home, I considered different ways to get Alix to tell me what she liked. By the time I reached home, I had a couple of ideas.

"Hi, honey, I'm home."

Alix came over, kissed and hugged me, and said, "Come sit down, I have something to tell you."

It must be something special, she's flushed and excited, I thought. "Sure, babe, shoot," I said as I sat down next to her.

She took a deep breath. "I'm pregnant. We're going to have a baby." Her shoulders tensed as she waited for me to respond.

Me, a dad. How could I be a dad? I wouldn't be good at it. I barely remembered my own father, and he turned out to be a bum. I gulped. "Wow, I don't know. I don't know anything about being a dad. I'm not sure I'd be particularly good at it."

I watched her face fall. "I think," she faltered, "you'll be a great dad." She looked down, dejected.

Oh, god, what have I just done? Suddenly I experienced a rush and my heart thumped. *A baby, our baby. Proof of our love. How could I be so stupid . . . it's wonderful news.* I laughed.

"Wow, a baby. What great news. Sorry I sounded so stupid a minute ago. It was just such a shock." I saw her shoulders relax and watched her face light up. Then I grabbed her and kissed her. "Thank you for this wonderful gift."

Then the questions came. "Are you okay? When is the baby due? What do I need to do?"

"Calm down, I'm fine. The baby is due either the end of April or the first part of May, give or take a couple of weeks. All you have to do is wait on me, hand and foot, rub my back and my feet daily, feed me bonbons and ice cream." She grinned from ear to ear. "Oh, yes, and fulfill my every wish."

"Of course, my darling, your wish is my command."

"Okay, so there's really not much for you to do. At least not right now."

"Will you still be able to graduate in December?"

"Oh, sure, no problem. I'm just having a baby, for heaven's sake, not dying of some dreaded disease."

"I don't mean to be stupid. It's just, what do I know about these things?"

"Well, I don't know much either, so I guess we'll learn together. Now let's have dinner and we can discuss it more later. Right now I'm starved."

We fixed dinner, but I barely ate. Alix ate like a horse. *God, if she continues to eat like this, she's going to be huge.* I smiled at the thought.

"What are you smiling about?"

"Nothing, just thinking about how you'll look with a big belly."

"You think that's funny?"

"Yes, don't you?"

"No, I don't." A tear trickled down.

"Why are you crying? What did I say?" I asked, alarmed.

"It's nothing, just hormones. Expect a lot of this."

THIRTY-NINE

THE NEXT COUPLE OF MONTHS passed uneventfully. We went about our lives as usual. When Alix began to show and felt the first kick, it hit me like an avalanche. My baby was going to have a pimp for a father. *This is not what I want. What am I going to do?*

I stewed, I fretted, I agonized about it for the next few weeks. What should I do? What could I do if I was no longer a pimp? I finally decided to talk it over with Alix. I waited until we had a free weekend. I took her to the movies and out to an early dinner.

When we got home, she said, "This was such a lovely day. I had a great time. It's been awhile since we had nothing to do and just had fun."

"Yes, it was nice," I said. "Come sit down. I have something to discuss with you."

She arched her eyebrows and gave me a questioning look. "Just buttering me up, were you."

"I like to butter you up."

"I know. Okay, so shoot."

"Well . . . I've spent the last couple of weeks worrying about the fact that our baby is going to have a pimp for a dad. I've been trying to decide what I could do. Then I realized that I need to talk it over with you. We both need to decide what to do."

Alix let out a big sigh, hugged me, and giggled and cried at the same time.

"Whoa, what's this all about?"

She dried her eyes. "I've been worrying about it too, but I just didn't know how to say anything to you. It's your business. How could I ask you to give it up? My heart has been feeling heavy with the thought. Do you have any ideas?"

I ran some of my ideas past her. "I've considered selling the business to the girls and going into the remodeling business. Or maybe construction. Or maybe real estate. That is where my interest is, but I want to hear what you think."

"I'm guessing that remodeling would work best for you. Look at what you've done with all the apartments and my house. You're terrific. Now, I'm not really worried about money, but how would selling the business affect us."

"We'd be okay, I think, for quite a while. I've got quite a bit of money put away, plus both apartment buildings bring in a little money. And, if I am able to sell the business, we'd have that money too."

"Plus we do have the money from the sale of the house," Alix offered.

"Oh, honey, I wouldn't want to use that money. I know you want that for a house."

"Having you out of the business is more important to me than any house."

"Right. I guess I'll start by doing research and talking to people in the industry."

"Sounds like the right approach to me."

"Yes, I'll get on it. Our baby is gonna have a dad he can be proud of."

"He?"

"Or she."

"Okay. Can we go to bed now? I'm tired."

"It would be my pleasure." I winked at her.

"Oh you devil."

⚊ ⚊

OVER THE NEXT FEW WEEKS, I spoke with several people who dealt in real estate, both buying and selling. I visited several construction companies and had numerous discussions with different owners. I also spoke with quite a few guys who did remodeling.

Then I went to the library and found as many books as I could about all three areas. The holiday season was rapidly approaching, so I had to cool it for a while. Business always exploded during the holiday season, and I needed to spend my time running my various enterprises.

Shortly after Thanksgiving, Tony dropped into the office.

"Hey, Eddie, I know how busy you are, but I wondered if you have time to have a drink with me. I have some things I want to discuss with you."

My guess was that he wanted to talk about Abbey. About time. "Sure, Tony, how about tomorrow night? I'm free if you are."

"I am. I'll swing by here say about six and we can go over to the Aladdin Bar."

"Good, I'll see you tomorrow then."

After Tony left, I sat there thinking about Abbey. *She's been looking very happy lately, so I suspect things have progressed with Tony. I sure hope so. She deserves a good man and a happy life. I've been so busy with my own life that I haven't taken time to talk with her lately.* I decided that after I found out what Tony wanted, I'd be sure to make time for Abbey. Besides, I wanted to run the idea by her of selling the business to the girls.

══ ══

TONY MADE SMALL TALK AS we drove to the bar. Once we were seated and had ordered a drink, he said, "I'm sure you've noticed that Abbey and I have been going together."

I nodded my head. "I have," I answered noncommittally.

He took a deep breath. "On New Year's Eve, I'm planning on asking Abbey to marry me. I'm fairly sure she'll say yes. The problem is that I'm not sure what to tell my folks about Abbey. On Christmas Eve, we have this big family dinner. It's a big hoo-hah, and I'm bringing Abbey to meet my family."

I thought about it for a minute and then said, "I think you need to do what Alix and I did. Get a story together about how you met, keeping it as close as possible to the truth. Then practice it until it feels like the truth to you. About Abbey's family, tell the truth. That she basically ran away from an abusive home and hasn't been in touch with them since then."

"Thanks, those sound like good suggestions."

"Just remember, don't do anything to hurt Abbey. You do, and I'll kill you." I grinned. "What I mean is that Abbey is very special to me and I want the best for her."

"I know that, and you're special to her too."

"Good, keep me posted on what happens. I wish you the best, Tony."

⸺ ⸺

ALIX AND I HAD A quiet Christmas at home. We opened our presents on Christmas Eve and then we watched *Miracle on 34th Street* for the umpteenth time. Christmas Day we spent relaxing and watching TV.

"This is our last quiet Christmas, you know," Alix sighed as she snuggled into me. "Starting next year, it's going to be chaos all the time."

"I know. And I'm looking forward to it."

The next day was back to work and routine. Alix finished up her final projects for graduation, and I was busy working on everyone's schedule for New Year's, when Tony and Abbey came in. I could tell by looking at them that everything had gone well. Abbey was sparkling and Tony was smiling from ear to ear.

"I take it things went well on Christmas Eve."

"My mom and dad loved Abbey. My dad said to me, 'Now son, I don't know why Abbey would want the likes of you, but don't screw it up and lose her.' The whole family was simply crazy about her. Do you know what she did?"

"I can't imagine."

"After dinner, Abbey threw my mom out of the kitchen. She told her that she'd worked hard all day and now she should enjoy her guests. Then Abbey and I did all the dishes and cleaned up the kitchen."

"We had fun doing it, didn't we Tony? And I loved his family too. I had no idea families could have so much fun together. They have all these games they play and then they sing carols. It was a blast."

As happy as I was for them, I couldn't help feeling a little sad for Alix and me. Neither of us had any family to celebrate with. "I'm glad for both of you that things worked out."

"There's something else, Eddie," Abbey said.

"Oh?"

"Well now that Tony and I are really a couple . . . well . . . neither of us could have sex with anyone else now. So Tony will be quitting and I—"

"Abbey, I understand. I hope, though, that you'll stay and help me with the girls and the office and the convention work. There's plenty to do without you being one of the girls. And I really need you around until Alix has the baby."

"Sure, I'll help out until the baby is born. Then I need to quit. You do understand that, don't you?"

I breathed a sigh of relief. "Of course I understand. I really do appreciate that you'll stay until Alix has the baby, though. Tony, I know I'll be seeing you around, even if it's not to work for me, so I'll just say congrats and I'll see ya."

The rest of the holiday season was total craziness. My crew was busy morning, noon, and night.

As Tony had planned, he and Abbey were engaged on New Year's Eve. Abbey was stunned. She didn't know everything was going to happen so soon. She called me on New Year's Day and asked if she and Tony could come over so she could show us her ring.

When I hung up, I went to find Alix. "I just talked to Abbey. She and Tony are on their way over."

Alix jumped up from the sofa. "Oops, I'd better get dressed and tidy up a bit."

"Don't worry. They're so excited they wouldn't notice if you were naked."

Alix giggled. "You're probably right, but just the same."

"Yeah. Do you think I should break out a bottle of champagne?"

"Absolutely. We've been saving it for a special occasion and this is it."

I got the champagne and glasses ready, along with Alix's beverage of choice: ginger ale. Tony and Abbey arrived within the half hour and we drank a toast to their happiness. Then Tony and I went off to the den to watch football and left the girls to discuss wedding plans.

═ ═

IN EARLY JANUARY, ALIX WAS notified that she'd passed all her classes. She was graduating with honors, a huge accomplishment. I was so proud of her.

Because of the lull that always came after the holidays, I was able to finish my research too. I decided that I wanted to start out remodeling and see where that might eventually lead me. I sat down with Alix and discussed my thoughts.

"I think I've done all the research I can. I want to start out remodeling. If things go well, I can always expand into construction. I found that I need to take some classes before I even get started."

"Classes? What kind of classes?" Alix wanted to know.

"Electrical and carpentry, mainly. I need to get certified in those. I probably need to take a class in some basic architecture, too."

"You're going to be one busy boy, daddy-to-be. I know I can help you with the architecture one, since I had to take classes in that too. By the way, I've been exploring my contacts. I've decided that I'm going to set up my own little interior design business here at home."

That surprised me. She hadn't mentioned anything to me. "Really? When do you plan to start? And, aren't you going to be too busy what with the baby and everything?"

"I plan to start right away. I'm only planning to do things in a small way to begin with. I'll play it by ear and see how it goes."

I could see that she was excited about doing this, so I wasn't going to throw any cold water on her idea. "Sounds great, honey. We can help each other. Going back to school scares the hell out of me, so I guess I'll need all the help I can get."

Alix threw her arms around me and gave me a big hug. "I'm so excited, honey. We're going to be a big success, I know it."

"I'm going to sign up for a couple of classes right away. They start next month, so I'm planning to talk to the girls sometime this week about buying the business."

Alix gave me a worried look. "How do you think the girls are going to take all this?"

"I don't know. We'll just have to wait and see."

FORTY

I CALLED A MEETING FOR ten o'clock. When I arrived, the girls were gossiping as usual. As I looked around at their faces, I knew that this was going to be harder than I thought. Eager as I was to leave the business, it had been a good business. And these girls, as much as they sometimes drove me crazy with their pettiness, selfishness, and gossiping—they were my girls. Attractive, sophisticated, and every inch professionals. They were bound to me. Now, ironically, I was going to abandon them. What a strange turn of events.

I cleared my throat. "Ladies, I have an announcement to make." Everyone quieted down. "At the end of April, I am leaving the business."

Shock reflected in their faces and gasps of dismay came from their mouths. "Just wait. There's more. I have two choices to tell you about. I can either shut the doors and you all can go find new jobs, or I can sell the business to all of you." I held up my hand for quiet as they all began talking at once.

"I'm clear that you are the only ones I would sell this business to—I don't feel comfortable entrusting it and all of you to anyone else. So let me present my proposition. Then you can think about it. I want $200,000 for the business. That means around $10,000 per person if you all decide to participate. This would be paid out over a period of five years. If this is what you all decide to do, I will have my attorney draw up all the paperwork that will need to be signed." I could see the looks of surprise as I scanned the room.

I continued. "I will still own the apartment buildings, so you will not have to move. And you will still have access to the rooms here, including the office and the special back room. Now I know this is a lot to think about, but I will need to have this finalized by the end of the month, at least to know whether or not I need to close our doors. Since, on the event side of the business, we have people who are ready to book for late spring and summer, I need to be ready to tell them as soon as possible if I'm going to close the business."

I could see that the enormity of the situation had begun to sink in. "Because I want all of you to have a chance to talk together and to really think about this, I'm going to end our meeting now without any discussion. I know you have questions, and I'm sure you'll have more once you talk as a group, so let's plan to meet again in two days to talk. No matter what, I want you all to know that you are the best group of women any pimp ever could have worked with. You are all true professionals, and I'm proud to have worked with you."

Before I got too sappy or they had a chance to respond, I motioned for Abbey to follow me into the office. She'd already known about the plan, so I wanted to get her take on the meeting. Once we were settled in the office, I shot her a questioning look.

"Quite a bombshell," she said. "But I think after the initial shock wears off, the girls will want to buy the business."

I breathed a sigh of relief. "I hope so. They'd have something lucrative to continue . . . plus I could use the money to keep me going while I establish my new business."

"No matter what they decide, Eddie, I know you. You'll be a success. That's just who you are."

I hugged Abbey and gave her my goofy grin. "Damn, girl, we've been together so long, I don't know how I'm going to get along without you."

"Just fine. You have Alix now and a new baby about to be born. And I have Tony. And you do know that we'll always be friends."

I hugged her again. "Yes always. Now scoot, I have work to do."

<hr/>

WITHIN A COUPLE OF WEEKS, quicker than I'd dreamed possible, the deal was set. The girls decided to become the owners and operators of the business. Abbey began working with them regarding the daily activity and the many ins and outs of the business.

Life seemed to be moving extremely fast. At the beginning of February, I started my classes at the technical school, so soon I was juggling my remaining business responsibilities with school and planning for my new business. By late February, Alix had also put into motion her business as an interior designer. Through her contacts, she landed her first client. Initially, she just wanted to get her feet wet and do a good job so that she would build credibility. As she neared the end of her pregnancy, this was about all she could handle anyway. She was ginormous and getting more uncomfortable with each passing day.

⚒

I WOKE UP TO ONE of those special days in Colorado. I could taste spring in the air. Even though it was only early April, it seemed as though nothing but blue skies and warm days lie ahead. As a Coloradan, though, I knew that this kind of day was just a teaser. Within hours, we could have the blizzard of the century.

As I lay in bed, I mentally went over the list of things I had to do. Alix had a doctor's appointment at eleven-thirty. I had decided to take her so that I could drop her off at the front door. Alix was having difficulty walking too far since she was in her final weeks. The baby could be born any time now.

I turned over and kissed her on the back of her neck and whispered, "Are you awake?"

"Only for the last two hours. Your baby has been doing a ten-rounder in my stomach, punching and kicking."

"Oh, so now it's my baby?"

"Okay, our baby. Would you rub my back just a little?" She sounded so whiny, I wanted to laugh.

"Of course, honey." I rubbed her back and then said, "I have to get up now. I have a ton of stuff to do before I come home to take you to the doc."

"Okay, come around and haul my sorry ass out of bed."

Now I did laugh. "Okay, I'd love to haul your sorry ass." I went around the bed and carefully helped her get up. I truly felt sorry for her—she was so miserable.

Alix was still sitting at the breakfast table, reading the paper, as I was ready to leave. "I'll be home around eleven to get you." I kissed her on the cheek. "Later."

She promised to be ready, waved goodbye, and went back to reading the paper.

I was still spending a few days a week at the office, and when I got there, Colleen was at the desk. "Susan called in sick, so I came in to answer the phone."

Susan was our regular receptionist and hadn't been feeling well the last couple of days, so I wasn't surprised that she was out. "Thanks, can you stay? I have several things to do and I have to leave by a quarter to eleven to take Alix to the doctor."

"No problem. Don't worry. We'll work it out."

I went into the office and found Abbey making a list of supplies needed for the weekend French Maid and Little Red Riding Hood scenarios. The girls' scenarios continued to be in high demand.

She glanced up, and when she saw it was me, she asked, "Anything you need while I'm out shopping?"

"Nothing I can think of. When are you leaving?"

"Probably not until around eleven. I have stuff to do around here to get ready for the weekend. I don't want to leave until that's finished in case I find something else I should pick up."

Abbey finished her list while I sat and worked on my paperwork. Before I knew it, it was almost eleven. I cleaned off my desk and prepared to leave.

Kim, Tracy, Sam, and Cassie were all out front working on a new French Maid and Red Riding Hood script. The scenarios were so popular that several of the guys kept coming back for more, so we finally decided we needed an ongoing script for our regulars.

"How's it going?"

"We're having a blast. Got a bunch of new ideas this week," Cassie said. Then they all started giggling.

"Okay, have fun. I'm off." I turned to Colleen. "I'll check with you later. Make sure everything's okay."

"Okay, boss."

"You know you're going to have to stop calling me that in a few weeks. You might want to start practicing," I said with a smile.

"Okay, boss."

⌐= =⌐

I LEFT ALIX AT THE doctor's office building and went to park the car. When I came into the lobby, I didn't see Alix amidst the other women—apparently she was already in the examining room. I found a chair in the corner and buried my face in a magazine, not wanting to face all those pregnant women. It was a scary sight.

Soon Alix came out with a big grin on her face. "Let's go."

"What's the grin about?"

"You know the ten-rounder I told you about this morning? Well, the doctor says that's the baby starting to turn. It won't be long now."

Suddenly I felt lightheaded. *This is really going to happen. I'm going to be a dad.* I clutched Alix as we walked out of the building—more for my support than hers. "That's fantastic, honey. Wait here while I go get the car."

I attempted to regain my calm as I walked toward the car. After a couple of deep breaths, I felt a little better. Thank goodness I had to get the car. I didn't want Alix to see how anxious I was.

⚊ ⚊

As soon as I opened the door to our apartment, the phone started ringing.

"Get that will you, hon? I have to go pee."

She always had to pee. "Got it," I answered. I picked up the phone. "Hello?"

"Is this Eddie Anderson?"

"Yes, who's this?"

"I'm Detective Tom Jackson with the Denver Police. There's a problem here at your office. Could you come over immediately?"

"What? What kind of problem? What's happened?" The sweat poured out of every pore of my body, and I could feel my heart thumping.

"I'll explain when you get here. Just come as quick as you can."

"What's wrong, you look awful?" Alix asked me as she came back from the bathroom.

"I'm not sure. Something at the office. Now you just lie down and rest, and I'll call you as soon as I know anything."

Alarmed, Alix said, "I want to come with you."

"Sorry, hon, since I don't know what's going on, I want you to stay here—safe and sound. I'll call as soon as possible." I grabbed the keys and ran out the door.

Fortunately, the office was just a couple miles away. When I drove up, I saw total chaos: three police cars, three ambulances, police officers, paramedics, media trucks, and yellow tape all over. Then I saw a group of the girls standing around crying.

Shit, shit, shit. What's going on? Frantic, I looked for a place to park. A policeman came up to me. "This is a crime scene, you can't park here."

"I'm Eddie Anderson, the owner of this complex. Detective Jackson called me."

"Sorry, just leave your car here. I'll take care of it."

"I have a parking space in back if you need to move it," I yelled as I ran up the sidewalk.

A tall, thin, almost bald man wearing glasses and a vest that said DPD motioned to me. "Are you Eddie Anderson?"

"Yes, what happened here?"

He led me over to a body lying on the grass. Shit, it was Goldilocks. He'd been shot several times, and his body was so bloodied it made me shake.

"Do you know this man, Curtis Brown?"

Curtis Brown? That was Goldilocks real name? I never knew his real name. "Yeah, I know   of him," I said. "What happened?"

"When we arrived on the scene, we heard screaming and shots. We called for the shooter to put down his weapon and come out with his hands up. Instead, he came running out shooting. We then shot him."

Abbey arrived at that moment. She ran up to me with tears streaming down her face. "Oh my god, Eddie, what happened? I was just coming back when I heard about a shooting here."

I put my arms around her and held her, both of us shaking. "I don't know yet. Detective Jackson here was just explaining. Detective Jackson, this is my office manager, Abbey."

"Miss," Detective Jackson acknowledged Abbey before continuing, "When we entered the apartment, we found two women dead."

Abbey screamed. It was then that I noticed the two gurneys. "Who?" He led us over to the first one and lifted the sheet. "Tracy," I cried. Then he took the sheet off the second one. "Kim, oh, my god, Kim." There was so much going on that I hadn't really had a chance to take in everything. Then it hit me. "Colleen and Sam, are they okay?" I suddenly remembered that Cassie had been one of Goldilocks's girls too. *Oh god, no.* "And what about Cassie, is she okay?"

Detective Jackson pointed to two other gurneys. "Two other women are currently being treated."

I saw that Colleen was being attended to by paramedics. I heard one of them say she was ready to be transported. Detective Jackson looked at his notes. "That's Colleen. She took a shot to the shoulder. We're sending her to University Hospital. She should be okay."

"What about Sam and Cassie?"

Once again, he checked his notes. "Samantha took a couple of shots to her leg. It's pretty messed up. We're transporting her to Rose Hospital. Cassie is in critical condition. She was hit twice in the chest. We've already transported her to Rose Hospital."

I raised my hand for him to stop. I needed to get myself together and take charge here. I ran over to the girls standing near the door. "Lindsey, Beth, Jan. They're taking Colleen to

University Hospital. Go there and stay. I'll get over there as soon as I can. The rest of you go to Rose Hospital. I'll be there when I can." I ran back to the detective.

"Can you tell me anything more about what happened?" I asked.

"We were able to talk to Colleen and she said that Mr. Brown came charging through the door pointing his gun. He pointed directly at Tracy, called her a bitch, and told her if she wasn't going to work for him, she wasn't going to work for anyone. Apparently Kim tried to cover Tracy or knock her down, and Mr. Brown shot them both. Samantha and Cassie were trying to get away and he then shot them. Colleen was trying to call us when he shot her in the shoulder. Then we arrived and you know the rest."

The breath seemed to have left my body. I sagged. If Abbey hadn't grabbed me, I probably would have fallen. Abbey hung on to me, crying uncontrollably. I tried to comfort her as I spoke. "What can we do, Detective?"

"I will need information on next of kin and where to reach them so I can call and advise them of what happened."

"Sure." Looking over at Abbey, I knew that giving her something to do would help calm her down. "Abbey, could you go into the office and get the detective the information he needs?" Obviously visibly shaken, she nodded and headed for the office.

"Is there anything else you need immediately, Detective? If not, I'd like to call my wife and let her know that I'm okay. Then I'd like to go check in at each of the hospitals."

Abbey came running out of the office, carrying a couple of sheets of paper. "Here Detective, here's the information you need."

"Thanks," he said. "I think that I have everything I need for now. I'll get in touch if I need more information."

I nodded and waved as I ran into the office to call Alix. When she answered, I could hear the hysteria in her voice.

"Eddie, is that you?"

"It's me, honey. I'm okay. Are you okay?"

She cried, "I've been watching on TV. Oh, Eddie, it's just awful. How did something like this happen?" she sobbed.

"I wish I knew. It's hard for me to have to tell you this, but Tracy and Kim were the two killed. It was Goldilocks."

"Oh my god, Eddie, I can't believe it!"

I wanted to comfort her, but I also was in a rush to get to the hospitals. "It's unbelievable and horrible for sure. Listen, honey, I need you to try and rest and take it easy. Colleen is at University Hospital and Sam and Cassie are at Rose Hospital. I want to get over to both places to check in on them. I'll call as soon as I know anything."

"I'll come to the hospital too."

"No, you need to stay home. The rest of the girls will be covering between the two hospitals. I can't have anything happen to you, so please try and rest. I don't want to have to worry about you going into labor too."

She sniffled. "Okay, but call me as soon as you can."

"I will. Bye, honey, I love you." I hung up, then took a minute to try and stop shaking and get control of myself. As I walked out, I saw Abbey waiting for me by her car.

"What do you want me to do now?" she asked.

She seemed to have regained control over herself. "You go to University Hospital and check on Colleen. If everything is okay there, then have one or two of the girls stay with Colleen and the rest of you come to Rose Hospital."

"Okay. See you later." She jumped in her car and drove away.

I walked over to the officer who had taken charge of my car. "Officer, I'm ready to leave. Can you tell me where my car and keys are?"

"Yes, I have your keys right here." He pulled my keys out of his pants pocket. "I parked your car in back."

"Thanks," I said, as I took the keys from him and headed around to the back. It didn't take me long to get to the hospital. I found the girls huddled in the waiting room.

"Any news yet?"

"Sam is out of surgery," Marty said. "She's in recovery. Her leg is pretty messed up, but the doctor said she'll be okay. She'll probably be here for several days and then have to have a lot of physical therapy once it heals. It's too soon to know, but he said she might need more surgery. We'll be able to see her once they get her into a room."

"That's good news. What about Cassie?" I asked.

Marty sighed. "No news yet. She's still in surgery."

I found a chair and sat down to wait. I wondered if Goldi-locks had found out about Cassie working for me too. *Maybe that's why he went ballistic . . . but we'll never know.* I needed to let it drop for all our sakes.

As we sat together, everyone was subdued. Most of the girls were crying quietly. I knew I needed to find some words to com-fort them, but at the moment, I just couldn't seem to find any.

After a while, I said, "Let's all hold hands and pray silently for everyone." I couldn't even say their names. It was just too painful. I wasn't usually a praying man, but figured it could only help . . . *all of us.*

We sat around like that for what seemed an eternity. Finally a doctor came out and approached us. "You're here about Cassie?"

"Yes," I said.

"All of you?"

"Yes."

"Okay, well she's out of surgery but still in critical condition. We have her stabilized as well as we can. She's in intensive care. The next few hours will be critical. We'll just have to wait and see how she responds. Do you have any questions?"

My heart dropped. "Will we be able to see her?"

"You can all wait in the intensive care waiting room and check with the nurse every half hour. You may be able to see her through the glass one at a time if the nurse thinks it will be okay. They'll keep you informed."

I stood up and shook the doctor's hand. "Thanks for doing everything you could."

We hurried to the elevators. Just as the door was about to shut, Abbey came running up and jumped in with us. "Glad I caught you," she said.

"Me too. How's Colleen?" I asked.

"She's doing fine. They have her doped up fairly good, so she isn't in that much pain right now. I left Beth with her. Lindsey and Jan had jobs, so they left."

Once we reached the ICU waiting room and the girls all seemed to be settled, I told Abbey to come with me, and we'd see if Sam had been transferred to a room yet. We stopped at the nurse's station and found out that Sam was in room 205. Before we got on the elevator, we stopped for a moment and Abbey and I just stood there hugging each other.

"We've got to be strong," I told Abbey. "So paste a smile on your face and be prepared to tell Sam she's going to be fine."

We rode silently down the elevator, and as we approached Sam's room, we once again took a deep breath to compose ourselves. When we walked into the room, Sam seemed to be asleep.

She looked so pale it was scary. She was covered up, so we couldn't see her leg. Abbey went up to the bed and took Sam's hand and squeezed it. Sam squeezed back.

"Oh! That surprised me," Abbey whispered.

Sam opened an eye. "I'm not really sleeping right now. I was just trying to get enough strength to buzz for the nurse. I'm so thirsty and my head hurts."

I reached over and poured a glass of water and handed it to Abbey. "Can you raise your head a little? Here's some water."

Sam raised her head and took a sip. "Thanks."

Abbey picked up the buzzer and buzzed for the nurse. The nurse arrived and, ignoring us, quickly took Sam's vitals. "What can I do for you?" she asked Sam as she continued to check monitors and adjust things.

"My head hurts something awful. Can you give me something?"

The nurse checked Sam's chart. "You had some painkiller about two hours ago, so I can't give you much, but I'll do what I can. I'll be back in just a moment."

She returned with a hypo and administered it to Sam. "Hopefully this will help." She then acknowledged us and said,

"With luck, this will put her to sleep. Are you planning to stay with her?"

"I'll stay for a bit," Abbey said.

"Good, call if you need me."

Abbey sat down by the bed and took Sam's hand and began to talk quietly to her. It didn't take long before Sam was asleep.

"You go back upstairs. I'll stay with Sam for right now. If she stays asleep, then I'll come upstairs."

"Okay," I said as I kissed Sam softly on her forehead. Then I left. When I joined the girls upstairs, I found that nothing had changed. We dozed in our chairs. Around three-thirty, a nurse nudged me.

"I just wanted to let you know that Cassie seems to have turned the corner. She's stabilizing well and is resting comfortably. She's still critical but stable. Time for you to go home and get some rest. If one of you will leave me a number, I'll get in touch with you if there's any change."

I jotted down my number for her, and then we picked up our stuff and prepared to leave. I turned to the girls. "I'll let you all know if there's any change. I'll be back here tomorrow."

They nodded in agreement and we all left in a group.

FORTY-ONE

WHEN I ARRIVED HOME, I found Alix sleeping on the couch. As soon as I sat down by her, she woke up.

"Oh, Eddie, thank god you're home. What's going on?"

I helped her sit up and then told her everything that had happened. "So now we just have to wait and see."

"I'm so sorry. What an awful thing. How could Goldilocks do that? I just can't imagine anyone wanting to kill someone for such a stupid reason."

"Me either. Life's too short. But we'll get through this. I know we will. For now, we both need to sleep. I'm exhausted."

"Of course you are. Let's go to bed."

THE NEXT WEEK TURNED OUT to be a nightmare. Kim's family lived in Goodland, Kansas. They came to identify her and then had her body sent back to Kansas for burial. All of us went down to the morgue to meet with them and express our sadness. They refused to speak to us or even see us. It devastated the girls to be treated as though they were lepers.

Tracy's family who lived in North Dakota refused to even come down and identify her. Her mother didn't want to have anything to do with her. "You can bury her in a charity grave for all I care. I don't give a damn what you do with that filthy girl's body."

Once again, we wept at the cruelty. I couldn't let that happen to Tracy, so I paid for and planned the funeral. Afterward, we all came back to our apartment. Abbey and Alix had put together a nice buffet lunch for everyone. We all ate and spent the rest of the day talking about both girls, laughing and crying at the stories we shared. Everyone was relieved that Colleen was doing well and had already come home. Sam and Cassie's recoveries were also going well. Surprisingly, they both were expected to go home within the next week.

"Okay everyone. This has been an awful week. I want everyone to go home, rest, and recover. We'll have a meeting on Thursday. Make it ten-thirty. Take care of yourselves and I'll see you all then."

After they left, Alix and I collapsed on the couch.

"Thank you for being so strong this week. I couldn't have done this without you." I put my arms around my wonderful wife and hugged and kissed her until I felt satisfied.

She couldn't say anything. She just hugged me back. Then she whispered, "Let's go to bed now so you can hold me all night long."

We slept late the next morning. We were wiped out and spent the day resting and trying to recover from the horrors of the recent events.

⇒ ⇒

EVERYONE WAS DRINKING COFFEE AND talking when I got to the office. Considering what had happened, they all seemed to be doing okay.

"Thanks for coming everyone. What I'm going to say next is extremely difficult for me. With just a few weeks left until I'm supposed to leave and with what's happened, I understand if you want to close the doors. With Tracy and Kim now gone, that changes things. And with the news reporting what took place here, I know that's had an impact on business recently.

"I know you have difficult decisions to make and they need to be made quickly. If you decide you'd rather close the doors, I completely understand. If you decide to all go your separate ways, then I'll close the office and back room and remodel them. And if you want to leave the apartments, I will re-rent them. I just want you to know that you are under no obligation to stay."

Colleen spoke up. "We've already been talking, Eddie, and we've decided to keep things going, in honor of Tracy and Kim . . . and of what you created. We will split Tracy's and Kim's debt between the rest of us. We know it means the paperwork has to be redone, so we hope that's okay with you."

I couldn't believe my ears. I really thought they'd want to walk away. I couldn't blame them if that's what they decided. There would always be the memory of what had happened here, at least for a time to come. But these girls were incredible. Each of them had become a true class act.

I teared up but tried to hide it. Too late. Within seconds, we were all in tears.

⟨═ ═⟩

ON FRIDAY MORNING, I GOT up and decided I'd go to class. I'd missed more than a week and was ready to get back to some sense of normal.

After we finished eating breakfast, I asked Alix if it would be okay with her if I went to class. She hesitated for a moment and then said, "Sure. I think it'd be a good thing for you to do."

"Okay, then. I'll call between classes and check in to make sure you're doing okay."

She came around the table and kissed me. "You're just such a good guy. I love you so much. And, you're going to be a great dad!"

I kissed her back, got up, got dressed, and went off to class.

⟨═ ═⟩

WHEN I WALKED IN THE door, I smelled good things cooking. I went into the kitchen and found Alix frosting a cake. The sink was full of dirty dishes and pots and pans. The aroma of chicken cooking wafted through the air from the stove.

"My god, woman, what have you been doing? The kitchen looks like it's been attacked by some kind of hungry hoard."

She giggled. Her face was rosy with sweat and she had a spot of flour on her nose. "I felt so good after you left that I decided to do some cooking. So I made soup, your favorite chicken rolls, and then I baked a cake. And now I'm pooped."

"How could you not be? Have you had lunch yet?"

"No, I was waiting for you. I made us a shrimp salad, and I also made the Louis dressing you like so much."

She finished frosting the cake and put it on the cake plate and covered it.

"Go sit down on the couch and rest. I'll clean up in here and then bring lunch to you."

"Oh that would be wonderful. Thank you. I should sit down. My ankles are pretty swollen."

I cleaned up the kitchen and made a couple of trays with the shrimp salad and warm pan rolls. I also made iced tea. When I brought the tray into the living room, Alix was sound asleep. I didn't want to wake her, since I knew she was beat. I put the tray down and was about to head back to the kitchen when she snored so loudly it woke her up.

"What happened? Was I asleep?"

I had to bite my lip to keep from laughing. "Yes, you were. Since you're awake now, here's your lunch. I'll just go into the kitchen and get mine and be right back."

After I cleaned up our lunch dishes and came back into the living room, Alix was once again sound asleep. I saw this as a good opportunity to spend time studying the regulations I would have to know in order to pass the exams to be licensed.

Later that night, we enjoyed the delicious dinner Alix had created, watched TV, and went to bed early.

About three-thirty in the morning, I felt an earthquake. "Eddie, honey, wake up."

"Huh, something the matter?"

"My water just broke and I've started having contractions."

I jumped up. Rattled, I wasn't sure what to do first. "Are we ready to go to the hospital?"

"No, not yet. The contractions are still pretty far apart and not too bad. I think we should just stay in bed and start to time them."

I broke out in a cold sweat. *Shit, can't we just go to the hospital? Now?* I knew Alix wasn't ready, so I resigned myself to do as I was told.

After about two hours, the contractions had become much stronger and were about three minutes apart. I couldn't stand it any longer. "I think it's time to go."

She took a deep breath. "I think you're right."

We dressed and were ready to go within ten minutes. Fortunately, Rose Hospital was just a few blocks away. When we arrived, the nurse immediately put Alix in a wheelchair and took her. I checked her in and followed the nurse's directions to the maternity floor.

I found her room and sat down by her side. "How ya doing, honey?"

"Hanging in. Hold my hand please."

Just then a contraction hit, and I thought she'd tear my arm right out of its socket. "Pretty bad?"

"Um," she choked out.

Within a few minutes, the doctor came in to check her. "It's not going to be long," he said. "If you're going to come in with her, it's time for you to change."

I gave her a questioning look. She nodded yes. "Okay, then."

By the time I changed, the pains were coming quickly. I swear ten minutes hadn't passed before she screamed so loudly I thought I'd go deaf. A nurse came running in to check.

"It's time," she said and got everything ready to move her to the OR. I followed, my heart thumping so loud I thought everyone on the floor could hear it.

After that, everything became a blur. The next thing I heard was the doctor saying, "It's a girl." Then I heard my daughter announce her arrival in the world with a loud cry. As I kissed and hugged my wife, I felt such an overwhelming sense of joy that I thought I would burst.

≈ ≈

IT WAS EARLY AFTERNOON, NOT yet twelve hours since we'd arrived at the hospital. Alix slept soundly in her hospital bed—she'd worked hard. Sitting in a chair beside her, I looked down at our baby girl who slept soundly in my arms. Smiling, I felt peaceful. After all these years, I'd at last found my home. I would never ever be alone again.

I raised my head and look upward. "Thanks Mom, Mr. G, Ches, Jeff, and Abbey for helping me become a man," I said as tears of gratitude streamed down my face.

When one door closes, another opens, I thought. The doorway was now wide open and standing there were the two beautiful women I planned to share my life with—my beautiful wife and daughter. This was not about endings. This was a whole new beginning.

ACKNOWLEDGMENTS

To my husband, Herb, my number one supporter. To my consultant, Susie Schaefer with Finish the Book Publishing, who guided my journey from beginning to end and helped me finish the book. To Donna Mazzitelli, The Word Heartiste, who always urged me on to be the best writer I could be. To Pam McKinnie, Concepts Unlimited, who perfected my cover ideas and made them come to life.

And to all the other people who made this book possible, my heartfelt thanks. It really does take a village to publish a book.

ABOUT THE AUTHOR

ROCHELLE PADZENSKY worked in several areas of the financial field, where she had considerable public contact. She soon realized that everyone had a story and every story had a life-changing moment. Fictionalizing and telling these stories has become her passion.

Rochelle has lived in Denver most of her life. Married with two children and four grandchildren, she is now retired. She enjoys writing and is a member of Rocky Mountain Fiction Writers. She loves to travel, cook, and spend time with her friends while enjoying all Colorado has to offer.